To my sisters: Jen, Cindy, Lizz, and Crystal
I love us.

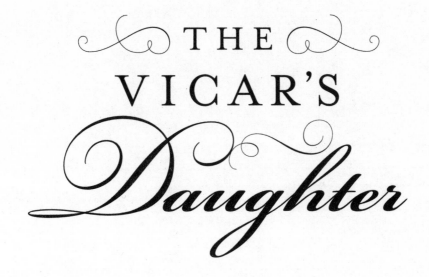

THE VICAR'S *Daughter*

PROPER ROMANCE

Josi S. Kilpack

SHADOW
MOUNTAIN

Visit us at ShadowMountain.com

This is a work of fiction. Characters and events in this book are products of the author's imagination or are represented fictitiously.

Library of Congress Cataloging-in-Publication Data
Names: Kilpack, Josi S., author.
Title: The vicar's daughter / Josi S. Kilpack.
Description: Salt Lake City, Utah : Shadow Mountain, [2017]
Identifiers: LCCN 2016029521 | ISBN 9781629722801 (paperbound)
Subjects: LCSH: Letter writing—Fiction. | Man-woman relationships—Fiction. | Sisters—Fiction.
 | GSAFD: Regency fiction. | LCGFT: Romance fiction. | Novels.
Classification: LCC PS3561.I412 V53 2017 | DDC 813/.6—dc23
LC record available at https://lccn.loc.gov/2016029521

Printed in the United States of America
Lake Book Manufacturing, Inc., Melrose Park, IL

10 9 8 7 6 5 4 3 2 1

Chapter One

Cassie fidgeted with the skirt of her day dress and said a silent prayer: *Please help me remain calm*. If only "calm" were a virtue of character she possessed without having to appeal to the heavens.

"It's not fair," Cassie said with a forced, even tone. There was so much more she wanted to say, but avoiding a tantrum was paramount if she wanted Mama to listen. "I should be seeking my future rather than gathering dust here in the vicarage for another season."

Mama did not look up from her sewing—a new shirt for Father she wanted done by Sunday's sermon, even though it would not show beneath his cassock. "It is as it has always been, Cassie. Your father and I did not change our mind for your sisters, nor did your protest sway us last year."

"But I am twenty years old now." Cassie's voice remained even, but she spoke through clenched teeth and her hands were balled into fists at her sides.

"As were Rose and Lenora when it was their turn to enter society."

"Elizabeth and Mary were seventeen, and Victoria barely eighteen. Yet *none* of my sisters were forced to wait through *three* seasons. You are resigning me to become an old maid, Mama. Surely you can lift this antiquated rule."

"It is not antiquated." Mama continued to weave her needle skillfully through the layers of white linen. "As the family of a vicar, we will apply ourselves to the propriety of our tradition." She paused in her sewing and looked up at her youngest daughter, locking Cassie with the green-gold eyes several of her children had inherited—Cassie included. "You are not on the shelf, my dear, and a lovely girl like you will have no trouble securing a good match after you debut."

"It is not *my* match I am worried about." Cassie heard the tightness in her voice and prayed again for calm. "Only that I have to wait for *her* to make one first. A prospect which seems less and less likely every passing year."

"You are being unkind to your sister."

"She controls my destiny!"

Mother lifted her eyebrows and cocked her head. "And now you are being blasphemous. God controls destiny—every soul is counted as the sparrows." Her expression softened following the reprimand, and she settled her sewing into her lap, a kind of surrender showing in the relaxing of her shoulders. "You *must* have more faith, Cassie, and greater compassion. Lenora will find the right man through the hand of Providence when the time is right—just as your sisters have and just as you will. You'll see."

"She will not even *go* into society anymore!" Cassie threw her hands into the air to emphasize the enormity of this fact. Had Lenora not gone to their sister's home for the afternoon, Cassie would never have spoken so boldly to her mother. Cassie truly did not want to hurt Lenora's feelings, but Lenora was *not* there and Cassie could no longer restrain the passion of her soul.

Last year Cassie had made a similar argument on a similar afternoon, but she had been nineteen, and it was only the start of Lenora's second season. Mama had assured Cassie that Lenora would make a match that season and *this* year would be hers. The prophecy proved false, and Cassie had since entered the third decade of her life. Her increased age, and the attention of a certain man in town, had spurred her anxieties to the point of confrontation. Cassie was determined to be heard this year, but Mama was giving little consideration. There was only one option left: increased fervor. Whatever calmness Cassie had mustered was cast to the wayside as she allowed the contained passion to flow freely through her veins.

"Sitting at home and playing that insufferable pianoforte day and night will not find Lenora a husband, Mama, and so I am to be relegated to spinsterhood, despite—as you yourself said—my charms that would recommend me so well to the very company she despises. Under the circumstances, I find it unfair that I am not allowed to debut until she is married. She and I could be out at the same time, and my future would not be on hold as it has been these last *three* years while I have waited for her to secure a match she does not seem the least bit eager to pursue!"

Mama put her sewing aside completely and the lines of her face became hard. She'd heard enough. Cassie prepared herself for punishment while wondering if her having been born the daughter of a vicar was a sign that God had a sense of humor. Her independent nature was a trial for her parents, who put great stock in their family being the paradigm of proper manners and virtue. Their determination was an increasing trial for *her*.

"Now you are being cruel." Mama's voice was as sharp as her gaze. "You will go to your room, transcribe the fifth book of Matthew, and present it to me and your father before dinner. It is the meek and the mild who will inherit, Cassie, not the argumentative and unkind."

Cassie should have lowered her head in a show of humility, but she was fuming and her head would not bow.

"Mama," she fairly growled.

"To your bedchamber before I think of another punishment you most certainly deserve! I have listened to all the argument I can stand, and I have said all I am going to say. See that you return in time to help set the table."

Still clenching her teeth, Cassie turned on her heel and stormed up the stairs. When she reached her room, she slammed the door so hard it shook the walls, and the watercolors tacked to the walls trembled. One of the straight pins she used to hold them up fell to the floor, leaving that particular painting askew.

"It is not fair!" she said to the windows of her bedchamber. Her fingers itched to pick up a brush and easel and transpose her feelings on paper—harsh lines and raging colors. But if Cassie didn't present the Bible chapter by dinner, there would be an added penalty. Mama might even forbid Cassie from attending dinner at the Mortons' tomorrow night. The Wiltons always dined with a family of the parish on Thursday evenings. Cassie knew she had already put her invitation at risk by addressing her mother so vigorously. The swirling storm began to ebb, yet part of her wanted it to remain. There was a certain comfort in raging against injustice.

"It is still not fair."

Cassie crossed to her writing desk and removed the well-worn Bible from the bottom shelf. Every Wilton child received an individual Bible at the age of twelve—the same age Jesus was when He addressed the scholars in Jerusalem. Cassie had made a cover for hers out of a scrap of royal blue silk and embroidered an elaborate cross and her name on it in silver thread. Usually the bright color cheered her, but today it may as well have been the drab black leather cover beneath the embellishment for all the joy it gave her. The book of scripture was well used; today was not the first time she had been required to transcribe chapter and verse. She lifted the front cover and turned the thin pages toward the first Gospel of the New Testament.

The Wilton girls—all *six* of them—were raised with the understanding that having one daughter out in society at a time would ensure full attention on each during her debut, allow the family to better bear the expenses of turning out a daughter properly, and keep the sisters from being competitive with one another during any given season. Such consideration was sensible for a modest family with so many daughters. Reasonable. Cassie would even say that as far as general policy went, the rule was *fair*. But if ever there was a reason to make an exception, it was *Lenora*.

Lenora had been out since Rose had married two and a half years ago. Though lovely, talented, and well-bred, Lenora had never enjoyed society events and often declined invitations. While Cassie ached to wear beautiful dresses and attend garden parties and soirees, Lenora worked herself into such a fit of nerves every time she was forced to accept an invitation that she would end up with a headache or stomach pain, which usually necessitated an early return from the party. Six weeks ago, she had vomited just after stepping down from the carriage at the Carters' ball. She had been brought straight home, but a significant number of guests had seen her disgraceful act. She had not attended a single event since.

Cassie was sympathetic toward Lenora's anxious nature and hopeful that the hand of Providence Mama had cited would bring a kindred spirit, albeit male, into her life. But when? After three years, the passing of her twentieth birthday, and Mr. Ronald Bunderson's increased attention, Cassie's patience had run out.

Last week in town, Mr. Bunderson had asked Cassie if she would be going to the Dyers' ball. There was usually one ball a month in Leagrave or Luton during the season, and anyone of marriageable situation and genteel birth received an invitation. Cassie, however, had to tell him that she would not be attending. All the way home, she'd fantasized of what it would be like if she *were* going.

Why did she have to be the youngest of six daughters? Why did all five of her older sisters have to acquiesce to her parents' rules? Why could she have not been born a boy? Her brother Christopher was one year older than she was, and Harold two years younger, yet *they* were not dependent on Lenora for their destinies. *They* could attend school and see the world and seek their own futures. It was not fair.

Cassie reached chapter five of Matthew's Gospel. Some years ago, she'd decorated the page with a vine of ivy that wrapped around the edges of the text. The artistry did not bring her any joy today. What did margin drawings matter when yet another season would pass her by? The walls of the vicarage became smaller by the month, it seemed.

Dancing.

Mr. Bunderson.

Gowns.

To be the one invited.

To be seen as a woman in her own right, not just the vicar's youngest girl.

Cassie wanted to flirt and sip lemonade and dance with Mr. Bunderson. She was ready to become a woman of the world and secure her future.

But instead of batting her eyelashes and sharing coy glances with handsome men, she was in her room, writing about the poor in spirit who would inherit the earth. She didn't care about inheriting the earth. She only wanted a pair of dancing shoes, inherited or otherwise. Did that make her so very wicked?

Chapter Two

The night of the Dyers' ball marched closer. Cassie did not bring up the topic or even remain in the room when the conversation turned in that direction. She was being treated unfairly and made sure her parents knew her displeasure by adopting a pouting disposition whenever in their company.

To distract herself from her continued irritation, Cassie settled into a routine. Spring weather in Bedfordshire was moderate but unreliable at best, so when it rained, she painted watercolors of the vibrant landscape awakening with the season or worked on the green ruffle along the hem of her striped day dress in hopes the extra splash of color would brighten her mood. When the skies were clear, she rode the old mare, helped with the needs of the parish, did her chores around the vicarage, visited her two sisters who lived in the village, or tended to her nieces and nephews.

Twenty years old and life had not changed a drop since she'd stopped her formal schooling at the age of thirteen. How had the stagnation of her circumstance not driven her completely mad before now? A young woman's priority in life was to secure a match, and although Cassie had learned every household skill and proper manner required for such a pursuit, she was shut up in the vicarage waiting for Lenora to clear a path.

For her part, Lenora kept to herself as she always had and played her pianoforte as she always did. The only times Lenora left the house were to visit one of their sisters' homes for an afternoon. Once a week, she taught pianoforte to Victoria's ten-year-old daughter.

Lenora spent the most time with Rose. They were only a year apart in age and shared a similar temperament—shy, soft-spoken, and pious. Rose had married Wayne Capenshaw—a yeoman farmer—two and a half years ago and was increasing with her first child. Lenora visited Rose nearly every day under the guise of helping her with household tasks.

On the afternoon of the Dyers' ball, Lenora was home, playing Beethoven's *Pathetique Sonata*. Cassie felt the heavy tones could only make Lenora's anxiety worse. The mournful music certainly did nothing to improve Cassie's mood. If only Lenora would play Mozart instead, surely the livelier notes would improve her mood rather than darken it.

Around five o'clock, Mama came into the parlor, dressed and ready for the ball. She wore a silvery purple gown with a silver turban sporting two ostrich feathers that floated lazily in the air when she moved her head. Though still pouting and sulking, Cassie could still appreciate her mother's striking presentation—but was careful not to say so. "Young is awaiting you in your bedchamber, Lenora," Mama said. "We shall need to be on our way by six."

Lenora looked slightly pale as she rose obediently from the piano bench and took heavy steps toward the stairs as though she were walking to her execution. Cassie shook her head in irritation and focused on the sketch she was doing of the window and curtains. It was too cold for her to find distraction out of doors. Her long and miserable walk that morning had proven that too well; Cassie was still trying to get warm.

She thought about the evening ahead of her, and it soured her all the more. There would be something simple for dinner at the vicarage—soup or something equally bland since it was only Cassie in need of the meal.

Cassie would eat alone, and then sketch or sew or read in the drawing room alone. Maybe she would work on the handbag that matched the new ruffle on her dress, only she'd been working on the embroidery for a week now and her enthusiasm was waning.

In earlier years, Cassie had often spent such evenings playing games with her brothers, but they were both away at school. All of her friends in the village—every one of them—would be at the ball. It was tempting to resurrect the argument from two weeks ago now that she and Mama were alone in the parlor, but it would be useless. The acceptance of the invitation had been for three, and Mama was unrelenting once her mind was made up. Papa said that Cassie and Mama were often at odds with one another because they were of similar temperament, but Cassie did not see it. She would never be so unbending as her mother. Never.

Cassie looked from her sketchpad to Mama, who had settled on the other side of the fireplace. She had picked up a piece of knitting while she waited for Lenora and Father to get ready. Scarves and gloves were still a welcome item in the spring, and Mama filled one of her duties as the vicar's wife well by keeping members of the parish in constant supply.

Mama was a handsome woman. She had borne ten children, eight of whom had survived infancy. Her thick brown hair was peppered with gray, but it added distinction to her features, and her eyes were as clear and snapping green as they had ever been. She was nearly fifty years old, and had worked harder than most women of the class into which she'd been born, but continued to look regal and aristocratic. Especially when she was dressed for an event such as this one.

Cassie sometimes wondered if Mama regretted marrying a clergyman, which had lowered her station—Mama's father had been a landholder of some distinction—but Cassie felt guilty as soon as the thought entered her head. Her parents had fallen in love, and nothing else had mattered.

Ever. Perhaps Cassie could be as blessed . . . if she was ever given the chance to enter society.

Mr. Bunderson would be at the Dyers' ball. He would dance all night, but not with her.

"You *could* help your sister," Mama said.

"Young can get Lenora ready well enough." Cassie had never helped Lenora before, and it felt too cruel to consider helping her sister prepare for an evening Cassie was forbidden from enjoying.

Cassie returned to her sketchpad, wishing it was six o'clock already so she might be alone after all. Her own company was preferable to the tension she felt in her parents' presence of late. If the fireplace in her room were larger she would spend more time shut away from everyone.

"I didn't mean help Lenora prepare for the evening," Mama clarified, settling her knitting in her lap. "At least not in regard to hair and dress. What I meant is that you have the confidence she lacks. I have been thinking of the discussion we had regarding tonight's ball and have wondered if you could encourage Lenora to hold herself in such a way that will keep her discomfort from taking over, especially as this is the first event she will be attending after the Carters' ball and her embarrassment there. That you have been keeping your distance from her has not gone unnoticed by any of us."

Cassie keenly felt the accusation of her mother's comment, but reminded herself that she did not deserve *all* the blame. She and Lenora had never been close. Then again, they had never been *this* distant.

"Or," Cassie ventured, "you could let me debut so that I might serve as her companion at these events. I would be far more helpful to her if I could advise in a moment of need."

Mama let out a breath and returned to her knitting without saying another word.

Cassie returned her smug attention to the sketch where she began to add the feather-soft lines of the sheer curtains that fell in graceful folds beside the diamond-paned windows. The unique architecture of the vicarage—built nearly a hundred years ago and meticulously cared for ever since—presented endless scenes worthy of sketching.

After a few moments of self-satisfaction regarding her clever comment, Cassie's hand began to slow as her thoughts began down a different road, one unexplored amid her fits of frustration.

Could I help Lenora?

She rested her pencil in her lap and stared unseeingly at the unfinished drawing before her. Cassie was comfortable around strangers and felt buoyed up by crowds. Lenora, on the other hand, preferred small parties with familiar people, if she had to socialize at all. She would never find a husband that way, but what if Cassie could help Lenora overcome her anxiety? What if, instead of pouting and grumbling, Cassie helped Lenora make a match? That would free Cassie to pursue a match of her own.

The idea came with a rush of invigoration, an eagerness to do something—*anything*—to change the situation she found herself in now. The possibility that Cassie could take action of any kind on her own behalf was like taking a breath after holding it as long as she could.

Cassie put her sketchpad and pencil on the end table and rose without saying anything to her mother. She did not want Mama to take credit for this decision. Mama's eyes followed her across the room, however, and Cassie rankled at the sense of victory she felt emanating from the other side of the room. Such victory wasn't as important as what Cassie was going to do, however, and so she refused to let Mama's ownership of the suggestion dissuade her.

Cassie headed to the second floor in search of her sister. Embarking on this new plan felt something akin to crossing enemy lines, but the end justified whatever means, humility, and effort were required on her part. Her parents were stubborn and unbending, but *she* would prove herself just the opposite by helping Lenora do what she could not do on her own.

Chapter Three

When Cassie was a child, the vicarage had been bursting at the seams—three sisters to a room while her two brothers shared a room—and it had been impossible to find individual space, which was what often drove Cassie to find activities outdoors. Now that only Lenora and Cassie lived at home, the house sometimes felt overly spacious. The sisters had their own bedchambers—for which Cassie was grateful—but as she approached Lenora's door, she wondered if their physical distance had led to loss of intimacy and affection. The consideration increased Cassie's determination to help her sister if she could. It was exhausting to feel so bitter all the time.

Cassie knocked on the door, and Lenora gave the invitation for her to enter in an anxious voice. Young was fastening the buttons of Lenora's dress—the mush-colored one Cassie had thought ugly when she'd first seen it two seasons ago.

When each Wilton daughter had her season, she was outfitted with a reasonable selection of gowns and accessories that would present her appropriately. Typically Mama sewed the family's clothes, but not when it was a daughter's season.

Lenora had met with a dressmaker, a milliner, a glover, and a cobbler and yet had ended up with what Cassie considered the most lackluster wardrobe she'd ever seen—a wardrobe that Lenora had not added to in two years beyond a few things Mama had made. All the gowns Lenora owned were in muted shades with minimal trims and adornments.

This particular dress looked as though it should be either white or gold but had gotten stuck in-between. It had a high neckline, tulip sleeves, and an unadorned hem that brushed the floor. The string of pearls at Lenora's neck only managed to enhance the plainness. She looked like a sheaf of wheat, and in an instant, Cassie knew exactly how to help her sister. Cassie not only possessed confidence and manners, but her love of color and design could do Lenora some good. Hadn't Cassie thought so a hundred times? Now was the time to act upon her God-given gifts for her sister's benefit. And, ultimately, her own.

"You should wear Victoria's pink ball gown with the sheer sleeves," Cassie said as she approached.

Lenora wrung her hands while looking from her reflection to Cassie's, her eyebrows pulled together. She said nothing.

"Remember the ball gown Victoria wore during her season? With the silver rosettes and sheer sleeves." The older sisters often left a few gowns behind for their younger sisters' use—dresses they would no longer wear for one reason or another in their married lives. The styles were sometimes outdated by the time a new sister was ready, but Mama would change the neckline here, or fashion a new sleeve there, and another sister would get her turn with a dress the family did not have to pay for. Victoria's pink dress was both lovely and timeless—Cassie had had her eye on it for years—but it was not something Lenora would consider for herself.

"I couldn't," Lenora said, shaking her head nervously. "It is too fine and hasn't been fitted."

"You are near enough to Victoria's measurements that it would fit,

I think, and you *are* going to a ball. You won't feel out of place in a ball gown at such an event as that."

"It is too . . . bright."

Cassie laughed. "It is the color of Mama's lilies and perfectly appropriate."

"It would be . . ." She looked at the floor and took a breath. "Noticed."

The sincerity of her comment pricked at Cassie's heart. "You are *supposed* to be noticed." Sympathy rose in place of the judgment that had clouded her vision for so many weeks, and she realized how cruel she had been for considering only her situation. Though she'd come up here for her own benefit, she felt her heart turning. She truly wanted to help Lenora for her own sake.

Young stepped back from the mush-colored dress, and when Cassie met the maid's eye, Young nodded her agreement. Cassie was glad for the support.

"May I be honest with you, Lenora?" Cassie asked, cocking her head to the side and looking deeply at her sister.

Lenora paused as though the question required great consideration, but then nodded.

"This dress"—Cassie waved her hand up and down—"does not flatter you."

Lenora's cheeks instantly reddened, and Cassie hurried to stave off the embarrassment she had inflicted. "I know you like the dress because it does not stand out, but I fear it draws *more* attention to you than another dress more appropriate for the occasion would. A ball is a formal event, and though there will certainly be a spectrum of presentations, you want to look your best, don't you?"

Lenora looked down at the dress as though aware of its lack for the first time. Cassie met Young's eyes and gave her a quick nod. The woman who served as kitchen, chamber, and personal maid to the household turned and left the room. The pink gown was kept in a wardrobe in their brothers' room with a handful of other gowns Lenora had never even looked at.

"I feel so . . . *loud* in colors," Lenora admitted, and Cassie felt an additional rush of tenderness for her sister. Despite Cassie's irritation, whatever Lenora felt was real inside her own head and heart.

"*You* are not loud," Cassie said. "And I think you will feel more comfortable if you present yourself like the rest of the girls."

"What if I disgrace myself again?" Lenora glanced from beneath her lashes and then let out a heavy breath, dropping her arms to her sides in surrender. "Oh, Cassie, I can't stand this type of evening! All those eyes on me feel like knives. I know everyone thinks me quite addled. The stupid vicar's girl who cannot make decent conversation. I feel as though I might fall from the edge of a cliff at any moment."

Cassie lifted her eyebrows. Could a ball truly feel so menacing? It was exciting to have people notice you, compliment you, want your company. How could those things be painful? But Lenora's sincerity testified that this was exactly what she experienced. Cassie reached for Lenora's hand and led her to the window seat beside the rain-streaked glass. They sat, facing one another. "What is it, exactly, that is frightening? Can you separate the specific portions that feel threatening?"

"I don't know," Lenora said, shaking her head as she looked at her hands now pleating the mush-colored dress. The fabric was soft with age and no longer held the crispness of its original design. The softening likely made it more comfortable to wear, but it did nothing to improve the appearance. "I feel as though everyone knows I do not fit, that everyone wishes I hadn't come. I feel so very judged, especially after what happened at the Carters' ball."

"Such fear of judgment is not true. And everyone is ill from time to time. I'm sure that is all they think—that the evening was an unlucky one for you. The Carters' ball is a distant memory if it is a memory at all for anyone there. Everyone loves you, Lenora. Your gentle spirit is acknowledged and appreciated among our friends and family."

Lenora wiped at her eyes. "If I am behind a piano or in my own home I am well enough, but when I walk into a room, I am like a simpleton who can't find words or manners so I say nothing at all rather than risk saying the wrong thing."

"I'm sorry it is so difficult," Cassie said, more sincere than would have been possible half an hour ago. "I wish I knew a way to help you."

The comment seemed to soften Lenora's fears, and she looked up at her younger sister. "You do?"

Cassie nodded, saddened that her treatment had led Lenora to question their sisterly affection. "You're my sister. I would do anything I could to help."

Young returned with the pink ball gown draped over both arms.

Lenora immediately began wringing her hands, her brows pulled tightly together as she inspected the dress as though she had to eat it rather than wear it.

"Just try it on," Cassie said, standing and pulling Lenora to her feet. "If it does not fit well enough, you don't have to wear it, but I think you'll find yourself feeling *more* comfortable when you are equal to the others in attendance. And I am sure the color will brighten your mood—color always does for me."

Lenora was hesitant, but with Cassie and Young encouraging her, she surrendered without a fight. The dress was somewhat tighter at the bust than it had been on Victoria, but Cassie downplayed Lenora's complaint—every asset must be employed this evening, even if she was a vicar's daughter. The dress was also an inch too long, but Young found a pair of shoes in the back of Lenora's wardrobe that had a thicker sole than the typical dancing slipper.

Cassie loaned Lenora her pearl headband and helped set it in her hair. Young avoided the rather severe bun that was often Lenora's style of choice, and instead created a softer chignon that, even to Cassie's critical eye, was perfect for the shape of Lenora's face and eyes. By the time they had finished, it was too late for Lenora to argue her way into a different choice.

Lenora stood before the looking glass and bit her bottom lip. She looked entirely different than she had with her dowdy hairstyle and mush-colored dress. The pink brought out her blue eyes—like Papa's—and matched the color in her cheeks.

"You look beautiful," Cassie said in a quiet voice.

Lenora started to turn away, wringing her hands. "I don't think I can—"

Cassie took Lenora's shoulders and faced her directly. "You *are* beautiful, Lenora. And smart and good and kind. Any man would be lucky to have your attention tonight." Not for the first time, Cassie found it odd that Lenora was the older of the two.

Lenora looked at her like a desert flower, desperate for rain. "Do you really think so?"

"I know so," Cassie said with a nod and a smile, hoping her words might sink into the root of Lenora's fears. When Lenora's brow smoothed and the smallest glimmer of a smile appeared upon her rosebud lips, Cassie continued. "Now, in addition to knowing that you look beautiful and are equal to every woman there, remember to be mindful of your breathing—don't hold your breath when you feel nervous. "

Lenora let out the breath she had already been holding and nodded, eager for the advice from her younger sister with no society experience.

"And smile." Cassie smiled by way of example. "Not only will you feel more comfort, you will have the added benefit of helping to put those around you at ease as well. Everyone will be nervous tonight; your calmness will be a blessing to all."

"Breathe and smile," Lenora said as though the words were a Bible verse she needed to memorize. "Breathe and smile."

"I have a very good feeling about this ball, and I cannot wait to hear all about it. You *must* come to my room when you return; wake me if I'm asleep." Cassie had never made such a request before, but she liked the idea of building a different relationship with her sister. They were both grown women now, and should work together for each other's good.

"Alright," Lenora said, nodding quickly and looking at herself in the mirror once more. She pulled at the flowing skirt, then took a deep breath and let it out slowly. "Breathe and smile," she said quietly to her reflection. She met Cassie's eyes and lifted her chin with the most confidence Cassie had ever seen in her before. "I can do this."

Chapter Four

Evan Glenside watched the footman fill his uncle's wineglass a fourth time and wished he could suggest it be his last. But up until a year ago, Evan had only known Uncle Hastings by name. He was actually Evan's great-uncle, and they had met for the first time when the man had shown up unexpectedly at the London accounting office where Evan worked as a clerk. In the year since, they had corresponded a great deal, and this was Evan's third visit to the estate that would one day become his own. Still, Evan did not feel comfortable enough to comment on the man's drinking.

Three heirs presumptive between Uncle Hastings's estate and Evan's humble circumstance in life seemed like secure insurance against Evan taking the position. However, the untimely demise of all three heirs over the last five years had changed Evan's future dramatically. He was intimidated, but grateful for the opportunity, eager to rise to his new circumstance, and heartened by his uncle's accepting nature. But he wished Uncle Hastings was not a drunk. A kind drunk, by any measure, and a good man, but a drunk all the same.

"You will enjoy the Dyers," Uncle said with the familiar evening slurring of his *Rs*. "They are good people with deep roots here in Leagrave.

Lady Dyer was a great friend of your late Aunt Lucy." He paused and stared into his wineglass, which he swirled to form a funnel in the middle of the glass. "A finer woman there never was—my Lucy." Like the slurred speech, Uncle ruminating about his late wife was familiar. The sentimentality would lead to tears in a few more swallows. "It's a shame you never met her."

"Indeed," Evan said. "I look forward to seeing the Dyers again. Remember, they had us to dinner last week."

"Oh, yes, last week."

Evan wondered if Uncle truly remembered it. He'd been drunk that night too. At the dinner, the Dyers had invited Evan to the annual ball they held prior to their exodus to London along with the other politically and socially obligated members of central Bedfordshire's upper class. Evan had accepted the invitation as was expected by his new position as the Glenside heir, but he wished he could have refused. Providence and tragedy had made Evan part of this society, and along with his inheritance of status, land, and a fine estate came certain responsibilities he was expected to fulfill. Therefore he would attend his first country ball among gentry even though he knew no one but the hosts.

"Are you sure you would not like to accompany me?" Evan asked, not for the first time. The Dyers had also pressed Uncle to come, but he'd refused them.

Uncle waved his hand through the air with great flourish, grunting in response. He shook his head, and some of the hair he had combed over his baldpate fell over his forehead. He pushed the wayward strands back, causing them to stick up like a rooster's tail.

Evan pinched his lips together to keep from smiling.

"Dancing is for the young." Uncle Hastings lifted his glass and drained the contents in a single swallow. The moment the glass hit the table, he beckoned the footman to fill it again.

Evan cleared his throat to draw his uncle's attention away from the burgundy liquid filling the glass. If his uncle would attend him to the ball, the regular routine of drinking himself unconscious in his study would be thwarted for a night. "The Dyers said there would be cards for those men—and women, I suppose—who are not inclined to dance. I plan to take a few hands myself in order to meet some of the local men." Stating his goal of the evening aloud made him want to run for London. Would these people accept him? Would they see him as out of place as he felt?

Uncle waved his arm through the air again. "Pish posh. There is nothing at such an event for a man like myself. Now, if my Lucy were here, well, then things would be different." He sighed, his eyes glossy. "Oh, Lucy was a magnificent dancer. Why, the first night I saw her was at a ball back in '85. She was dancing a reel with my best friend, Malcolm . . ."

Evan remained at the table, listening politely to a story he had heard half a dozen times during his earlier visits. Uncle's feelings for his lost bride were certainly the reason behind his overindulgence. He seemed lost without her.

When Evan's father had passed twelve years earlier, Evan had felt a similar sense of loss from his mother, though she did not remedy her despair with liquor. The mother from Evan's youth had been buried alongside his father that day, and though the woman left behind was kind and dedicated to her children, she was not whole. There was sadness in her eyes and a slowness to her smile that reminded Evan of his responsibility as man of the family now. Mama may never find joy again, but he was dedicated to her comfort and the security of his sisters.

Evan's position as Uncle's heir provided greater prospects to his family than they'd ever have otherwise. That was why he would go to this ball among strangers who, a year ago, would not have met his eye on the street. He would go for his mother and for his sisters, and be grateful for the unexpected hand fate had dealt them all.

"Oh, Lucy," Uncle Hasting said after he lost his place in the story. He covered his eyes with one hand, but his trembling chin still showed.

Evan felt the man's regret, deep and heavy. Hastings and Lucy had been married for fifteen years and given up on ever having children. So Lucy's pregnancy seemed a miracle to them; a reward for years of Christian charity and devotion to each other. But then Lucy died in childbirth, and the infant had not survived the night. Lucy and their son were buried in a plot just west of Lucy's favorite rose garden on the estate.

Uncle Hastings visited their graves every afternoon before coming back to the house and pouring his first drink of the night. His glass would not be empty until he lost consciousness. It had been seven years since their deaths, but Uncle relived that sharp pain every day of his life. Though Evan had never met his Aunt Lucy, in a very odd way he missed her.

It was another ten minutes—and the last of the dinner wine—before Uncle pushed himself up from the table, teetering enough that both Evan and the footman stepped forward to steady him.

Uncle waved them off. "I'm keeping you, my boy," he said to Evan. "To the ball with you!"

Without waiting to see if Evan followed his instructions, Uncle turned toward the doorway that would lead him down the hall to his study and the decanter of brandy he kept there. When Evan had arrived at Glenside Manor three weeks ago to begin his permanent residence, Legget, Uncle's butler, was bearing the responsibility of helping his master to bed each night after Uncle passed out in his study.

Within the week, Evan had taken over the task. It seemed the least he could do. Legget was sixty years if he was a day, and though he resisted at first, once he understood Evan's sincere desire to be of assistance, he relented. Uncle had no idea that Evan was the one to help him every night, and Evan had not felt it necessary to tell him for fear it would embarrass his uncle to know.

Evan remained standing, listening for the door to Uncle's study to close. When the familiar click sounded, Evan turned his attention to the footman hovering in the hall. It seemed there was always some servant lurking about. Unnerving, really. "I shall return by midnight, Jeremiah, and help my uncle to bed."

"Yes, sir."

Evan made his way to the foyer. Jeremiah followed and assisted him into his coat and hat. Evan had to bite his tongue to keep from insisting he could dress himself. Would he ever get used to his loss of independence?

Worry for his uncle faded as worry for the night ahead rose. How Evan wished he were not going. In London, he had been comfortable with working-class people who preferred ale to wine and purpose to idleness. He and his friends made cracks about the aristocracy, the landholders, the rich—and now he was one of them.

A year ago, he'd been a clerk at an accounting office, he'd lived in a four-room house with his sisters, and he'd found an hour or two each week to work in what used to be his father's carpentry shop. The equipment belonged to Evan, but since his father had died before he'd been able to properly train his son in the craft, Evan rented the shop to a man with enough skill to make a living who did not mind Evan making use of the tools when he could. Evan enjoyed making a piece of simple furniture from time to time, but his hobby was frowned upon by the new society of which he was a part. Gentlemen did not work with their hands.

The memories of his former life left him hollow. Sometimes it seemed as though he had to give up everything that once made him who he was to become an entirely new person—*the heir*.

The heir had responsibilities.

The heir must act his part.

The heir was tired even though he had only just begun this journey.

It will get better, he told himself, though it was his mother's voice he heard in his head.

Jeremiah opened the door, and Evan nodded his thanks because Uncle had explained that it was beneath him to verbalize his gratitude to the servants. Evan stepped onto the porch and shuddered despite his many-caped coat Uncle had purchased for him in London. He bowed his head against the wind and hurried down the steps to the waiting carriage. It was too bad a ball could not be cancelled on account of the weather, though the icy rain that had plagued the day did seem to be easing. A garden party could be canceled for rain, Uncle had explained, but not a ball. Never a ball. Too much went into its creation, and the gentry would drive from miles to attend.

A warm brick had been placed on the floor of the carriage, reminding Evan that there were luxuries of this new life he appreciated very much. Hopefully the comfort would chase off the longing he felt for the life he had left behind.

The carriage pulled forward, and Evan took a deep breath, inviting calm and the ability to act well his part for the night. He would live in the small hamlet of Leagrave for the rest of his life, and in a few months— once the dowager cottage was set to rights—his mother and sisters would be joining him. The people he met tonight would be his friends and neighbors forever. He would one day marry and raise his family here. *This* world with its rules and expectations and, yes, comforts, would be all *his* children would ever know. He looked out the window and tried to focus on the gratitude of being in this place. He thrummed his fingers upon his knee.

Evan had been thirteen when his father died. Through the help of a benevolent cousin on his mother's side, he'd become an apprentice to a clerk at an accounting office. He didn't have the standing to attend University, but he worked hard to do his best and earn the respect of his colleagues. Now, twelve years later, he had been presented a new opportunity. So many people depended on him. Once again he was being thrust into an unfamiliar world. He would do his very best to be equal to it.

This would be his first ball, but it would not be his last. He had to find his place here, and the sooner the better.

Chapter Five

Evan's new boots pinched his heel. He had eight additional pairs of shoes at Glenside Manor, three of which he had never worn. In London, he had worn the same pair of shoes for two years at a time. Such comparisons were heady.

"It is a pleasure to meet you, Mrs. Holdsworth." He straightened from a bow he hoped was elegant and smiled in a way that he hoped hid how out of place he felt.

The woman of quality smiled before turning to the young woman standing beside her. "Allow me to introduce my daughter, Margaret."

"Pleased to meet you, Miss Holdsworth." Evan bowed again, only over the young woman's hand this time.

He had expected a country ball to be a small affair made up of snooty people. He could not have been more wrong. First, he'd never been to such a large event in his life; he felt sure he'd met a hundred people to-night. Second, the distinction between the few titled and obviously wealthy guests and the typical genteel class was not nearly so pronounced as he'd expected. Beyond that, they made a lively group. No one sniffed in boredom or acted as though it were a privilege for the hosts to have them.

Rather they were gracious to their hosts, eager to see old friends and, in his case, make a new one.

"I am pleased to meet you as well, Mr. Glenside," Miss Holdsworth said, looking up at him with such unabashed interest that his neck became hot. Amid the other unexpected aspects of this evening was the interest the young women—and their mothers—had in meeting him.

In London, Evan had been considered an eligible bachelor among the third class of society. He worked for a living, but with his mind not his hands. He was not too fat or too thin, nor were his teeth askew or his nose too pointy. He did not dress with great flair, nor did he comb his hair in a Brutus or some other style of the day, but he was no worse turned out than many other bankers or lawyers. Beyond those recommendations, he did not put his foot in his mouth often, nor did he have a tendency to ogle young ladies, laugh too loud, or gossip, gamble, or drink too much.

A handful of women in London had showed their interest in him over the years, even though he had not been inclined to marry until his younger sisters found good situations. However, he had *never* encountered such eagerness from such lovely ladies as he'd had tonight. Knowing that the attention was due to his new status gave it an air of artifice, but he did not have to wait for his sisters to marry now. He could support the family of his birth *and* a family of his own at the same time.

After so many years of putting the needs of his family before his own, however, it felt selfish to consider his own interests. Never mind that he could now consider a match with women who had been out of reach just a year ago. Women who would never have solicited his attention back then.

Miss Holdsworth blinked and cocked her head coyly to the side. Was it his imagination, or had she also pushed her bosom a bit higher?

The opening strains of a dance began, and Evan was glad for the diversion. He had made it through a quadrille and the minuet already, then spent an hour in the card room, where he'd met a handful of men. Mr. Ronald Bunderson had been particularly welcoming and was near Evan's age. He had suggested they hunt pheasant together, and Evan had agreed, though he'd never fired a gun in his life. He'd eventually left the card room to face dancing again. Running out of words seemed as good a reason as any to take the floor a third time.

"Would you care to dance, Miss Holdsworth?" At least it was a country dance. He'd danced a lower version for years, and it would not take nearly the concentration the earlier dances had demanded.

"I would be honored," Miss Holdsworth said. She *was* pretty, with a nice smile and eyes the color of hazelnuts. Could he imagine himself married to her? It bothered him to know that if he asked her she would likely say yes even though they'd only just met. He was a wealthy man, or would be one day, and that was all the recommendation a great many people needed.

Evan masked his thoughts with a smile as he led Miss Holdsworth to the floor where they took their places with the other dancers. Before he'd come to Leagrave, Mr. and Mrs. Mundy had tutored him on etiquette and dance. They lived in the same London parish as Evan and had been in the service for a titled family. He made a mental note to send them a letter expressing his thanks. Without their help, he could never have felt this confident on the dance floor—country dance or not—or at the dinner table for that matter.

The dance began, and Evan managed the first few minutes rather well. He unobtrusively watched the other men and tried to imitate the way they held their chins up, raised their knee higher here, dropped a shoulder there. They did hold better form than he was used to from the dances he'd attended in London.

Evan was feeling good about his skills until he went left when he should have gone right, colliding with a woman who let out a squeak of alarm. He reached out to steady her, only to be kicked from behind by another dancer who had not seen him fall out of form.

The woman immediately moved to find her place again. Evan looked for where he was supposed to be and tried to ignore the heat shooting up his neck.

Miss Holdsworth nodded to her left, her eyes wide with embarrassment, and he quickly ducked back into place, but his heart was racing and he could feel the looks from the other dancers.

You recovered well, he told himself, but the tension remained. *No one will fault you for missing a step.* But it was the simplest dance he knew, for heaven's sake! Many of the other guests were aware of his humble place in society before coming here. Some of them likely disapproved of his rise, and he hated to validate any objections.

Chin up. Smile. Try not to draw additional attention.

When the dance finally ended, he breathed a sigh of relief and escorted Miss Holdsworth back to her mother.

"Would you care to join us for a glass of punch?" Mrs. Holdsworth asked.

"Thank you," Evan said, thinking fast, "but I am promised elsewhere for the next set."

Both women frowned, and he felt a prick of guilt for the white lie but restated his regrets. He also thanked Miss Holdsworth again for the dance and her generous patience with his mistake. She kindly said that everyone missed a step now and again, which he appreciated. However, he still needed escape. Just for a few minutes.

Once he extracted himself from the women's company, he scanned the room for any doors that would lead outside, hoping the Holdsworth women would not notice when he did not take the floor for the next dance.

It was cold on the veranda, but the heat of the ballroom coupled with the heat of his embarrassment made the chill a welcome relief. The earlier rain was gone, and the cooler temperatures seemed to have kept the other guests inside. All the better.

Evan took a garden path and soon found himself at a fork. He was still near enough the house that the path was illuminated by the light pouring from the numerous windows. The direction he could see led to a bench beneath an arbor threaded with vines and climbing foliage bright with spring. But the bench was in view of the house, and Evan needed to hide. He took the path that wrapped around the back of the arbor only to find the same scene—another bench beneath another arbor. No, it was actually the same arbor. Back-to-back benches with a bramble of foliage to hide the one from the other and a canopy that protected both benches from the earlier rain. This bench, however, was out of view of the house. Private, removed, and perfect.

"Praise the heavens," Evan murmured as he took a seat on the cold stone, rested his elbows on his spread knees, and dropped his head in his hands. He could renew his energy, recover from his embarrassment, and restore his confidence.

As the minutes ticked by, the tension drained from his shoulders, and he found the idea of extending his reprieve more appealing than returning to the ballroom. He fell into a rather virulent argument with himself regarding whether or not to return at all. He looked at his pocket watch: 11:15. He had ordered his carriage to be ready at 11:45, which meant he had half an hour left before he could make his excuses to the hosts and leave.

But how should he spend that last half an hour? If he returned to the ball, he would have time to dance another set, but with whom? He couldn't ask any of the girls he'd danced with already. The attention would seem too particular. The other girls he had been introduced to earlier in the evening had since blended in his mind to the point that he could not sort one from another.

He could play more cards and shore up his acquaintance with the men. But was half an hour enough time to spend at the tables? Would making a short appearance be worse than making no appearance at all? Were there rules about that sort of thing?

Mr. Bunderson had been dancing last Evan saw him, having also thrown over the card games for companionship of a gentler kind.

Evan shook his head. Would he ever feel as secure in this new world as he'd felt in the one he'd known before?

Footsteps on the path caused him to go perfectly still. No one knew him well enough to come looking for him, but would anyone come out in the cold for another reason? The steps paused—likely at the spot where the path forked. To go right would lead the interloper to the first bench; to go left would bring the person around to where he sat.

Go right, he said in his mind. *Please go right!*

The newcomer seemed to have read his thoughts—or preferred to avoid the more shadowed portion of the garden—and moved to the other bench.

Evan surmised through the cadence and softness of the step that this new arrival was a woman. He was glad that her choice of the other bench meant he did not have to explain himself or attempt awkward conversation, but he was also rather stuck. Returning to the house would bring him in view of her. With his new understanding of the manners and expectation of the noble class, might he create some question regarding her virtue or his character if they were found together?

In his past life he would expect to explain the situation and suffer some jeering from his friends. Amid these new customs he had no such assurance. Things were so formal, so certain and proper. Surely this woman would rest a few moments, be overtaken by the cold, and then return to the ball. All he had to do was wait.

Two minutes. Three. After *five* minutes, he was reconsidering his situation. His carriage would be ready soon. If he didn't appear, would the coachman ask for him? He'd never had his own carriage but assumed that since he had said to have the carriage ready for him by 11:45 it would be ready by 11:45. Would his waiting carriage interfere with other people's carriages if it was parked for him out front? Might he cause all kinds of havoc if he didn't arrive precisely when he said he would?

His anxiety was rising when his company—who did not know she was his company—sneezed.

Evan looked over his shoulder, and though the wooden scaffold of the arbor was mostly covered with foliage—wisteria, he thought—he could see a few gaps. An elbow moved on the other side of the arbor, startling him—an elbow clad in pink satin with a sheer cuff of some kind. The woman was very close to him, perhaps three feet away. If *she* looked through the same gaps he had found, she would see him. What would she think of him having sat silent as a church mouse for five full minutes? Could he explain that he was trying, as best he knew how, to be a gentleman?

She sneezed again, then sniffled. Was she . . . crying? Raised in a noble class or not, Evan knew what was proper when a man encountered a woman in tears. Besides, if he did not make himself known, and she realized he'd been there all this time, he might find himself in quite a predicament. Hoping his chivalry would work in his favor, he reached inside his coat and pulled out a handkerchief, one of a dozen his mother had given him before he left London. Mama had embroidered each one with his initials in one corner. He shook it out, took a breath, and then turned toward one of the larger gaps in the arbor. He cleared his throat to reveal himself.

She gasped and he cringed. He was most certainly doing this all wrong.

"I beg your pardon, miss." He stretched his hand through the gap between their two benches. He could think of nothing more to say so held his breath until the scrap of cloth was taken from his hand.

"Thank you," a soft voice said.

It was a pleasant voice, a kind voice, and he felt a shared sympathy with the woman behind it. They had both made their escape only to find themselves alone . . . together. "Forgive me for having not revealed myself when you first arrived. My name is Evan Glenside. I was unsure what to do when you came upon me. There are so many bits of etiquette I don't fully understand." He winced at his lame attempt at explanation and shook his head in self-reproach. He was more eager than ever to get back to his drunk uncle and put this evening behind him.

"I . . . I am Lenora Wilton."

He didn't think he had met her tonight. If so, then they had not had a proper introduction, which was vital. Without one, they should not be speaking to one another at all. Evan was muddling everything. "I was just leaving when you arrived but worried I would frighten you if I made myself known."

"Please don't let me keep you." She sniffed again.

"Are . . . are you all right?"

"Yes, thank you," she said nervously. "P-please do not stay on my account."

Evan was still unsure what to do but increasingly anxious that his carriage was already waiting for him in the drive. If only he knew the rules of how he was supposed to behave in such a situation. "Are you sure you are well, Miss Wilton?"

"Please do go in. I am well, and thank you, again."

Feeling as though he had no other course, he stood and made his way back to the house. When he reached the fork, he looked back and saw the skirt portion of a pink gown with silver roses. Miss Wilton's face was hidden by the arbor, but it was just as well. He doubted he would remember anyone from tonight well enough to recognize them later. Though he could appreciate her desire to be alone, he feared she was freezing in only a ball gown. He would tell the Dyers about her in case she needed aid.

As he reached the steps of the house, Evan squared his shoulders. Lifted his chin. Took a deep breath and let it out slowly while reviewing all the things he had done *right* tonight. He had made his first public appearance, presented himself well—for the most part—and made himself known to the society of this place. He had met any number of women, young and otherwise, played cards with the men, and been given a genteel welcome. The one dance had not gone perfectly, but it could have been so much worse. And, best of all, the entire event was now over.

Regardless of the night's imperfections, Evan would never again have to attend his first ball in the town he would now call home. That was something to be grateful for.

Chapter Six

Country balls were known to last until the early hours of the morning, but the vicar's family rarely stayed so late. They were always home by two o'clock in the morning, or earlier if Lenora's nerves got the better of her. Cassie had high hopes that her advice to her sister would help her through this particular evening and was therefore disappointed when she heard the carriage arriving home just after midnight.

Cassie quickly blew out the candle she'd been reading by even though Mama would have seen the light already. She listened to the sound of movement and hushed conversation downstairs, then footsteps moving upstairs and along the hall until she heard two bedroom doors open and close. Only when the hallway had been silent a full minute did Cassie get out of bed and tiptoe across the hall to Lenora's room. She had told Lenora to come to her, but her eagerness to hear about the ball made Cassie unable to wait. She slipped into the room, startling Lenora, who was sitting at her vanity. She had removed the pearl headband and begun taking the pins from her hair; Young would help their mother before she would attend a daughter.

"How was the evening?" Cassie gestured for Lenora to stand and then began unfastening the buttons down the back of the gown. They had once helped each other in and out of dresses on a regular basis, but Cassie couldn't remember the last time either of them had asked the other for assistance.

"It was lovely," Lenora said, stepping out of the dress.

Cassie laid the gown over the foot of the bed and began working to release the high stays. Lenora could likely have managed on her own—all the Wilton girls were embarrassingly self-sufficient—but as Lenora was not waving her away, Cassie continued to help.

"Did you feel sick?" Cassie asked.

"No," Lenora said, with enough surprise in her voice that Cassie moved around to face her.

"You didn't?" Cassie asked. "But you're home so early."

"Papa was the one who felt ill." She grinned.

"But *you* were well?"

Lenora nodded quickly, then looked around as though someone might overhear them. She leaned closer to Cassie and spoke in a whisper. "I met a gentleman."

Cassie slapped her hand over her own mouth to keep from shrieking. Lenora smiled wider than Cassie thought she had ever seen her do before, not even when presented with a new piece of music.

Once Cassie could contain herself, she grabbed Lenora's arm and led her to the window seat. "Tell me *everything*," she demanded.

"I did what you said and focused on my breathing and keeping a smile on my face. I didn't expect it to come to much, only hoped it would keep me from being ill."

Cassie nodded quickly and waved for Lenora to continue.

"So what happened first was that Mr. Capenshaw asked me to dance—he is always so kind."

Wayne Capenshaw was their brother-in-law, and with Rose unable to dance due to her pregnancy, it did not surprise Cassie to hear that he had sought Lenora out as a partner.

Lenora continued. "Then Rebecca Glanchard sat beside me and complimented my dress. I told myself we were just at church and talking beneath the yew trees while we waited for our mothers. I didn't think of anyone watching me, and I felt so much better!" She put a hand on her stomach, making Cassie realize that Lenora wore only her shift, but they were sisters so it was of no matter. "I had butterflies, of course, but not the snakes roiling around in my belly like I usually do. We took some refreshment together, spoke with some other ladies near the tables, and then went back to where Mama and Rose were sitting. After a while, Rebecca was asked to dance." Her smile fell. "And then I felt conspicuous because I was sitting alone—Mama and Rose were on the other side of the room talking with Mrs. Burbidge, who is so overbearing I couldn't imagine approaching them and having her turn her attention on me. I didn't know what to do, and the butterflies got so heavy I decided to go into the garden to clear my head. No one had ventured out due to the cold, and I was glad for the solitude. I sat on a bench, still in view of the house, and it was a lovely reprieve until I realized it was wisteria along the arbor above the bench."

"Wisteria?" Cassie asked. Who cared about the wisteria? When would they talk about the gentleman?

"I'm terribly allergic to wisteria, you know."

"Oh, yes," Cassie said, though she did not know that about her sister. Or at least, if she had known it she'd forgotten.

"And so I sneezed." Lenora smiled as though her reaction had been a happy surprise. "And when I sneezed a second time, a handkerchief was suddenly thrust toward me from behind the bench. A hand came out of nowhere." She punched her hand forward as though demonstrating. "Just like that."

Cassie pulled her eyebrows together, terribly confused. "A handkerchief from behind you?"

Lenora nodded quickly. "I had not realized there were actually *two* benches separated by the arbor. A gentleman had escaped the ballroom just as I had and was sitting on the bench behind me." She put a hand to her chest and shook her head. "Of course I was horribly embarrassed to realize he'd known I was there while I did not know *he* was there, but I accepted his handkerchief through a space in the arbor and thanked him and he apologized for not revealing himself."

Cassie waited expectantly for several seconds before she realized that Lenora was finished. "Is that all he said? Did you speak to him face to face? Is he handsome?"

"He was such a gentleman," Lenora said with an accompanying sigh. "He could have easily just sat there, taking his repose and letting me sneeze like a cat, but he didn't. As someone who well understands the difficulty of social events and the need for solitude now and again, I am touched by his generous nature."

"That *is* wonderful," Cassie said, but inside she was shaking her head. This is what Lenora called "meeting a gentleman"? This was nothing.

"He had such a lovely voice, Cassie. Low and smooth. I wonder if he sings."

Sings? "But you were not introduced to him? You do not know his name?"

"His name is Evan Glenside, nephew of Mr. Glenside and recent heir to the estate. He is here to become familiar with the estate and the village so as to be in a better position to inherit when the time comes."

So they *had* conversed beyond the exchange of the gentleman's handkerchief. "He told you all of this on the bench?"

"Oh, no, I told Mama about him when she came to find me, and she asked Mrs. Preston. It seems he is a most eligible man." Lenora's eyes sparkled.

"Yet he hid in the garden." This meeting was far less impressive than she had expected. Then again, hadn't she wished for the hand of Providence to bring a man as socially awkward as Lenora into her view? Perhaps Cassie had received *exactly* what she'd wished for.

Lenora nodded, her eyes twinkling. "He is unused to this level of society, that is what Mrs. Preston says, and does not know many people. There was also some unfortunate turn in a dance or something." She shrugged her shoulders. "But look at this."

Lenora hurried to her dressing table where she picked up a white square of fabric. She returned to the window seat and handed the handkerchief to Cassie. Cassie held it gingerly; it had been given to Lenora for necessary reasons, after all. It was an ordinary handkerchief, not coarse but not overly fine, and no lace edge. The initials EGJ were monogrammed in gray thread in the corner.

"Did you ever get to see his face?" Cassie asked, setting the handkerchief between them. What if he were a troll? Lenora was allowing her emotions to carry her too far.

"Only briefly," Lenora explained, still grinning. One would think she'd been kissed under a full moon for how excited she was about sneezing beneath an arbor. "We were collecting our cloaks and gloves when a man was leaving the vestibule. I'd never seen him before. He nodded toward us briefly and then left. After he was gone, Mrs. Preston came to find us and tell us that she'd heard Mr. Glenside had just left, perhaps we had seen him? And so we *had* seen him. What remarkable providence that we were all there at the same time, don't you think?"

Cassie kept smiling politely and looked at the handkerchief. Remarkable providence? Not nearly. *But it* is *progress*, she told herself. Comparatively. It would be counterproductive to Cassie's goals to be the least bit discouraging. She must help Lenora make the most of this. With those objectives in mind, Cassie felt a plan developing.

"And so you must return Mr. Glenside's handkerchief." She lifted a hand and tapped her chin. "I don't believe Papa has yet made his welcome visit to Mr. Glenside. If he were to do so tomorrow, perhaps we could attend with him. Then you could properly thank Mr. Glenside for his kindness to you."

Everyone knew Mr. *Hastings* Glenside. He owned one of the larger holdings of land between Luton and Leagrave and was well respected, even if he kept his own company and didn't interact with the village very often. She had heard he had a nephew who would inherit the estate, but knew nothing else about him—certainly not that he was unmarried.

"Oh, I couldn't," Lenora said, standing quickly and snatching the handkerchief from between them. She looked at it longingly, then glanced at her sister. "It would be so forward."

"It's not forward to call on a man who left you with a token," Cassie said. "It is good manners."

"But it would seem as though I were using his kind gesture as an excuse for an introduction."

"Yes, that is exactly how it would seem because that is exactly what you would be doing. Father or Mama visit every new member of the parish. You'll just be attending with them—we both will. You are not trapping him, only returning what he so generously loaned you in your time of need."

Lenora started pacing, clenching the handkerchief tightly in her hand. "I couldn't," she said. "It wouldn't be proper."

For heaven's sake! Cassie forced herself to take a breath and find another approach. "So you would *keep* his property instead? His *monogrammed* property, no less. You would decline an opportunity to thank him for his kindness and instead *steal* his handkerchief?" She tsked and shook her head as though disappointed. "That does not seem charitable to me, Lenora."

Lenora stopped pacing and stared at the stolen article. Cassie could fairly hear the thoughts looping in her sister's head. Afraid she might press too hard if she stayed, and hopeful that Lenora would choose the better course if she were not forced to defend herself, Cassie stood. She crossed to her sister and gave her a quick embrace. When she pulled back, she smiled. "I know you'll do the right thing. I shall see you in the morning. Congratulations on a most excellent evening."

She left Lenora standing in the middle of the floor, staring at the handkerchief and, quite likely, searching her soul. Cassie smiled all the way back to her room.

Chapter Seven

The next morning, Cassie slept later than usual. She assumed that because of the ball the entire family would sleep late—except Father, who never did—and took her time getting ready. She threaded a red ribbon through her braid before wrapping it into a bun. The red ribbon matched her favorite red shoes that went rather boldly with the sky-blue dress she'd chosen to wear. Sometimes the beauty of a thing was best noticed through the contrast of its accessories.

But the main reason she took her time was to give Lenora ample opportunity to be convinced of the only good and proper course regarding Mr. Glenside's handkerchief.

Cassie could see exactly how things would play out: Once Lenora chose to do the right thing, she would talk to Mama, who would explain to Papa the need to visit the Glensides and convince him to take his family along. Lenora would return the freshly laundered handkerchief and share her stuttering thanks for the younger Mr. Glenside's generosity. The awkward Mr. Glenside would be so charmed by sweet Lenora that he would court her for a few weeks, decide it was silly to waste time, and propose marriage. Lenora would make a lovely bride—perhaps in June, or even May. By fall, Cassie would be allowed to attend local social functions, and in the spring, she would have her official debut. By this time next year, she herself could be engaged. To Mr. Bunderson, perhaps, or maybe another gentleman who caught her eye or whose eye she caught. All because Cassie had decided to help her sister. Truly, service *was* good for the soul.

By the time Cassie came down for breakfast, several platters had already been cleared; apparently she had dawdled too long. She had settled herself with some toast and jam when she heard Lenora's pianoforte. There was a rule about no music before 9:30 and just as Cassie had supposed, it was exactly 9:30. That Lenora had chosen Mozart seemed a good omen.

Cassie finished eating and found her sister in the music room. Gone was the easy hairstyle of last night's ball and the tight bun was back in place—though it *was* braided. Improvement was improvement. Lenora wore her light-green morning dress with the high ruffled neck and long sleeves. It went well with her eyes, at least.

Lenora finished the piece and looked up at Cassie, who was sitting across from the instrument. She gave Cassie a nervous smile and straightened her sheet music.

Cassie's eyes narrowed. Something was wrong; something Lenora was nervous to talk about.

"Lenora?" she said, unwilling to beat around the bush. "Is everything all right?"

"Everything is just as it should be," Lenora said, tapping her papers into place. Her eyes gave away her lie, however.

Cassie cocked her head. "You are acting strange."

Lenora took a deep breath and finally met Cassie's gaze with a guilty expression. "Please don't be cross with me."

"Why would I be cross with you?"

Lenora looked away. She played a single chord on the pianoforte.

Cassie stood and took a step closer to the piano. "Why would I be cross, Lenora?"

Lenora moved her hands from the keys to her lap. She did not meet Cassie's eyes. "I asked Papa to take the handkerchief back for me," she said quickly. "He shall go this morning after he finishes his work at the church office."

Cassie clenched her jaw while Lenora's words continued to pour out of her. "I thought a lot about what you said, Cassie, and you were exactly right that not to return Mr. Glenside's handkerchief would be a great offense. I was so ashamed at having considered keeping it—so mortified by my lack of character—that I couldn't sleep. I rose this morning and washed and pressed the handkerchief myself then begged Father to take it to Mr. Glenside first thing as part of his official parish visit."

Cassie lowered herself into a chair and tried to smooth her expression. "If *you* had returned it, *you* would have been able to be introduced to the man."

"It felt wrong." Lenora shrugged her slim shoulders. "To use his kindness as an excuse to ingratiate myself is disingenuous."

"No, it isn't," Cassie said, losing patience. Frustration edged her words. "It would have been *courteous*. Now he will think you didn't want to meet him."

"No," Lenora said, though she didn't sound convinced. "He will simply know that I am not out to manipulate his goodness."

Cassie took a deep breath and let it out over the course of five counts but feared it was not long enough to keep her ire in check. "Have you not considered, Lenora, that Mr. Glenside will be highly sought after now that he has presented himself to the society here?" Her voice rose in pitch, and she did not try to remedy the terseness. "And if you take just two seconds of thought, you will realize that there are a great many women who will pursue him this time of year as many of the bachelors are heading to London for the Season. Mr. Glenside was kind to you, he left you with a token, and you have slapped away the chance to use it as an opportunity to know him better." Filled with indignation, Cassie stood from her chair and began pacing. "You say that crowds make you ill, but here was the chance to meet Mr. Glenside without anyone but the people who love you best in attendance and you ruined everything!" She threw up her hands. Her perfect vision of the future—*her* future—shattered like glass, the shimmering shards of what was once beautiful shooting in every direction.

When Lenora didn't respond, Cassie stopped pacing and faced her, only to find Lenora's chin trembling and eyes swimming with tears. Cassie's rant dissolved on her tongue. A little.

"I knew you would be cross." Lenora stood and fled the room.

Cassie should go after her, but what for? Lenora had bungled everything. Who knew when she would accept another invitation for an event where Mr. Glenside would attend, and by then both Rebecca Glanchard and Margaret Holdsworth—eighteen years old to Lenora's twenty-*three*—would most certainly have found a way to make his acquaintance. He would have no lack of admirers now that his situation was known throughout the village. That he had sought refuge in the garden at the Dyers' ball just as Lenora had—and then left the ball early—showed that he was uncomfortable too. The shared discomfort could have been a place for them to build a relationship with one another. Instead, he would get a visit from the local vicar who would hand him the handkerchief as an aside topic of their meeting and every opportunity would be lost.

In nearly three years of eligibility, Lenora had only ever shown interest in one man. This man—Mr. Glenside. If no one intervened, she would throw this opportunity away, and who knew when she might have another. Surely if she remained unmarried in another two or three years their parents would have to consent to let Cassie have her debut—but she would be the same age then that Lenora was now. Not on the shelf, *yet*, but competing for attention with girls five years her junior. Mr. Bunderson would surely have married by then. Such thoughts made the edges of Cassie's vision shimmer with frustration.

"I shall be an old maid forever," Cassie grumbled as she left the music room and climbed the stairs to her bedchamber as though crushing each step underfoot. Her mother's words rang back to her: *"You could help her."*

Cassie snorted as she entered her room and closed the door behind her. She *had* helped, and Lenora had rejected the perfect opportunity to further her acquaintance with an eligible man! "She needs far more help than I could give her," Cassie said to her paintings. Still fuming as she crossed the room, her eyes fixed on her writing desk and her mind spun toward a new possibility.

Was there another way she might *help* her sister?

With a slower step and a more focused mind, Cassie moved toward the desk. She ran her fingers across the worn wooden surface while a new—and rather desperate—idea began to build itself brick by brick in her mind.

A slow smile spread across Cassie's face. The confidence Lenora needed would only come through success gained through action she was too nervous to take. Cassie, however, could take that action and write letters on Lenora's behalf.

She sat at the writing desk and extracted a fresh sheet of paper.

The first obstacle would be learning to write in Lenora's same hand, but for a woman of artistic talent who could draw nearly anything it did not seem too much of a challenge. The second obstacle would be the delivery of the letter without her parents' or Lenora's knowledge. Young could help there; she was a trusted confidant among the children and had protected Cassie from trouble with her parents before.

Cassie would have to confess after the exchange of just one or two letters, enough to intrigue Mr. Glenside and give Lenora the feeling of being "known" by him. Cassie would be disciplined for her deception if her parents learned of it, but if that confession came on the heels of a young man's interest in Lenora, who would come alive in her letters . . . well, then, Cassie would accept whatever penalty might come. And once her penance for the act—not quite a sin since her intent was good—was complete, Cassie would have the chance to truly live her life.

Dancing.

Gowns.

Mr. Bunderson.

Oh, and Lenora's happiness, of course.

Chapter Eight

When Evan had come to Leagrave a few weeks earlier with the intent to stay on permanently, Uncle had surprised him with his own desk in his own study. The area had once been a sitting room that connected with Uncle's study, so a few mornings a week, the men worked with the door open between their spaces, Uncle visiting with his steward, housekeeper, or solicitor, while Evan either studied past ledgers or helped Uncle with matters of accounting. His history as an accounting clerk made him feel capable of at least part of this responsibility. Uncle's solicitor had even complimented Evan's attention to detail and fine hand.

Today, Evan was in his study—sparsely furnished with the desk, a nearly empty set of shelves, and two chairs that faced the desk—reviewing a county farm report. He would share the more pertinent details with Uncle before the weekly meeting with the steward tomorrow morning, where they would forecast the upcoming season. Evan could hear his uncle scratching about with his own records, or perhaps correspondence, though Uncle seemed too solitary for much connection to other people.

Evan had finished his breakfast and written to his mother before Uncle appeared on his side of the door. He asked after the ball the night before, and Evan gave him an honest report: fine company, excellent music; thank goodness the awkwardness of his first social event was complete. The men returned to their work, but Evan noted that Uncle was unusually subdued. Perhaps he had drunk more than usual the night before.

Evan heard a knock at the front door and greetings exchanged in low tones. Uncle didn't receive many visitors, and Evan listened as Legget showed the visitor to the drawing room and then came down the hallway toward the men's studies. Evan continued working on his report.

"Mr. Wilton to see you, sir," Legget said, entering Uncle's room.

"What business would the vicar have with me?" Uncle grumbled.

"He is also here to see Master Evan."

There was a pause, and Evan straightened in his chair. A visitor for him? From the local vicarage?

The name Wilton was familiar, but it took a few moments before Evan remembered that he'd shared a bench with *Miss* Wilton last night in the Dyers' garden. Was her father the vicar? Evan had told Lord and Lady Dyer about Miss Wilton being in the garden prior to his leaving the ball last night. They had thanked him and said they would see that someone make sure she was well. He hadn't done anything wrong, had he?

Uncle appeared in the doorway between their offices. "Seems we have to make the pretty," he said darkly, his mouth pulled into a scowl. "Shouldn't take upwards of ten minutes or so, I should think."

"I'm happy to meet the vicar," Evan said, hopeful that acting enthusiastic would improve Uncle's mood regarding the visit. "I didn't have a chance to meet him last night." He stood from the desk and followed his uncle through the study to the hall and into the drawing room.

A thickly built man with a round face and blue eyes stood when they entered. He wore the simple black coat and white neck cloth of the clergy, and Evan realized he had seen this man as he was leaving the ball last night.

"Good morning to you, Mr. Glenside," the vicar said to Uncle Hastings before turning to Evan. "And to you, Mr. Glenside. Welcome to our fine county."

Evan shook the man's hand in turn and thanked him for the welcome.

"My apologies for not making your acquaintance last night at the Dyers' ball," Mr. Wilton said as the men took their seats. Uncle called for tea. "I'm afraid I was having some trouble"—he put a hand on his stomach—"necessitating that we leave earlier than planned. However, we were glad to catch a glimpse of you, Mr. Glenside, as you raced into the night."

Evan smiled, though he had a difficult time reading Mr. Wilton. He was kind enough, and welcoming, but there was a reserve about him as well as an aura of judgment. Perhaps that was not too surprising; he was clergy, after all.

"I hope you are feeling better," Evan said, wondering if the man should be making calls if he were unwell.

"I am, thank you," Mr. Wilton said, nodding. "Nothing a good night's rest and a good breakfast couldn't remedy. I'm glad to have found you both at home so I might introduce myself." The vicar reached into his coat pocket and extracted a square of fabric. "I do believe you met my daughter last night, Mr. Glenside. She asked that I return this to you— washed and pressed—with her sincere thanks."

Evan took the handkerchief from Mr. Wilton. He hadn't expected a return, necessarily, but certainly not the day after the ball. Miss Wilton must have prepared it first thing this morning. Was there some unwritten rule amid the gentle classes that dictated a prompt return of a proffered handkerchief?

"Thank you," Evan said, placing the perfectly pressed square on his knee. How much did Mr. Wilton know about his exchange in the garden with Miss Wilton? Should Evan be apologizing for something?

Before he could determine the proper protocol, Mr. Wilton turned his attention to Uncle Hastings. Evan noted the tiniest bit of tension enter the vicar's face.

"And how are you faring, Mr. Glenside? We miss you at services."

Uncle bristled, and Evan found himself instinctively tensing as well. "Don't waste time waiting on me to show. I haven't been back and I won't be," Uncle said with a snort at the end.

"I understand," Mr. Wilton said, smiling though it didn't look completely natural. "But I want you to know you are always welcome."

Uncle narrowed his eyes. "I don't want your welcome, Vicar."

Mr. Wilton did not seem surprised. "Yes, well, it is my job to extend the invitation."

"It's not your job to be pressing me."

Mr. Wilton looked at his knees, perfectly lined up side by side.

"When are services?" Evan said before the vicar was forced to defend himself again. Evan had never heard his uncle talk to anyone so harshly, except perhaps the servants after he'd had too much to drink. "I can't promise weekly attendance, but I would like to become familiar with the congregation. My mother and sisters will be joining us in a few months, and they are faithful churchgoers."

"The congregation would embrace you and your family, Mr. Glenside," Mr. Wilton said with a relieved smile.

Uncle snorted, causing Mr. Wilton to tense again. He kept his eyes on Evan and continued. "Services begin at ten o'clock on the Sabbath. We have a children's class on Tuesday afternoons, choir that evening, and a study hour on Wednesday evenings."

"A study hour?" Evan had never heard of such a thing. "What do you study?"

"Themes found in the Bible, mostly," Mr. Wilton said. "Some parishioners bring their older children to teach them to read the language, and then we have open discussions about ancient practices and how they transpose to our daily lives."

"Do you discuss Job?" Uncle said.

Mr. Wilton and Evan both looked at him.

Uncle continued, glaring at Mr. Wilton. "Do you talk about the way God made a deal with the devil and ruined the life of a good man? A worshipful man?"

Mr. Wilton cleared his throat uncomfortably. "We have discussed Job, yes."

Uncle kept his eyes fixed on the vicar. "And do you tell your congregation that we are all playthings in the hands of a callous God who wants nothing but His own entertainment at our expense?"

"Uncle," Evan said in surprise. He might not attend services on a regular basis, but he did not insult his Creator.

"No, it is all right," Mr. Wilton said. He seemed to pull himself up as he looked back at Uncle with confidence. "There is balm in Gilead, and Christ can help you bear your sorrow if you will but exchange your burdens for His."

Uncle's face began to redden and Evan shifted in his chair, but Mr. Wilton did not stop. "All He asks of us is a broken heart and a—"

"My heart *is* broken," Uncle hissed through his teeth, leaning forward in his chair. "My wife and child are dead, but I have received no solace or comfort or balm in all these years. You want me to come to church and worship a vengeful, hateful, and cruel God who would take the best a man has and sentence him to hell on earth?" Uncle rose from his chair, and Evan did too, hurrying to put a hand on his Uncle's arm. He'd never seen Uncle like this and feared he might strike the vicar.

"Uncle," Evan said quietly, "he means no offense to you."

"He offends me with every word he has ever said from that blasted pulpit!"

"Uncle," Evan repeated, with greater emphasis this time. He moved to block the vicar from view. "Why don't you return to your study. I shall finish conversing with Mr. Wilton and join you shortly."

Uncle finally turned his eyes to Evan, who forced a sympathetic smile in hopes of diffusing the stifling tension in the room.

Silence prevailed for several seconds before Uncle took a breath, looked at the ground, and then glanced at the vicar. "My apologies, Wilton. Not a good day for me."

Mr. Wilton gave a wavering smile as Uncle turned and left the room. Only when the door closed behind his uncle did Evan face the vicar.

"My most heartfelt apologies on behalf of my uncle, Mr. Wilton," Evan said, trying not to show his own embarrassment. "I'm afraid he has endured a great deal of pain."

"I did not mean to add to it," Mr. Wilton said, finally standing. "I have struggled all these years to find a way to connect with him, and perhaps help him connect with God once again, yet I continue to go about it badly, it seems."

Evan was quiet a moment as questions began to list themselves in his mind. He worried he would overstep a boundary he ought to know, but if Evan were going to make a mistake in etiquette, a vicar seemed likely to forgive him. "I don't know if you are aware that I only met my uncle a year ago, when the previous heir—his cousin—succumbed to a lung disease quite unexpectedly. I know very little of his life before now, and the only thing he talks about is my Aunt Lucy, and only then when he has had perhaps more to drink than is recommended."

"Your uncle is a fine man," Mr. Wilton said with a nod and softening expression. "I would daresay he and I were even friends up until Lucy's passing."

"But not after?"

"I tried to convince him to have them buried in the churchyard. Lucy was devout, and her family was buried there. Your uncle was not in a good . . . state of mind for the discussion and took great offense to my pressing, which I admit I took too far. He asked the vicar in a neighboring village to officiate. I took some offense to that and did not attend the funeral." He let out a heavy breath. "I have prayed mightily for forgiveness for my pride, and though I believe the Lord has forgiven me, your uncle has not. We are usually cordial with one another when our paths cross, but, as you saw today, there has been little healing between us." He was quiet again for several contemplative seconds, and then he met Evan's eye. "I also stand by what I said: God can help him find solace if only he will humble himself."

It took some effort on Evan's part not to bristle. It had never sat well with him when churchgoing folk acted as though every ill could be mended with a prayer and a smile. "I admire your concern for my uncle. Though he and I are only newly acquainted with one another, I have found him to be a kind, hardworking, and admirable man. He seems to enjoy my company, and I believe our continued relationship will improve him as time moves forward. I think . . ." He paused, unsure if he should continue. The eager eyes of Mr. Wilton spurred him forward. "I think my uncle is very lonely."

"Something the congregation could remedy as well."

Evan was unimpressed by the man's stubborn insistence that the church had every solution. "Obviously he is not prepared for such connections, but I do think my being here is a positive change for him. In a few months my mother and sisters will be joining us at his invitation. I believe it will help him to have family around him."

Mr. Wilton nodded. "I hope he might one day return to the church. Perhaps your mother and sisters will make a good change upon his habits."

Evan reminded himself that a vicar's occupation was to bring people into his fold and so he tried not to be offended by the man's determination to solve Uncle's problems with worship. What Uncle needed was genuine friendship. Maybe it was only Evan who could supply that for now. "I shall begin attending services when I can, Mr. Wilton, and you will find my mother to be quite pious. With any luck, our example might encourage him."

"I understand," Mr. Wilton said, seeming to accept Evan's subtle request that the vicar not press Uncle Hastings about church again. "If you ever feel that I might be of service, you need but ask."

Evan nodded his thanks and walked Mr. Wilton to the door. Once the door closed, Evan returned to the drawing room and saw the white handkerchief on the rug. It must have fallen off his knee when he'd stood. He picked up the cloth and wondered at Miss Wilton's eagerness to rid herself of his handkerchief. He did not wonder for long, however, and stuffed the article into his pocket before leaving the room.

Evan found his uncle at his desk with a glass of brandy in his hand. A bad sign as he rarely drank this early in the day.

"I have no place for God," Uncle said as he swirled the liquor in the snifter. He eyed Evan with suspicion. "And if you think you and Mr. Wilton will change my mind, you'll find our relationship much different than it's been thus far, my boy."

"You think I would conspire against you?" Evan said, raising his eyebrows. "I only stayed in that room to uphold the manners of your household."

Uncle remained suspect. "Did you apologize for me?"

"I did," Evan said. "But only after you apologized for yourself."

Uncle's brow softened, and he raised a hand to his forehead. He closed his eyes as his shoulders fell. "Wilton didn't know," he said softly, as though talking to himself. "He couldn't have known."

Evan furrowed his eyebrows. "Know what?"

"Today would have been the twenty-third anniversary of the day Lucy and I were married." He sniffled, and his eyes became glassy with more than the drink. "The days that should be celebrations mock me and pull me into the depths of despair." He scrubbed his hand over his face, then took a swallow of brandy.

Evan let out a sympathetic breath. His mother found such days equally difficult—Father's birthday, the day he died, their wedding anniversary. "I am sorry." Evan wished he knew how to help.

Uncle shook his head. "It's certainly not your fault."

"Nor is it Mr. Wilton's," Evan said, earning a glare from his uncle. "I could explain it to him, if you like. He told me of the disagreement you had when Lucy passed—regarding her burial. He regrets handling it as he did. He said you were once friends."

Uncle grunted and poured himself another drink. Evan stepped forward and when Uncle put down the bottle, Evan moved it to the sideboard, out of reach.

"It is a very fine day." Evan pretended not to notice his uncle's scowl or the way his nostrils flared. "Would you walk the grounds with me and tell me of my aunt? Perhaps we could put some flowers on her grave to mark this day."

The expression on Uncle's face changed from anger to surprise, perhaps even eagerness. Evan realized that though he had heard a great deal about Uncle's wife, he had never been the one to request the stories.

"Please, Uncle," Evan said, latching onto the possibility of this idea. "I can think of no better way to celebrate the joy you and Aunt Lucy shared."

Uncle rose from the desk, not even finishing his brandy, and moved to the door. "Let me change my boots. I shall meet you in the foyer in quarter of an hour."

Chapter Nine

April 10

Dear Mr. Glenside,

I was glad to hear that your handkerchief found its way to you without incident—my father assures me it was successfully returned—but I have felt unsettled since it left my possession for fear that I had not taken the opportunity to properly express my gratitude for your having lent it to me. I hope that your opinion of me, though limited due to our short connection, is not diminished in the boldness of my letter. However, it is an unfortunate matter of my character that I am very ill at ease with people in person, especially at crowded events, and until I feel known by them, and know their natures as well, I seem only able to adequately express myself in writing. Therefore I pray your forgiveness and understanding for any lack of manner this letter might reflect upon me.

On the night of the Dyers' ball, I found myself alone and uncomfortable in the ballroom, and so I made my way to the garden, only to fall prey to my nemesis of nature: wisteria. One would think that a girl so unfortunate as to have anxiety at social events would not be additionally cursed with such a negative reaction to a pretty flower, but alas my condemnations seem to have no bounds. Therefore my escape became another matter of discomfort, and your handkerchief became the greatest boon of the night.

I realize that you had also sought respite and yet you unveiled yourself in order to help me. Such compassion was most kind, and I shall ever be grateful for it. I would imagine a gentleman with such tender generosity is often at the ready to help a woman in distress, and perhaps you do not even remember how many times you have offered such aid, but I wanted to make sure you knew the change you made for me that night. Whereas I often leave events such as a ball with a pain in my stomach and gratitude for escape, that night I returned home to confess to my dearest sister, Cassandra, how very kind you were. It was a new and wonderful experience for me to be so invigorated at the end of an evening, and I have you to thank for such a change.

Though I have no expectation of a response to this letter, should you do so, would you kindly address your response to my maid, Edith Young, and have it delivered through the kitchen? My parents would not fault me in expressing myself as I have—though it would certainly surprise them—but they would tease me regarding communication with a gentleman and that is something I cannot bear any better than I can muster through the fair wisteria blossoms that so vex me.

Most kindly yours,
Miss Lenora E. Wilton

Evan read the letter over breakfast on Saturday the week following the Dyers' ball. The letter seemed unorthodox considering the social expectations he was trying to learn, but he could not ignore the sincerity of Miss Wilton's words, both of gratitude and her explanation for why she had been in the garden. That she wanted to avoid her parents' teasing was something else he could appreciate. He felt the pressure of his mother's hopes for him to marry and assumed what Miss Wilton felt was much the same.

Still, the letter surprised him. Evan had felt sure when he closed the door after the vicar's visit last week that the chance of furthering his acquaintance with Miss Wilton was at an end. The history between Mr. Wilton and Uncle felt too wide a gap to bridge, not to mention how uneasy Evan was regarding his recent elevation of position. And then Evan had been unable to attend church services the following Sunday due to some spring flooding in the lower field. Faced with such obstacles, Evan convinced himself that he didn't want to further the acquaintance with Miss Wilton anyway.

But then she was bold enough to write this letter, which he found refreshing. And she'd admitted her anxiety, which he could relate to. There was also something in the words on the page that expressed a different confidence than he expected from a girl who chose to hide in a freezing garden rather than dance at a ball. Though ill at ease in a crowd, she was *not* ill at ease in her letter and that intrigued him. So often since coming to Leagrave, he felt like one man on the inside and another on the outside. So often he felt as though no one, not even his uncle, knew, or truly cared, who he really was. This letter seemed a reflection of that same battle—someone trying to rectify two different parts of her person.

Would he also come across with greater clarity in a letter?

That she'd initiated contact seemed proof that such correspondence was not inappropriate. Would it be rude if he didn't respond? Dare he invite a worse opinion if it should become known that, following his uncle's bad behavior to the vicar, Evan had behaved badly to the vicar's daughter?

Evan folded the letter and tucked it into the inside pocket of his coat. He was riding out with the steward this morning to circle the fields, and he wanted to arrive early to the appointment so he could get comfortable in the saddle before they took the tour. He'd never ridden in his life before coming to Leagrave, and he envied men, like the steward, who seemed to take to horseback so easily.

He would revisit the letter with greater attention this afternoon. Perhaps by then he would have a better idea of what to do about it.

Chapter Ten

The Wilton girls had always helped on washing day, and since it was the time for spring cleaning, Cassie's help was required for longer than usual. Fortunately, the day was warm enough to allow line drying instead of filling the house with drying racks. At least that.

Lenora was in a pleasant mood, and the sisters talked more comfortably than they had of late. Cassie offered up the gossip from the village, and Lenora relayed more details of the Dyers' ball. At first the topic was awkward. The last they'd spoken of it, Lenora had run from the room after Cassie berated her for not returning the handkerchief. But now that Cassie had that situation in hand, she felt no ill will toward her sister. In fact, she felt internal satisfaction at being a better sister than even Lenora knew.

The sisters were hanging a sheet on the line while Mrs. Ashby, the laundress, fished a hot sheet from the washing pot when a man came around the corner of the house, startling the three of them. Lenora immediately stepped behind the hung sheet as though hiding.

"Beg yer pardon," the man said. He inclined his head slightly at Cassie, who had stepped forward. "I've a letter for Miss Young."

"Young?" Cassie said, instantly alert as she hurried to dry her hands on the apron of her skirt before taking the letter.

"Who's it from?" Mrs. Ashby asked with cheeky suspicion.

Lenora was nothing more than the bottom of a skirt and a pair of shoes beneath the hung sheet.

"Glenside Manor," the young man said.

"I'll see that she gets it," Cassie said with a smile. She gave a quick nod. "Thank you."

"See that she gets what?"

Cassie spun around to see Mama, holding a basket on her hip. Cassie blinked, feeling caught until she remembered that the letter was not addressed to her. "A letter, I suppose. For Young." She feigned boredom as she looked over the envelope. The script was very fine, with flourished curves and excellent form. It had to be from Mr. Glenside, and the idea filled Cassie with a nervous anticipation she could not allow her mother—or Lenora—to see. She slid the letter into her apron pocket with a shrug just as Lenora peeked around the sheet and let out a breath.

"I'll give it to her when we finish here," Cassie said, then took the basket from her mother. "Are these ready for the pot?"

Mrs. Ashby finished removing the hot sheet, and Cassie traded her the dirty linens in Mama's basket for the tub that held the laundered sheets. She moved toward the ringer and Mama followed. The work required two people to make sure nothing landed in the dirt.

"When did Young begin receiving letters?" Mama asked.

"I don't know," Cassie said, but her stomach tightened. She did not want to lie to her mother directly. Lenora fished another sheet from her basket and threw it over the line, silently glancing between them as the conversation continued. In her own way she was curious, Cassie knew, but she would not assert herself.

"Where was it from?" Mama asked.

Cassie pretended she hadn't heard Mama as she put the basket down on the table to which the ringer was bolted. "I hope the weather doesn't turn on us," she said, squinting up at the sky that, while overcast, was not heavy with rain clouds.

"Said he was from Glenside Manor, marme." Mrs. Ashby picked up the basket and dumped the dirty linens into the hot water. The women had worked together for so long that the movements were nearly a dance between them. She picked up the paddle and began to agitate the items.

"Glenside Manor?" Mama separated out the first sheet to feed through the machinery. "It's all the way on the other side of the village. Who would Young know from that house?"

Cassie tried to keep her breathing in check. "Surely it isn't any of our business, Mama. What interest do we have in who she knows from anywhere?"

Mama began to feed the fabric through the ringer, and Cassie turned the handle, which pulled the fabric through, squeezing out a great deal of water.

"As her employer, I most certainly do have interest. And as a family of the church, we have certain expectations beyond those of a typical house." The first sheet was finished, and Mama reached for another. "I shall speak to your father about it."

Cassie managed a laugh. "You act as though receiving a letter is a sin."

"If it is only a letter, then of course it is of no consequence, but we can all benefit—Young included—from reminders now and again of what is appropriate and what is not. Besides that, secrets can be destructive. I certainly won't pry into anyone's privacy, but your father and I deserve the assurance that those under our care are behaving as they ought. Now, Cassie, keep turning the handle."

Cassie did as she was told, swallowing the discomfort Mama's words presented. If Mama was this concerned about Young exchanging letters, what would she think of Cassie doing so? She reminded herself that she was doing this for the greater good, and she even dared think that her parents, in the end, would be impressed with her cleverness. But she would need to keep Young from getting in trouble as well. Already this was becoming more complicated than she'd anticipated. But surely that was only because she was so unused to deception.

It was another two hours before the sisters were dismissed. Lenora went to the music room—she practiced for hours every day—while Cassie hurried to her bedroom. She tried to ignore her scalded and aching hands as she removed the letter from her pocket. She looked over the script again and felt a rush of excitement until she remembered that this letter was meant for Lenora. Cassie was merely a facilitator.

Reminded of her role in this exchange, Cassie unfolded the letter and settled on the window seat to read what it was Mr. Glenside had to say in response to her letter . . . rather, *Lenora's* letter.

> *April 13*
> *Dear Miss Wilton,*
>
> *I thank you most kindly for your letter and wish to assure you that I did not in any way disapprove of your boldness. Rather, I found it intriguing enough to respond—as you can see. Finding myself in new society has been an unsettling experience, since until now I could always count myself among people I was acquainted with from my youth. I do not mean to disparage my situation—it is certainly a blessing for me to be in the place I am, and I am quite enjoying Leagrave—but it is very different from East London, and I have found it rather lonesome, though I enjoy my uncle's company a great deal.*
>
> *You rightly accuse me of having sought refuge in the garden*

the night of the Dyers' ball, and I am grateful for your explanation as to why you were there too. I feared my offer of my handkerchief had startled you and made you uncomfortable. Though I do not suffer the effects of spring myself, my mother is sorely afflicted. I worry how she shall settle into the country when she and my sisters come to Leagrave themselves, but I hope that the country air will be enough of a relief to compensate for any other discomfort. I am glad to hear that you are recovered so well.

I found your letter in very good humor, and it was restorative of my own spirits. I addressed this letter as you suggested in order to be certain you knew how appreciated your thoughts were on my behalf. I believe I saw you a few days ago in town, coming from the apothecary shop with another young woman— perhaps the sister you referenced in your letter? Cassandra, I believe. Were you wearing a blue bonnet, by chance? I believe your sister's bonnet was a straw chip with multicolored ribbons about the trim. Do you have more than one sister? I would hate to presume an identity and be incorrect.

Best Regards,

Mr. Evan J. Glenside

Mr. Glenside had seen them in the village? Cassie bit her lip. Why that should fill her with excitement she could not say. They always saw a great many people in town, but he had seen them without her knowing it. And she still had no idea who Mr. Glenside was since he had not come to services on Sunday, much to Papa's regret. Had Mr. Glenside watched the sisters for some time in town? Had he looked between the two and tried to figure out which was Lenora?

Upon reflection, Cassie remembered that Lenora *had* been wearing her blue hat the day they'd gone to the shops together, so Mr. Glenside had rightly guessed who was who. What did he think of Lenora's sister?

Had he referenced Cassie's bonnet—which she'd redone just last week—because he found it particularly fetching?

Cassie shook her head. That was of no consequence. What was important was that he had noticed Lenora. Cassie's plan was working!

She read through the letter again and then, knowing she would be undisturbed until dinner, she hurried to her writing desk. It would not do to appear too eager, so she would wait until next week before she sent the response, but she would write the letter today and date it for the future while she enjoyed every delicious moment of this adventure. Surely if Lenora knew how it felt to receive particular attention from a man, she would not let her anxiety keep her isolated. Cassie didn't know Mr. Glenside and wasn't even the true recipient of the letter and yet *she* was invigorated. She could hardly wait for the day when Lenora would feel like *this*.

Chapter Eleven

April 18

Dear Mr. Glenside,

I was so glad to receive your letter. My maid is most discreet and seems to find the role of secret envoy rather thrilling. That she has never expected this of me seems to lend greater assurance that she will keep our communication private. I have never had a secret before, and it is rather exciting. I appreciate you allowing our communication to continue in this way.

You asked after my family and so I shall explain. I am blessed with five sisters—four older and one younger—and two brothers set on either side of Cassie, the youngest girl, in birth order. My older sisters are married; two of them live here in Leagrave. My brothers are away at school, leaving only dear Cassie and myself here at the vicarage. It is strange having so much space after years of being packed in like a toffee box at Christmas, but I enjoy the improved privacy.

I am flattered that you noticed my bonnet enough to use it as an identifying aspect of my person last week. I was with my dear sister, Cassie, as you guessed. She is such a good friend for me, and she was indeed wearing a straw chip she adorned herself just the week before. She is an artist and adores color so much that she will often have some bright ribbon or flower of some sort about her person. You should know that she is the only person fully aware of my letters to you and therefore completely trustworthy should that be of any matter. She has just turned twenty years old, and I can only hope to be considered half as lovely and good-hearted as she is.

I am sorry to say I did not see you in the village that day, but I am often more focused on returning home than I am toward making acquaintances in town. Please do not take offense if I am similarly unaware of you in the future. I would appreciate your patience as I try to improve myself in this area. I feel that this exchange of letters is the perfect place for us to become acquainted with one another so that when we do meet in person, I shall feel as though I already know you.

I am particularly sorry for my personal limitations now that I know how lonesome you feel here. I could help to remedy that if I could get my own difficulties under better measure. I cannot imagine what it would be like to find myself in entirely new society. Why, it makes my heart race just to think of it. I imagine it is very different here than in London. I have only ever been to London to help Mama purchase items for my older sisters' weddings. It is such a big place, I cannot imagine how anyone can find their way about. You mentioned your mother and sisters—are they still in London? When will they come to Leagrave?

I understand that you are to inherit your uncle's estate and are currently helping with the management. What a good opportunity that seems to be, and I sincerely hope that you shall find improved comfort the more time you spend here. I wonder if you will be attending the May Day celebration on the first of May—the entire community is invited. It will be held in the pavilion of the churchyard, and my family helps with the serving. I might see you there. Pray forgive me if I act as though we are unknown to one another—I am the most vexing creature alive, I am sure.

I find myself wondering about you quite often and would love to know more about your work on the estate and what you do when you can pursue your own interests. For myself, I am a great lover of music and spend hours at the pianoforte. I am also very close to my older sister, Mrs. Capenshaw, who lives with her husband here in the village. I visit with her often. She will welcome her first child soon and being with her often makes me long for my own family one day. Until then I am quite content with improving my domestic skills such as sewing and household management.

Sincerely yours,

Lenora E. Wilton

Chapter Twelve

April 29

Dear Miss Wilton,

I apologize for the delay in this letter. I went to Manchester with my uncle on business and did not receive your letter until our return. I shall be certain to make an appearance at the May Day picnic knowing you shall be in attendance; thank you for the invitation.

In regard to church attendance, I assure you I am not a heathen, though you would not guess it since I have not yet attended services in Leagrave. It is my goal to be a more regular attendee as soon as I am better settled in. Spring seems to be a very busy time here in Bedfordshire, and I am attempting to keep up with all I have to learn about the management duties of the estate while also helping my uncle with a number of tasks the season presents.

I cannot imagine having so many brothers and sisters as you have, but it sounds as though it has been a blessing for you. As to my family situation, my mother and sisters will be coming to Leagrave by the end of the summer. I have two younger sisters—Camilla is seventeen years old and Natalie is recently turned sixteen. They live with my mother in London but shall be moving to the Dower House at Glenside Manor in a few months, once renovations are complete. Right now they are taking classes on etiquette and dancing. I hope they will be prepared for this new society once they arrive, though I wonder if classes alone are sufficient preparation.

My mother is remarkable. After my father's death, she took on printing invitations and such—she has a very fine hand—to make up for my paltry income as an apprentice clerk. I am eager for my family to join me here, and it is very kind of my uncle to have given them the invitation. He did not know any of us prior to my becoming the surprise heir to his estate, and he has been very generous and accommodating.

As to my interests and pursuits, I was an accounting clerk by trade and content with my place, but it seems the good Lord had a different course set for me. I am very grateful for this new opportunity. I am also rather good with my hands; my father was a skilled carpenter and taught me the basic points of that craft. Sadly, he passed away some twelve years ago. I find it difficult to fill the ache his loss left behind but have found satisfaction in my work since that time. Your father seems to be a good man. His visit was very generous, though I fear it was not very pleasant for him. I don't know if he would have told you about it, but my uncle was not quite himself that day.

I hope that one day I might listen to you play your music. If you devote hours every day you must be quite accomplished. I fear I have not had much exposure to great musicians, but I would be most eager for a change. I am artistically more familiar with design as it applies to the carvings I like to do in the evenings and such. I am impressed with how accomplished you and your sister seem to be.

I quite admire the solicitous connection you seem to have with your family. What a great blessing that is to you as well as a recommendation of your good character. It is affirming to know of your domestic pursuits; it is such an admirable application in a young woman.

I shall look for you at the social but will not press for an introduction since I know that might be difficult for you. A smile in my direction, however, would surely be welcome.

Yours truly,
Evan J. Glenside

Cassie had to pinch her lips together from squealing in excitement as she finished Mr. Glenside's second letter. The tiny spark of jealousy that his interest was so focused on Lenora was quickly doused with the acknowledgment that her plan was working. Better than she could have hoped. He was so candid. So open and comfortable talking with her . . . no, *Lenora.*

Cassie wished he had greater appreciation for music, since it was Lenora's greatest companion, but at least he was open to an education on the topic. His enjoyment of woodworking was interesting—it was not a typical gentleman's interest—and she appreciated that he felt secure enough to confide in her . . . well, in Lenora.

Another niggling of regret surfaced but rather than chase it into the corner as she usually did, Cassie decided to confront it. Yes, Mr. Glenside was a very kind, articulate, and interesting sort of man. Yes, if circumstances were different Cassie might have enjoyed getting to know him for her own interest rather than Lenora's. But circumstances were not different, and, should Cassie ever hope for the opportunity to get to know *any* man, Lenora must find a happy arrangement first. Every word she wrote was on Lenora's behalf, and therefore every word Mr. Glenside wrote in response was for Lenora's benefit, not Cassie's.

Besides, he could still look like a troll. She had yet to make his acquaintance, and although Lenora had said he was handsome, and the few people she'd heard comment about him had not said he was unattractive, he had also hid in a garden during a ball. Handsome men did not fall into such fits of anxiety.

If everything continued to go well, the day was coming when a face-to-face encounter between Lenora and Mr. Glenside would force Cassie to explain herself. Lenora would then read the letters intended for her. It was important that Cassie did not forget that fact.

She refolded Mr. Glenside's note and tied it, along with the first letter she'd received, with a ribbon she had taken from Lenora's room last week—Lenora's ribbon for Lenora's letters. Each time Cassie wrote a letter to Mr. Glenside, she made a copy for Lenora too. She was determined to present her sister with a full accounting. All of this was, after all, for Lenora.

For Lenora.

For Lenora.

For Lenora.

"Do not forget that," Cassie said to herself as she looked one moment longer on the stack of letters, and then pushed the drawer to her writing desk closed.

She allowed herself to revisit the fantasy of sitting beside Mr. Bunderson in the fall and sharing intimate conversation with *him*. Goodness, Mr. Glenside could be Cassie's brother-in-law by that time. The thought made Cassie's chest heat up; a good reminder that she must not entertain any tenderness toward Mr. Glenside. Her thoughts spun forward, and she wondered if Lenora would one day tell Mr. Glenside of Cassie's role in their relationship.

The idea made her heart race. *Why have I not considered such a thing before now?* The instant anxiety propelled her to her feet, and she began to pace from one side of the room to the other. She would be so embarrassed to have him know, and yet, she could not undo the connection now. It was too late. And he would only find out if he and Lenora made a match. But the fact that her plan was *working* had to be proof that there would be no negative consequences.

Cassie wished she had time to respond to Mr. Glenside's letter immediately. Unfortunately she was supposed to be at the pavilion helping to decorate for the social Friday afternoon—just two days' time. Young had delivered the letter with a sly grin just as Cassie was leaving the vicarage, which necessitated her hurrying to her room to read the letter that very minute. Now, however, she had to remedy her delay. The May Day celebration would be the first time Lenora and Mr. Glenside would be in each other's company since the beginning of the letter campaign. Thank goodness he was not expecting an official introduction, and yet he *did* hope for a smile from Lenora—a more than reasonable request.

Cassie smiled to herself. How hard could it be to ensure such a thing?

Chapter Thirteen

W here are you off to tonight, my boy?" Uncle asked as the footman served the dessert course. Lemon custard, it looked to be, and Evan's mouth began watering before he'd even spooned a bite. Genteel food was something he found no hardship in enjoying to its fullest.

"Mr. Ronald Bunderson invited me to a card game."

"Ah, yes, Henry's third son, I believe. Can't say I know him well, but Leagrave isn't such a big village as to *not* know anyone."

Evan had had almost this exact conversation last night when he'd told Uncle about the invitation, but Uncle had already been through a bottle of wine by the time they'd discussed it. He was only on his second glass so far tonight, however, which seemed promising.

"Seems an amiable man," Evan said. "We met at the Dyers' ball, and then conversed at length at the Yardleys' dinner party last week."

Uncle had been invited to last week's party as well but at the last moment said he did not feel up to the event. Evan had been uncomfortable going alone and had felt great relief when Bunderson arrived. By the end of the evening, Evan felt as though he was making good progress toward becoming part of this community. His origins had not been as much of a stumbling block as he had feared.

"You are welcome to join the card party, Uncle. The invitation was issued to us both."

"Only because I am the head of the house," he said, shaking his head. "I shan't crash a young man's party."

"His father will be there."

Uncle huffed but said nothing. Instead, he ate his custard, which Evan turned to as well. After a few bites, Evan broached a topic that had been on his mind.

"Uncle," he said, putting down his spoon. "This afternoon when David was showing me the tack shed, I noticed an antechamber connected to the stable. It held a variety of odds and ends but didn't seem to have a specific purpose."

"I can't say I know it off the top of my head."

"As I would expect, since its purpose is ambiguous. I asked the stable hand and he said it had been an office for the groomsmen until the new outbuilding had been built with better accommodations."

"Ah, yes, I do know the room, then. Must be used for storage now, yes?"

"Exactly," Evan said. "I wondered if I might . . . have use of it."

Uncle raised his bushy eyebrows. "For what purpose, my boy?"

Evan shifted slightly, wishing he was not so uncomfortable with this but determined to take this step of combining who he used to be with who he was now. Writing to Miss Wilton about his woodworking seemed to have awakened his desire to bring it into his new life here. "My father left me his tools when he died—I have since rented them out to another carpenter—but I wonder how you would feel about my turning that storage area into a shop. I should like to pursue the craft somewhat, if that would be acceptable."

"Carpentry?" Uncle said, leaning back in his chair. "A trade?"

"Not for occupation, no. More of a . . . a hobby, I suppose. My father taught me as much as a boy of thirteen could know, and I have spent what time I could manage to pursue it further these last years, but I should like to continue to use the skill. I realize it is not a typical pursuit for a gentleman, and—"

"I have no objection to your tooling about," Uncle said easily, returning to his custard. "Only I wouldn't like to see you setting up a shop or any such thing. To have my heir selling his work would be vulgar."

"No," Evan said, shaking his head and trying not to take offense at the inadvertent insult of his father's trade. "It would be for my own edification, that is all."

"Well, then, I see no reason the storage room can't be made to accommodate you. I shall have the grooms clear it out."

"I would be glad to clear it myself. In fact, I feel rather eager to do so."

Uncle looked up at him. "Why on earth would you want to do that? It's a filthy job."

"I don't mind working up a sweat from time to time," Evan said, smiling at how foreign the idea seemed to his uncle. "And then I could arrange the room just as I like." He also hated to add more work to the servants, who already seemed to do too much for the household. It would be nice to take on a task himself, with no help from anyone else.

"Huh," Uncle said. "Well, you shall need someone to attend to the reassignment of the items stored there, but I suppose if you truly don't mind the dirt and vermin and whatnot, I see no reason to prevent your taking charge of it."

"Thank you, Uncle," Evan said with a nod. "I appreciate your blessing very much." And he did. If Uncle had been uncomfortable with the idea, it would have been difficult for Evan to press him.

Uncle took the last bite of his custard and then gave Evan a thoughtful look. "Actually, what do you say to striking a bargain in exchange for that storeroom?"

"What kind of bargain?"

"Had you ever ridden a horse prior to coming to Leagrave?"

Evan cut out a bite of his dessert but did not lift the spoon. "I'm afraid there is little opportunity for horsemanship in Mile End."

"Yes, I imagine that's the case. I happened to watch you set out with the steward yesterday and thought you looked ill at ease in the saddle. You have been a very good sport about riding when it's been required of you, but I imagine you find yourself rather uncomfortable the next morning. When you live in the country, riding should be as natural to a man as walking."

Evan shifted and shrugged his shoulders. Indeed he was usually very uncomfortable after riding, but embarrassed to admit it.

"I shall agree to your use of the storage room and allow you to clean it out yourself, if you will allow me to offer you riding instruction."

"I don't mean to sound argumentative, Uncle, but riding instruction is for children."

"And for grown men who didn't learn when they were younger. You're a gentleman now, Evan, and will be required to ride for a great many activities. That you've been able to avoid it as much as you have thus far is surprising, but you don't seem to be improving much on your own. After this many weeks, you should not feel the saddle the next day."

"You will hire me an instructor from the village?" Evan said, making a face and feeling like a schoolboy. Would he become the topic of jabs and jeers when the working-class men gathered in the pubs at night just as he and his friends had done to the noblemen who crossed their paths in London? He could see jesting now as a way to equalize their situations with those of their betters, but he did not look forward to becoming the topic of such raucous discussions.

"No, I shall teach you myself. I think a few mornings over the next weeks will iron out the missing patches of education and lend to great improvement."

Having his uncle teach him was a much more attractive prospect. "And if I accept these lessons, I can have my wood shop?"

"Not a *shop*," Uncle corrected. "You might have your wood . . . room."

Evan smiled. "My wood room."

Uncle lifted his chin. "Yes, a woodworking room. In exchange for riding lessons that will save you a great deal of discomfort."

"Well, I can't see how I can lose in this arrangement," Evan said, spooning up the last of his custard. "I agree."

"Very good," Uncle said with a nod. He pushed back from the table. "Meet me at the stable at eight o'clock tomorrow morning."

"Eight?" Evan raised his eyebrows. Uncle was never up that early.

"Riding is best learned in the morning, before anything has spoiled the horse or the rider." He turned to Jeremiah, standing near the door. "I shall not retire to my study tonight, but please bring a single glass of brandy to the library. I should like to read for a time."

One glass of brandy? Evan wasn't sure his uncle could stick to such an ideal.

Uncle pointed at Evan while closing one eye. "Eight o'clock. Don't be late."

"Yes, sir," Evan said with a crisp nod. "Eight o'clock."

Uncle paused on his way from the room and turned back. "What time is that blasted church social?"

"Uh, it begins at two o'clock. Will you come with me, Uncle?"

Uncle grunted. "Not a chance, but I want to make sure we conclude your lesson in plenty of time for it. That's all." He left the room, turning left for the library.

Evan finished his custard with a smile on his face, optimistic about how things were turning out. Tonight, he was going to a card party with other men of the village, and tomorrow at the social he would see Miss Wilton in person for the first time. Within the week he would get started on his woodworking room. Better than those things, however, was the fact that his uncle was choosing time with Evan in the morning over time with the bottle tonight.

Chapter Fourteen

Lenora blinked her big blue eyes at Cassie as they sat in the parlor the afternoon before the May Day celebration. "You had a dream about me?"

Cassie nodded with reverence even while silently praying for forgiveness for this lie. A necessary lie to be sure, but a lie all the same. Their parents were out on parish business or Cassie would never have dared this conversation.

"And about Mr. Glenside?" Lenora asked further.

"The *new* Mr. Glenside," Cassie said, wanting to make sure that detail was clear. "He asked you for a kiss and you refused him."

"As well I should!" Lenora said, scandalized by the very idea.

Cassie hurried to redeem Mr. Glenside of his fictionalized action. "Then he said that he would be content with a token of your love, a lock of hair or scrap of lace, so that his heart might continue in patient waiting."

"Shockingly forward. Had we been introduced in this dream?"

"No," Cassie said, shaking her head. "But he was so ardent in wanting your attention. Finally, he said that if you could just smile at him from across the way then his heart would be filled and he would have the patience he needed to await your confidence in knowing him."

"Confidence in knowing him," Lenora repeated, looking toward the window and pondering the words.

It was low character for Cassie to use a dream against her sister—as the children of a clergyman, they took such things very seriously—but Cassie felt rather desperate. The more she had considered Mr. Glenside's request for a smile, the more she understood how important it was he receive it. He had made himself vulnerable through his letters, and it had become a heavy weight on Cassie's shoulders to realize how trusting he'd become. If Lenora ignored him after he'd shared such depth in his letters, Cassie could see the potential for him to retreat from this course altogether. He deserved validation of his connection; Lenora was the only reason he would even be attending the social.

As the mastermind behind the match, Cassie must make sure he left the social feeling confident and willing to continue their secret communications. And so here she was, the morning of the social, divulging a fictitious dream to her sister in the desperate hope that it would result in a smile shared between the two of them at the social.

Cassie had considered confessing the letters directly, but she dared not tip her hand too soon. The thought flashed through her head that she would miss her vicarious connection to Mr. Glenside once the truth was revealed, but she stopped that line of thought with a swift self-reprimand. Honestly, was she such a selfish girl as to covet what she wanted so much for her sister? Cassie wanted Mr. Bunderson's attention—*that* was her goal. The letters with Mr. Glenside were just the means to an end. Nothing more.

Lenora was still pondering Cassie's dream. "Confidence in knowing him," she said again, looking up at Cassie. "That is such an interesting turn of phrase. I'm not altogether sure I know what it means."

"It means that once you know someone, you can be comfortable with them—confident in their connection to you. Is that not how relationships work for you, Lenora? Once you feel as though you know someone you can be yourself. The eyes of family and close friends do not cut through you as a stranger's does."

"And Mr. Glenside understood this about me in your dream?"

Cassie couldn't meet the trusting expression in her sister's eyes and looked away. "That is what he said," she said, shoring up her own confidence while smoothing her skirt over her legs. "What's more, I could *feel* it. I could feel his sincerity, his goodness, and his true desire to have your friendship." That wasn't a lie. The impressions hadn't come from a dream, but from his letters. Cassie sensed Mr. Glenside's true desire to find his place here in Leagrave—and his place with Lenora.

Cassie took a breath and ignored the sinful nature of what she was saying and, even more, what she was *about* to say. "Lenora." She took her sister's hand in a display of affection and smiled. "I feel, in my heart, that the hand of Providence you have waited for is being extended. I feel that this dream is meant to encourage you, to help you break free from your nerves that might otherwise keep you from acknowledging Mr. Glenside. We know that faith without works is dead, and I feel that you need to make this effort in order to encourage Mr. Glenside as much as you can."

The longing in Lenora's eyes made it clear that she did want such a connection.

"But if that is so," Lenora said carefully, "why would God give *you* a dream about Mr. Glenside rather than send such a thing to me?"

Cassie blinked, but it only took her a moment to answer. "Perhaps because I would be more objective than you. I know how it frightens you to be around strangers, especially men. Perhaps my encouragement will help build your confidence." She paused a moment before continuing. "Remember how much better the Dyers' ball was after you and I spoke? You said you felt so much more equanimity and comfort."

Lenora frowned. "I still ran for the garden."

"But you were sociable until that time, and you came home with a much lighter heart, did you not?"

Lenora paused, then smiled. "I did feel so much better than at prior events, and I have reflected on that a great deal as we've prepared for the social. I think that confidence is why I can participate this year."

Last year Lenora had been unable to attend the social, even though the family had hosted the event for years and she had helped with preparations for days leading up to it. At home she was excited and optimistic, but the day of the event was a poor one for her nerves. She stayed in her room while the rest of the family made excuses for her absence. This year she had not shown the least bit of reluctance to participate fully.

Lenora continued, her voice animated. "Each time my anxiety has seemed ready to send me into a panic, I remember that I *did* sit and talk with Rebecca for several minutes at the ball, that I kept a smile on my face and did not feel so conspicuous. Because of that success I am hopeful that tomorrow will not be so difficult."

Cassie smiled and squeezed her sister's hand. "I am so glad to hear of your confidence. My hope is that you will feel well enough to share a smile with Mr. Glenside if the opportunity presents itself. Don't forget that it was not only Rebecca with whom you conversed that night; you also managed to speak with Mr. Glenside at the Dyers' ball."

"I spoke with him through the arbor," Lenora said, her eyebrows puckering. "And I was terrified he would come around and present himself."

"But he didn't. He respected your need for distance, which I think speaks volumes about his character. It is just a smile, Lenora. You have such a lovely smile—just let him see it. Let him *feel* who you are on the inside."

Lenora smiled a moment, but then it fell and she was instantly nervous again. "What if he comes over and requests an introduction?"

"Then you shall smile and breathe and get through it just as you did at the Dyers' ball, but I feel sure he will not do so. I am *certain* that a smile is the only interaction you can expect for tomorrow."

Lenora took a breath and straightened slightly. "Then I shall trust in your dream, Cassie," she said with a nod. "I will be brave and let your confidence in my ability to do this, and God's confidence in sending you such a dream, give me the strength I need."

Cassie forced her smile wider to cover the prick of conscience. "Good," she said, hurrying to stand, her guilt increasing now that God had been pulled into her charade. "Very good."

Chapter Fifteen

Cassie hurried from the house to the pavilion holding the tray of sand-wiches, her arms burning. She should have waited for a servant—Father had hired half a dozen to help the usual staff at the vicarage—but everything was behind schedule, and she thought she could manage the tray. She was almost running before she finally reached the table, and Mama took the tray from her arms.

"Goodness, Cassie, it's a wonder you didn't drop the lot of them."

Cassie shook out her hands, which tingled from the exertion. "You're welcome," she said tartly, then lowered her eyes when her mother gave her a look and an arched brow. "Sorry, Mama, I was only trying to help."

"Is the punch ready?" Mama asked, positioning the platter on the table.

"Almost. Timothy said he would have it out in a moment. What else can I do?"

Mama glanced at the skies, still thick with clouds. "Pray that we do not get rained out after already being delayed."

The morning's rain had been enough to delay the social, but not enough to cancel it. The Wilton family and a handful of other women from church had been working for days on the food. Canceling the

86

celebration outright would result in so much waste. When the rain stopped at nine o'clock, Mama decided that they would go ahead with the social and hope for at least two hours of fine enough weather that the preparations for the annual event would have purpose.

"At least the wind has died down and the day is warmer," Cassie said while Mama secured an oilcloth over the food to prevent it from drying out.

"Yes, at least that." Mama paused and smiled at Cassie while putting a hand to her cheek. "Thank you for looking for the positive."

Cassie shrugged as though she was always optimistic. Perhaps if she were better at looking for the silver lining she would get more praise from her mother. Mama went back to laying out the refreshments. The truth was that Cassie *needed* this social to not only happen but to go well. She needed Lenora to smile at Mr. Glenside across the park so as to keep the connection growing between them. That this was also Cassie's chance to see him for the first time was an additional incentive. She had been writing to him for three weeks and had never actually met him.

"Dear heavens," Mama said, drawing Cassie's attention to the road that ran alongside the pavilion. The Sherwood family had just come around the corner, the children running and laughing ahead of the parents. "We are not nearly ready."

"I shall see what else needs to come from the kitchen." Cassie turned back to the house and lifted her skirts so that she might hurry. Time was of the essence. The Sherwood children would be hard to keep at bay from the food.

In the kitchen, Cassie quickly helped load another platter with shortbreads. Servants and family—Rose and Victoria had come to help, though Rose was too pregnant to be of much use—were scurrying this way and that. Everyone was intent on one task or another to the point that Cassie didn't dare ask anyone to stop what they were doing and take the cookies to the tables. She was sure this tray would not be as heavy as the sandwiches, but when she reached the halfway point on the lawn, her arms began to tremble. She tried to speed up, but that made the tray unstable. She slowed her step, afraid she would not reach the table in time, when someone came up to her from behind.

"Let me take that," an unfamiliar low-timbered voice said as he slid his arms beneath the tray.

"Thank you," she said while releasing the breath she'd been holding. "I was near to dropping it."

"As I saw," he said.

Cassie rubbed her weary arms and looked up to thank her rescuer, only to freeze as she met the darkest blue eyes she'd ever seen. One instant she didn't know this man at all and the next moment she knew *exactly* who he was. Mr. Glenside. Perhaps the only man in town she would not recognize, and one of the most handsome men she had ever seen.

The realization set her toes on fire. "Th-thank you," she said again, forcing herself to look away from those lovely eyes and strong jaw and fine nose and . . . She took a breath for fortitude and met his eyes again. "I'm Cassandra Wilton. I do not believe we've met."

"No, I don't think we have." Was it her imagination that he was studying her as intently as she had been studying him? He broke eye contact and looked around them. "Is there someone nearby who could give us an official introduction?"

Cassie furrowed her brow, then remembered the letters where he'd talked about being unsure of all the protocols of this new society. She *should* wait for someone to introduce them, but who would that be? Mama was tending to the refreshments, Father was busy greeting the parishioners, and it appeared Mr. Glenside had arrived alone. Perhaps, between the near catastrophe his kindness had averted and the odd way in which they felt alone, there was little need for such formalities.

"I believe when a gentleman rescues a damsel in distress it is perfectly acceptable for the two of them to introduce themselves without a third party. Every rule must have some room for exception."

He smiled, and her toes began to burn again. This was the man she wanted for *Lenora*?

"Well, thank you for putting my mind at ease," he said, bowing as well as he could while holding the tray. "Would you be so good as to direct me toward the destination of these particularly fetching biscuits?"

"Yes, of course." Cassie moved a step ahead of him, though all she really wanted was to stay and stare. "This way."

He followed her to the tent, and she directed him where to set the tray. Mama was still there, unpacking plates and cups from their wooden storage crates. "Thank you, Mr. Glenside," Mama said, smiling at the man.

"You know him?" Cassie asked in surprise. It seemed strange that anyone could know this man and not have told her how breathtaking he was.

"Mr. Glenside introduced himself a few minutes ago and asked if he might be of help," Mama explained. "I sent him to the kitchen."

"And he found me instead, halfway across the lawn and floundering," Cassie said sheepishly. She looked at Mr. Glenside again. *Those eyes.*

"Shall I return to the kitchen and see what else can be done?" Mr. Glenside asked.

"I should forbid it," Mama said with an apologetic smile. "But the morning rain has set us behind schedule, and I cannot thank you enough for lending a hand."

Mr. Glenside left them, and Cassie turned to watch him depart. He was dressed in blue trousers and a lightweight, black coat, as appropriate for the party. His hair was short rather than worn fashionably long as many other men, giving a polished air she would not have expected from a working-class man. He cut a very fine figure, and she found herself wishing he would look over his shoulder and smile at her.

"Cassandra."

She turned to face her mother, whose knowing expression instantly brought fire to her cheeks.

"Guard yourself," Mama said while removing a set of plates from the burlap they'd been wrapped in. "Do not forget who you are simply because a man catches your eye."

"Yes, Mama," Cassie said, though she knew exactly who she was. She was the youngest daughter trying desperately to create a match for her older sister. She moved to a crate and began unpacking the glasses.

Each time Mr. Glenside returned to the tent, Cassie purposely busied herself with her back to him for fear that if she looked into those eyes again, or saw that smile once more, she would freeze and her mind would go blank. What was happening to her? She'd never experienced anything like this before and did not know what to make of it, think of it, or do about it.

Finally, her father climbed atop the wooden box he always used for his outdoor announcements and welcomed everyone to May Day—the first day of summer and the opportunity to celebrate the fertility of the land and livestock that was the foundation of country life. He introduced the Maypole and explained its significance while the younger children, girls mostly, began to move toward the front of the group. The festivities were a welcome distraction from the thoughts cluttering Cassie's senses.

When she had been younger, Cassie loved twining her ribbon around the Maypole, and she watched with delight as the children hurried forward to take hold of their special ribbon. Mr. Simpson brought out his fiddle and began to play while the children wove in and out of one another, laughing and shrieking as they braided the ribbons around the pole. Next would come the Morris dancers with their bright costumes and energetic dance, and then the Queen of May would be crowned, a symbol of another year of prosperity for the village.

"Cassie," Lenora whispered. "Is that him?"

Cassie followed Lenora's gaze to Mr. Glenside and felt an energy move through her like a breeze . . . or an arrow. He was laughing at the children's antics, his arms folded over his chest and his face bright. "I believe so," she said softly, then wondered why she was hedging. He was standing next to Mr. Bunderson and the contrast of her reaction between the two men was worrisome. Cassie had been pining over Mr. Bunderson for months, yet he looked quite ordinary next to Mr. Glenside.

"I don't think I can do it, Cassie." Lenora clutched at her arm.

"Do what?" Cassie said, tearing her gaze from the men and looking at her sister in confusion.

"Smile at him. Don't tell me you've forgotten your dream."

"Of course I haven't forgotten." The desire to remove and ponder on whether or not she should encourage Lenora toward Mr. Glenside any further tempted her. But no. She'd already made up a dream and written letters; she could not stop now. "Um, it's just . . . what I mean is, that you *must* smile at him. You promised me you would."

"But maybe it was just a dream," Lenora said.

Cassie considered telling her that it *was* just a dream and no smile was necessary, when Lenora's grip on her arm tightened.

Mr. Glenside looked their way, smiled slowly, and then tipped his head.

"Smile," Cassie said, smiling herself and elbowing Lenora in the side and talking through her teeth. "For heaven's sake, smile at the man before he thinks you a complete dolt!"

Lenora's eyes were wide as the saucers stacked on the table, but the corners of her mouth suddenly went up, snapping into the shape of a smile. It looked completely false and ridiculous, but it *was* a smile, and she couldn't chastise Lenora for the admirable effort. Not with Mr. Glenside looking their direction and a fake dream lying between them.

After a few moments, Lenora turned away, tugging at the corner of the tablecloth as though to straighten it. Mr. Glenside turned his head back to the Maypole, but at the last moment, he caught Cassie's eyes.

Goodness, she thought for perhaps the fifth time as warmth rushed into every empty space within her mind and heart. *He is so handsome.*

He gave her a nod. She smiled and nodded in return. He continued to hold her eyes until Mr. Bunderson leaned in and said something in Mr. Glenside's ear. Then it was Mr. Bunderson looking at her.

Cassie smiled politely and turned away. All of this—the advice, the letters, the dream—was because of Mr. Bunderson, and yet she no longer wanted his notice. The realization was terrifying.

Chapter Sixteen

So you have met the Wilton girls," Mr. Bunderson said, nodding toward the young women beneath the canopy.

"I met Miss Cassandra earlier today, but I have not been officially introduced to her sister." Unofficially, however, he felt he knew her quite well. The thought that Evan likely knew her better than Mr. Bunderson did gave him an odd sense of pride. No one here—except Cassandra—was aware of the connection he and Lenora shared. Perhaps that was why Miss Cassandra seemed so taken off guard when they'd met. What did she think of the letters?

"Not sure many people have had an *official* introduction to Miss *Lenora* Wilton," Bunderson said with a laugh. "She's a queer thing, shy as they come. Why, I've lived in Leagrave my whole life and am friends with Christopher Wilton and I have never had a conversation with Miss Wilton."

"To be shy is not a failing of character," Evan said with a knowing smile. "I would imagine she is improved in smaller groups."

"You would imagine, would you?" Bunderson said, grinning. "You've lived here, what, a week, and can already define Miss Wilton so confidently?"

"I have been here nearly six weeks, thank you very much." Evan took hold of his lapels and puffed out his chest, making Bunderson laugh loud enough that several people turned to look. He bowed as though he had performed just for them, while Evan dropped his hands, feeling sheepish for having drawn their attention. The onlookers turned away with varying degrees of amusement.

"Do I detect admiration in your assessment of Miss Lenora?" Bunderson asked, arching one dark eyebrow.

"Would it be so surprising?"

"Her family is very well respected, and while I can agree that her countenance is fine, it is certainly not to the level of her sister. I think Miss Cassandra ten shades prettier than Miss Lenora."

Evan couldn't help but consider Bunderson's assessment as he looked at the sisters, still busy with their work beneath the canopy. Cassandra was a bit taller than Lenora despite being younger, and she carried herself with more confidence. Both women had slender figures, but Lenora's was a bit more feminine. Evan felt guilty comparing them. Lenora was the one who had opened up to him in her letters, and despite the nervousness he saw in her now, there was a part of her that was as confident and self-possessed as her sister. "I think both sisters are equally pretty," Evan said diplomatically.

"Well, good, then. You set your sights on Miss Lenora and get her out of the way so I might try my luck with Cassie."

Evan pulled his eyebrows together. "'Out of the way'? What exactly do you mean by that?" And why did he call Miss Cassandra *Cassie*? That seemed rather familiar.

"The vicar only allows one daughter *out* at a time—there were once six of them, you know. One daughter is presented, makes a match, and then the next will be available."

"So Miss Cassandra is not out?" In Evan's prior society, it was typical for girls to be considered out once they reached the age of sixteen. They were not presented so formally as the Wilton girls would be, but Evan had never heard of anyone holding to the tradition of waiting for the elder to marry before the younger had her turn. Did not Shakespeare have a story with such a plot? He could not remember how it ended. "How old is Miss Cassandra?"

"Twenty," Mr. Bunderson said, shaking his head as though disappointed. "I can't imagine why she has not thrown an absolute fit at the arrangement. My sisters would never have stood for such heavy-handed rules. All three of my sisters were out at one time, and my second sister married before the eldest did." He shrugged. "It would be very difficult to be a clergyman's child, I think. Such expectations must feel oppressive. To say nothing about how ungenteel the girls have become."

"Ungenteel?" Evan asked. He didn't think he'd ever heard the term before.

"They do some of the cooking, cleaning. Even here, they're at the serving table rather than enjoying the party. I suppose with so many children and only a vicar's living it's difficult to manage a household appropriately. Still it's only their relationship to the church that elevates them at all." He shrugged again and turned toward the children, who had undertaken a new game now that the Maypole was finished. "I understand their mother stepped down some when she married."

Evan chose not to comment. He didn't see the women's efficiency as a drawback, but then he'd been raised in a home where his mother did all the cooking and cleaning; they had never employed a servant. Mama had often labored long into the night to make a hundred copies of an invitation to a ball, each one written in her perfect hand. The family needed an income after Father's death, and she'd taken pride in being able to contribute. Evan looked around this new company he kept and wondered if they would see his mother's skill as an embarrassment.

Don't think on that now, he told himself. The Morris dancers were invited to perform and while many people stayed to watch, others began moving toward the serving table where the Wilton girls stood alongside the servants, preparing plates for the guests. Bunderson suggested they get a plate and Evan agreed. A few minutes later, he found himself face to face with Miss Cassandra, who stood opposite him at the first table.

She looked up and her cheeks went as pink as the dress she wore. A bright yellow ribbon was tied around the knot atop her head, and a matching ribbon was tied in a bow at one wrist.

"Thank you," he said when she handed him his plate.

"You're welcome, Mr. Glenside."

She avoided his eye, and he found it amusing how like her sister she was in that moment, nervous and tongue-tied. Lenora was at a table further into the tent, her back to the crowd as she busied herself with some other task. Did Miss Cassandra disapprove of the letters? Is that why she seemed embarrassed to see him? He watched her until she met his eye once again, then smiled in hopes of getting some reassurance that she didn't think poorly of him for the secret correspondence. She smiled back, free and unrestrained enough that he took it as confirmation of her approval.

"Have a good day, Miss Cassandra," he said as he moved down the table.

"Good day to you too, sir," she said under her breath.

As he walked away, he felt sure she was watching him, and when he glanced over his shoulder, she darted her glance away. He began to smile, but then stopped himself. *Lenora,* he said in his mind as though reminding himself of which sister he had interest in.

He searched for Lenora again. She was still at the back of the tent but while he watched, she turned, a stack of plates in her hands, and caught his eye. She froze like a rabbit. He smiled. She didn't even blink.

He nodded, and finally she did too, a quick bob. She remained in place however, until he turned away, wondering if that might be the only thing that would get her moving again. When he glanced back, she was hurrying forward with the plates. Bunderson was flirting with Miss Cassandra, who showed none of the embarrassment she'd seemed to feel with Evan. Maybe she *did* disapprove of the letters.

Evan moved toward an empty table but thought of what Bunderson had said about Lenora's shyness. Though he still felt he knew her better than Bunderson did, he wondered what a woman afflicted with such shyness would be like as a wife. For a man who already felt out of place, would a wife unable to help him navigate through society pose an even greater difficulty?

Chapter Seventeen

May 9

Dear Mr. Glenside,

How wonderful it was to see you at the social last week. It seemed as though you were meeting some of the fine people in our village, and I hope you enjoyed yourself. I tried all afternoon to muster the courage to speak with you, but I am glad that I was at least able to share a smile with you as you had requested in your last letter.

My sister said that she did get an introduction. I hope you found her personable. She was quite struck by your fine manners and was eager to give me her report after we had finished clearing all the frippery of the event. I am glad the weather was so fine.

Cassie paused and laid down her pen before staring out the window toward the Glenside estate, though she could not see it from here. She sighed deeply and reflected on the exchanges she'd shared with Mr. Glenside at the social. There was not much to ponder on, and yet the few minutes she had spent in his company outshined every other moment of the day. She told herself the powerful feelings were due to her investment for Lenora's sake, but she worried that her own curiosity and interest was becoming a factor. Cassie had caught Mr. Glenside's eye a time or two, but wondered if she were smiling to further his good impression of her for Lenora's sake or for her own. She'd put off this letter almost a week because of her consternation.

Cassie stood up from the writing desk, but then sat back down. She wanted something else to occupy her thoughts, but she needed to finish this letter. Only after she wrote to him would he write her back, and she was increasingly eager to read his words. Would he share with Lenora what he'd thought about Cassie?

She wrote another line about the event, but her mind wandered once more and her pen went still.

Mr. Glenside had come to church on Sunday, sitting at the end of a row near the back whereas the Wilton family always occupied the second pew. When the family exited, he'd been talking with some of the other parishioners. She'd wanted to find a way to speak with him, and yet to do so would draw too much attention to them both. Instead she'd found herself talking with Mr. Bunderson and trying to find the pleasure in their conversation that she usually did. Unfortunately, it was as though all the invigoration and interest she had once had for Mr. Bunderson had disappeared. In its place was curiosity about Mr. Glenside. *Only curiosity*, she told herself.

Now she was writing him a letter and unable to find the right words. She had always felt as though she were writing from Lenora's heart, but it felt different now. Changed. But that was silly. *Nothing* had changed. Cassie was still doing all of this to help *Lenora*. That was her goal.

Cassie straightened in her chair and picked up her pen with resolution. She dipped it into the ink to ensure a fresh line before returning her attention to the letter. She needed to prove—to herself if no one else—how determined she was to do right by Lenora. And then, as she wrote, an idea formed as to how she could move the letter writing a step forward.

Thank you again for your kindness to me and for not requiring more than that smile. I have enjoyed our getting to know each other on paper. It has given me such an easy time of feeling comfortable. As a token of my thanks, I shall leave a gift for you in the glen behind my family's barn. If you come on the north lane toward the vicarage, you will see a copse of trees that hides a bit of grassland in the center. Cassie often goes there to read or paint. It is lovely. I shall leave the gift there for you Saturday morning. Pray do not arrive before ten o'clock; I cannot guarantee it will be there before then. I shall retrieve the basket later in the afternoon when I can get away unseen.

Your friend,
Lenora

Chapter Eighteen

May 13

Dear Lenora,

I must beg your forgiveness for the shabby presentation of this letter. I am right now sitting on the stool I presume you left in the middle of the glen, and I fear my penmanship will suffer for want of my desk. A pencil is not easy to navigate on a man's knee as it turns out. I am also holding the prize you so graciously left for me. I am a great lover of toffee, and, as I have already partaken of one of the offered treats, I can quite confidently compliment your cook for the excellent confection—unless you made it yourself, in which case I would be doubly impressed.

One of my fondest memories was visiting my grandmother in Thurst for Christmas and being spoiled by her excellent toffee. She would let us eat as many pieces as we could want, and there are few things more satisfying to a child unused to sweets than a belly full of candy. You do have the most charitable of hearts, and I consider myself quite privileged to have come to know you as I have.

I must admit that I am increasingly eager to become better acquainted with you and have spoken with my uncle regarding inviting your family for dinner. It would be a casual affair, not

too much of a crowd, but would give us a chance to spend more
time together. Please let me know if that is acceptable to you. If
it is, I shall pursue the arrangements with my uncle.

Best Regards,
Evan

Cassie sat on the stool in the glen and read the letter a second time. Mr. Glenside had held this very paper only a few hours before, when he'd come for the toffee she left for him in the basket. Toffee she had made herself. She had impressed him with her usefulness!

When she'd arrived, the basket had been empty save for his letter, filling her with a warm sense of familiarity toward the man who had enjoyed her treats. Enjoyed them because she had thought to move their relationship beyond letters. Letters that were from Lenora.

The pit opened in her stomach again, and she forced herself to focus on the next part of the letter—dinner at Glenside estate. Such a step was reasonable, even expected, and yet disheartening too. Cassie should show Lenora the letters. The thought drained every bit of energy through her toes, and she immediately began to formulate an argument.

Did she *have* to tell Lenora of the letters before the dinner party? Lenora would not end up having a private enough conversation with Mr. Glenside that he might mention their letters. Surely not.

Cassie picked up the basket and the stool, one in each hand, and turned back toward the house, pondering the situation. Knowledge of the letters would only increase Lenora's nerves—that was true enough—but that wasn't why she argued the point.

Cassie knew Mr. Glenside better than any other person in Leagrave, perhaps even better than his own uncle did. She knew his discomforts, his fears, and his hopes for the future. How could she simply hand such knowledge to Lenora? It didn't seem right, even though it was what she'd intended all along. So then why did it feel so right *not* to tell her the truth?

Chapter Nineteen

Cassie chose not to share the letters with Lenora, and the closer the family carriage got to Glenside Manor on the night of the dinner party, the tighter Cassie's stomach seemed to wind in upon itself. Had she ever been so nervous in her life?

She put a hand to her stomach and glanced at Lenora, seated across from her and staring out the window. Was this how her sister felt at every social event she attended? Equal parts eager and anxious, confident and insecure? Such feelings on a regular basis would drive anyone to madness. Cassie didn't know how she would eat let alone attempt any kind of conversation. Would she react to Mr. Glenside's rich blue eyes with the same dizziness she'd felt at the social?

"Are you all right, Cassie?"

Cassie looked across the carriage at her mother and forced a smile. "Of course."

Mama glanced at Cassie's hand pressed against her stomach. "You seem anxious."

Cassie moved her hand to her side while searching for an explanation. "I've never been to Glenside Manor," she said with a shrug. "I suppose I am a little nervous."

The dinner invitation, direct from Mr. Hastings Glenside, had arrived two days after Cassie had left the basket of toffee in the glen. The invitation had included an apology for Mr. Glenside's actions during Papa's visit last month. Papa had then recounted the visit, and Cassie could imagine the young Mr. Glenside heroically caught between the two men yet keeping his actions noble. The man's excellent character should put Cassie's mind at ease, but instead her thoughts began swooping and spinning at a fever pitch. Handsome *and* kind *and* noble?

"No need to be nervous," Papa said, looking up from the sermon he was reviewing. "Mr. Glenside was most apologetic in his note, and I look forward to making better acquaintance with his nephew."

Mama did not seem to believe Cassie's explanation and watched her carefully.

Cassie turned her attention to Lenora. "Are you not nervous too, Lenora?"

Lenora paled a shade lighter than she already was and nodded vigorously. "My heart is in my throat."

No one questioned *her* anxiety or gave her curious looks.

Instead, Mama patted Lenora's knee. "There is no need for anyone to be nervous about this evening." She included Cassie in her glance. "Mr. Glenside is a good man, deeply wounded by the tragic loss of his wife. I can't fault him for the pain he feels. That he is extending an olive branch is a remarkable thing." She smiled sideways at Lenora. "Perhaps his nephew is a good influence on him and that is why he has softened. I must say he is exactly the type of man parents dream of for their daughter."

Cassie swallowed while Lenora's pale cheeks flushed scarlet. Must Mama have used the word "dream"?

"I have never even spoken to him, Mama," Lenora said in a shaky voice. "What will I say if he attempts to speak with me?"

"I would not give too much thought to that," Mama said, patting

Lenora's knee. "Lucy played the pianoforte, so I suspect the instrument shall be available for you after dinner, and when I returned our acceptance of the invitation, I provided a seating arrangement that will keep you from sitting next to Mr. Glenside."

"Mama," Cassie said, shocked that her mother had taken the liberty of arranging someone else's dinner.

"It is not entirely unheard of," Mama defended, straightening her shoulders. "Especially in a home without a woman to pay mind to such details. Knowing that Lenora would . . . struggle, I suggested that she be seated next to me and that you, Cassie, be seated across the table beside the younger Mr. Glenside."

It was Cassie's turn to pale. "I am to sit beside the nephew? I am not even out."

"Says the girl who has thrown a number of fits about that very circumstance," Mama said, looking curious again. "Besides, this is nothing more than dinner with our parishioners. You are comfortable with conversation and easy with new acquaintances. It will be good for you to help facilitate good relations through this dinner as well as give Lenora an example for her own future interactions. We all have a part to play."

"As long as my part is at the piano." Lenora did not seem the least bothered that Cassie was being given the charge of entertaining the man the whole family seemed to have chosen for Lenora.

Cassie leaned against the side of the old carriage—older than she by nearly a decade—as it made the turn into the manor drive. There was no point in arguing, and she would be dishonest if the idea of close conversation with Evan didn't excite her more than a little. It also terrified her. What if she inadvertently spoke of something from the letters? What if she ruined everything? The briefest thought further shamed her: If she ruined everything for Lenora, might that leave Mr. Glenside available . . . for her?

Oh, she *was* wicked.

The carriage slowed, marking limited time remaining for Cassie to gather her wits. *Smile and breathe*, she told herself, repeating the advice she'd given to Lenora the night she encountered Mr. Glenside for the first time. Cassie could only hope the counsel would be as helpful to her now as it had been to Lenora then.

Chapter Twenty

Cassie's hands were sweating within her gloves when they were shown into the drawing room. Mr. Glenside and Evan stood, and Mr. Glenside stepped forward and extended his hand to Papa. The humility of the action distracted Cassie from her discomfort for a moment. Papa took Mr. Glenside's hand and they shook one time, firm and full.

"Thank you for coming," Mr. Glenside said, straightening his coat in a display of his own nerves. He rarely entertained, if ever, and was making great effort tonight. Cassie appreciated it.

"Thank you for having us," Papa said, bowing slightly. "I am humbled and very grateful for the invitation." They exchanged a smile and that was that. Men were far more simple in their resolutions than women, Cassie decided.

"You remember my wife," Papa said, beginning the introductions that included the rest of the family.

"Wonderful to finally meet you," she heard Evan say to Lenora.

"A pleasure," Lenora said, surprising Cassie. Her face was bright red. She was not looking into Evan's handsome face, but she'd spoken. That should feel like a success, but it somehow increased Cassie's nerves.

Cassie met Evan's eye when Papa introduced him to her. As soon as her gaze locked with his, it became hard to look anywhere else. Oddly enough, however, her nerves calmed, replaced with a comfortable willingness to be in his company for any reason at all—even as a decoy for Lenora's benefit.

"It is a pleasure to see you again, Miss Cassandra," Evan said, bowing slightly as though he'd been doing it all his life. She felt oddly proud of him.

Cassie curtsied without looking away. "As it is to see you, Mr. Glenside."

The smile he gave her was like a flash of sunshine catching the surface of Miller's pond, transfixing and glorious.

"Well, then, let's move on to dinner," Mr. Glenside said, leading the way in an informal manner. Papa put out his arm for Mama, but the rest of them kept their own company.

Cassie fell into step with Lenora out of habit, which had the added benefit of being behind Mr. Glenside and therefore being able to take in the form of him—long legs, broad shoulders. A soft sigh from Lenora reminded Cassie which of them *should* be noticing such things.

And which of them should not.

There was just enough tension between the older Mr. Glenside and his servants to prove that the entire household was unused to having guests. Luckily for Mr. Glenside, the Wilton family was used to a variety of households. They had eaten fine dinners in grand houses as well as mutton stew from bowls held in their laps in some of the humblest homes in the village. Cassie wondered if anyone but Mr. Glenside and his nephew had sat at this table since Mrs. Glenside's death, and the thought humbled her even more.

"Evan tells me that the May Day celebration was excellent," Mr. Glenside said.

Mama quickly picked up the subject and an easy conversation ensued. Cassie was only peripherally involved, which suited her just fine since it allowed her to concentrate on her dinner companion's every movement. He counted the forks under his breath before picking up the outermost, which made her smile, and then he held his soup spoon wrong for the first two bites before realizing his error and correcting his hold. Cassie didn't understand why his actions were so endearing, but they were.

"The soup is excellent," Cassie said to Evan, as though he had any part in its creation. Her parents and Mr. Glenside were in an attentive conversation about the new magistrate, allowing Cassie the chance for a side conversation. Lenora was intent upon her bowl.

"It is," Evan agreed. "Cream of asparagus, I believe."

"I do love asparagus."

"As do I," Evan said. He then paused, his spoon halfway to his mouth, and shook his head.

"What?" Cassie asked with a soft laugh. "What are you shaking your head about?"

He smiled and gave her a sideways glance. "Only that I'm having a conversation about asparagus."

"There are worse topics," she said with a teasing grin. "Once we spent most of the night discussing manure with a farmer in the parish."

He chuckled.

"It is no joking matter," Cassie said with feigned sincerity. "You would not believe the differences, and you should know that too much of the wrong choice could burn your crops straight through."

Evan raised his napkin to his mouth as he hid a laugh behind it.

Lenora glanced at him, but when he met her eye and smiled, her face went red and her eyes jumped back to her soup. Evan's laugh subsided. He watched Lenora a moment longer, and then returned to his dinner more subdued. When Cassie spoke next, she raised her voice so that Lenora could hear them more easily. *For Lenora, for Lenora, for Lenora.*

"I hear that your mother and sisters will be coming to Leagrave in a few months' time."

He looked surprised, and she raised her eyebrows, willing him to remember that "Lenora" had told him Cassie knew about the letters. Cassie nodded slightly in Lenora's direction, and he seemed to make the connection. His expression relaxed.

"Yes, in August, we hope." Evan also spoke louder in order to include the others at the table more directly. "Uncle Hastings has been very generous to offer them the Dower House."

"Only done right by my place," Mr. Glenside said sheepishly. "I'm ashamed I wasn't more aware of the family's situation before."

Cassie noticed Evan's shoulders tighten, but he did not drop his smile. "Very generous." He turned back to his soup.

"That reminds me," Mr. Glenside said, turning toward Papa. "I'm in need of a good plaster man. Do you know of anyone in the village? It's been some time since I've had need of such."

"Oh, yes," Papa said, clearly pleased to be consulted. "Marcus Holland does excellent work—he and his sons—and at a fair price."

"Howard Holland's son?" Mr. Glenside said. He offered up a story of childhood antics undertaken with this Howard Holland, whom Cassie had never heard of. He was likely dead, but alive in the memory of Mr. Glenside and her father.

Cassie turned her attention back to Evan. "You must be excited for your family to join you."

"I am." He took the last bite of soup, scraping his spoon against the bottom of the bowl, which caused the three Wilton women to share an amused look; genteel society did not make noise with their dishes. For Cassie, it was yet another endearment.

"Tell me about your mother," Cassie asked, eager for more information. "Our family will embrace her and your sisters, of course, so we would love to know more."

"She will be grateful for your friendship, as will I. I worry for their transition." He cast an anxious look at Mama, as though asking whether it was appropriate for him to bring up the topic.

"Transitions are very difficult," Mama said as a good vicar's wife should. "You must know we will help in any way possible. Like Cassie, I should like to know everything I can about your family before they arrive." She paused, then hurried to add, "Lenora is very interested in learning about them, too."

All eyes turned to Lenora, who again turned crimson. She stared into her empty soup bowl as though pretending she hadn't heard her name.

Oh, Lenora, Cassie thought with a sigh. *How can you be so uncomfortable with a man like Evan?*

Evan watched a moment, as though waiting for some commentary from silent Lenora, then turned his attention to Cassie. He began to speak of his mother with an affectionate tone that became yet one more point in his favor . . . *for Lenora.*

The comfortable mood of the meal continued through the dessert course—an excellent tart—at which point the party stood together. The women moved to the drawing room, which was somewhat strange since there was no woman of the house to host them there, while the men stayed behind for their port.

As soon as they entered the room, Lenora hurried to the pianoforte, sat in the chair, and began playing scales, something she often did to calm herself when her anxiety was extreme. Cassie sat down to wait for the men to join them. She hoped they would not linger too long over their drinks.

"Well, that went better than I expected," Mama said, sitting by Cassie with a satisfied smile. "I am so relieved."

Cassie nodded her agreement, but she cast a glance at the doorway, eager for Evan to arrive. The room felt almost chilly without his presence.

"You played your part very well, Cassie."

Cassie looked at Mama. "Oh, yes, thank you. Mr. Glenside is a good conversationalist."

"That he is. I hope he will be well accepted here."

"He seems to be thus far, and I'm sure he will only improve upon the village the longer he is here."

"Which makes this dinner even more important," Mama said.

Lenora transitioned from scales into something by Tchaikovsky, and both Cassie and Mama looked her direction. She'd calmed considerably, and Mama let out a relieved sigh. "He is perfect for her."

Cassie's smile tightened. She nodded because she knew she should, but she wanted to ask what made Evan perfect for Lenora. Was it because no man of their equal class would have her? That because he was new to this society, he would accept her failings? They were uncharitable thoughts to be sure, but Cassie told herself she was trying to look out for Evan as much as she was trying to look after Lenora. After all, a poor match would be painful for everyone.

The men entered the drawing room, and Cassie found herself sitting up straighter and wishing she'd taken the chance to check herself in the small mirror by the door to make sure she looked as pleasing as possible. A few pinches to her cheeks would have brought out the color. Why had she not thought to do as much? She'd worn her lavender evening dress—the one with the lace bodice and pleated hem. She loved it because of the small black stripe in the purple silk. Would Evan notice the stripe? Would he agree that the purple enhanced her green-gold eyes?

The conversation continued as easily as it had during dinner. Cassie thought it remarkable how well Mr. Glenside and Papa were getting on after so many years of discord. The seating was such that Cassie could not engage Evan in conversation, but it did not prevent her from watching him. Admiring him. Listing his numerous qualities in her mind.

After a few minutes of listening to the conversation between the older men, Evan moved to stand beside the pianoforte. A surge of jealousy took Cassie by surprise, and as soon as she recognized the feeling, she tried to talk herself out of it. But then Evan murmured something to Lenora, and she smiled—a tiny, nervous smile—and he said something else. Lenora smiled *again*.

Watching them together reminded Cassie that Evan believed Lenora was writing him secret letters and that Lenora believed he was interested in knowing her better because of Cassie's dream. There was no way for her to undo what she'd done. The proof was before her eyes. Even so, she desperately searched for some way to do just that, finally admitting to herself that she'd been searching for such an option ever since she'd met Mr. Glenside at the May Day celebration.

Chapter Twenty-One

Evan stood just behind his uncle as Mr. Wilton disappeared out the front door along with his daughters and his wife. After Jeremiah closed the door, Uncle turned to Evan, a smile on his face. "You were right to suggest I invite them over," he said graciously, clapping the younger man on the back. "It is a relief to feel as though any difficulty I might have caused when the vicar last visited has been remedied. I do not like contention, though one might find it hard to believe after how I behaved that day."

"You behaved admirably tonight. The evening seemed to be a great success."

"It did, didn't it?" Uncle puffed out his chest some, then laughed and began walking. "Join me in the study for a glass of brandy to celebrate."

Evan followed despite the fact that he didn't want to drink. Uncle had limited himself to one glass of wine at dinner and one glass of port after dessert, but he went straight for the sideboard and poured two glasses of dark brandy, handing one to Evan.

"To a successful evening," Uncle said, lifting his glass in a toast. He threw his head back and finished his drink in a single swallow as though it were whiskey not brandy, which was generally sipped.

Evan took a sip of his own drink, feeling the liquid burn down his throat. By the time he lowered his glass, Uncle had already turned back to the sideboard. Evan searched for a distraction to keep Uncle from pouring another drink.

"What did you think of the Wilton daughters?"

"Ah," Uncle said with a laugh, the decanter poised over his cup long enough for Evan to feel hopeful about Uncle's restraint. "I wondered when we might talk of them." He did pour his drink, however, and then turned to face Evan with a smug grin. "I thought your encouragement of this event might have an ulterior motive." He did not throw back his second drink, and instead sat on a leather-covered settee and waved Evan to the chair across from it. "I thought you seemed rather interested in the girl."

Evan looked into his glass, embarrassed to be the topic of this conversation and yet eager for his uncle's impressions. He pictured Lenora sitting at the pianoforte, so intent and composed. Nothing like the anxious, awkward girl she'd been before tonight. This new perspective of her gave him hope, and yet she still avoided him, using the piano like a shield and leaving him frustrated with attempts to engage her. She was so different in her letters, and he was eager to uncover that side of her in person. "She has an amazing talent for music. It is impressive."

"Do you mean the older Miss Wilton?"

Evan looked up, as much because of the words as the surprised tone. Had his attempts to be attentive to Lenora not been obvious? "Yes. Lenora."

Uncle shrugged. "Oh, yes, she is talented. Only I thought it was the younger daughter you found interesting. You seemed quite taken with her at dinner."

Evan swallowed. He *had* been rather taken with Miss Cassandra at dinner. Too taken. Realizing how much he'd enjoyed their conversation at dinner was why he'd tried to be more attentive to Lenora when they joined the ladies in the drawing room. She had already been at the piano-forte by then, however, and so there was limited chance to converse. But he *had* made a point to compliment her playing. By the end of the evening, she wasn't blushing with every look shared between them. That *was* progress. He could understand why it wouldn't seem like much to his uncle, however.

"Miss Cassandra was a lovely dinner companion," Evan said.

"But you prefer the older one?" Uncle seemed confused.

"I feel that behind her shy manner is a great deal to admire." Evan took another drink of brandy if for no other reason than to gain time to center his thoughts. The liquid did not burn nearly as hot as the first swallow, and he could feel a comfortable softening of his arms and legs. "And, besides, Lenora is out and Miss Cassandra is not."

"So it is a matter of availability?"

"What?" Evan didn't understand the question.

"If Miss Cassandra was out, would you consider her?"

"She is not out."

Uncle regarded him with a sharp look. "You're avoiding my question."

"Am I?" Not drinking hard liquor often left Evan easily muddled when he did. And he hadn't even wanted the brandy. He set the glass aside. "Forgive me, I do not mean to be avoiding anything. What was the question again?"

Uncle smiled with only half his mouth. "I asked if you would consider the younger girl if she were out in society?"

Evan thought about that. Cassandra was an excellent conversationalist and had a lovely laugh, which he'd managed to coax from her a time or two. Her attention to him felt sincere—not flirtatious or inappropriate—but it was Lenora he'd been writing to all these weeks. Talking to Cassandra had only increased his eagerness to get to know Lenora. He imagined the sisters would be very much alike once Lenora let down her guard.

"I have been exchanging letters with Lenora."

Uncle looked nearly as surprised to hear the confession as Evan was to have confessed.

Evan tried to grab on something other than the truth that he could offer as an explanation of his outburst; there was an understanding between Lenora and himself that their letters were a secret.

Uncle's eyebrows remained lifted. "I think you've something to tell me, my boy."

The letters were supposed to be a secret, but then Cassandra knew of their campaign. If Lenora's sister knew of the letters, what could be wrong about Uncle knowing as well? They both deserved a confidant, did they not? Evan took another drink, then opened his mouth and told the whole tale.

When Evan finished, Uncle leaned back in his chair and said nothing, his hands limp upon the armrests of the chair. The longer the silence stretched, the more uncomfortable Evan became. "You are displeased."

"I am neither pleased nor displeased," Uncle said with a shrug. He leaned forward and picked up his glass from the desk. He swirled his drink, then paused to take a swallow. "Only surprised, I suppose. Neither of you seem the type to conduct such an affair."

"Surely *affair* is too strong a word," Evan said, laughing too loud at what he hoped was an exaggeration. "I've made no promise to her."

"Oh, my boy, conducting a secret connection with a young lady— especially a young lady who happens to be the daughter of a clergyman— is very much an *affair*, promise or not."

Evan panicked. "No, the letters are simply the means to get to know each other better on account of her shyness. That is how she explained it when she first wrote to me."

"She first wrote?"

Evan nodded, not realizing he'd left out that information in his earlier explanation. He repeated how the letters came about, hopeful that the originating circumstance would soften Uncle's reaction. "Have I behaved badly?"

Uncle smiled, which eased Evan's anxiety, and shook his head. "You have not done wrong," he said. "Especially since it was Miss Wilton who initiated the exchange of letters. But that you allowed it to take place and have continued deceiving her parents is not something they will look well on if they learn of it."

"But they might not learn of it."

"But they might." Uncle leaned back in his chair again. "She is nearly twenty-five years old, is she not?"

Evan wasn't sure, but he remembered Bunderson saying that Miss Cassandra was twenty and there was a brother between the sisters in birth order. "I believe so," he said.

"An unmarried girl of twenty-five is cause of concern for her parents, and so they likely won't denounce you if they learn of the letters. I would caution you about continuing such a thing without having intentions toward her hand, however. It does not reflect well on you, no matter their daughter's situation. It will get her hopes up, mark my word."

"But she cannot speak to me in person," Evan blurted, the drink and his anxiety working against him in tandem. "You saw her tonight. The only time she spoke to me was to thank me for my compliments on her playing, and even those two words were stammered. I swear she played louder once I approached her." He hadn't realized just how frustrated he was by her lack of engagement, and he blamed the brandy for encouraging him to vent his emotions so undiplomatically.

"You have *never* spoken to her?"

Evan shook his head. "Only through the letters, but through those letters I have come to know her. I understand what hides behind that facade."

"A facade she does not lower even at an intimate dinner with only her family and your uncle in attendance?" Uncle pulled his eyebrows together. "That does not seem worrisome to you?"

Evan hesitated. He did not want to be critical of the young woman, but it would do no good to be dishonest either. Perhaps Uncle could help him resolve his concerns. "Yes, it does worry me some," he admitted and took another swallow of brandy, hoping the strong drink would relieve the guilt he felt at discussing Lenora's faults. Who was he to be critical of her? Without his uncle's entailment he was a clerk in a shop. He had no right to judge anyone.

"A wife can make or break a man in more ways than one, and, if you don't mind my saying so, you would benefit from a woman who can help you navigate this higher level of society. I'm not certain Lenora Wilton is that woman."

Evan blinked at how similar those thoughts ran to the ones he'd had following the May Day celebration. Those thoughts had prompted him to push for this dinner party so that he might have more time in her company. But his fears had not been relieved by their time spent together tonight. Not hardly. Still, his uncle presenting the same argument gave Evan reason to advocate for the opposite so that he might see the situation from every possible perspective. "She is the daughter of a well-respected, genteel family. That is a strong recommendation."

"And certainly to her credit, yes. But as one of the larger landholders in Leagrave, you will have a position in this village, Evan. You will be expected to entertain and conduct yourself in a public manner. I would suggest you find a wife who can strengthen that area for you, one who was raised with an understanding of how things are to be done since you were not."

Evan ignored the sting though he was well aware of the truth of his unfamiliarity with this new level of society. "I am hopeful that as Lenora becomes more comfortable with me, she will lower her defenses."

Uncle took a thoughtful sip of his drink. "Did you notice how her family allowed her to stay apart? They did not invite her to join in the conversation or offer that we all play cards or interact in some other way. They were as content to leave her behind the instrument as she was to remain there. To expect a woman of her age to change her character is a fragile hope at best." He paused. "Do you understand what I am saying?"

"That she is not a good choice for me." Evan stared at the carpet.

"That is not what I said," Uncle said quickly, causing Evan to look up at him. Uncle smiled. "If you love her, then her shyness would be but one defect in an otherwise worthwhile connection."

"I do not think I *love* her," Evan said, shocked that his uncle would suggest it. "I am certainly intrigued by her—by the duality of her letters and her persona in public. I feel a sense of challenge to break through her barriers, and, I admit, I feel a sense of freedom to be myself in the letters, too."

"I can see the benefit for both of you in that regard, but, again, I must caution you against exchanging many more letters. For one thing, it may become the only way to be true with one another, which would not bode well for a marriage at all. Additionally, if her parents were to discover this secret liaison, it would very likely force your hand to make an offer already implied—however unintentionally."

Evan's stomach rolled, and he set his glass on the side table. Was he already obligated? "What can I do?"

"At the very least, I suggest you spend more time with her. Take her for a drive or some such and see if she does become the woman from her letters."

"What if she cannot connect with me in person as she does in her letters? What if, like you say, it is the only way we can be true with one another? If I court her openly then I *will* be obligated."

"It would be better to take the young woman on a drive or two and part ways than to set up greater expectation and find it does not translate into a good match. Those letters are setting up an expectation, my boy. To believe otherwise and continue them would be foolish. You must now develop a relationship based on interaction."

Evan considered every word of counsel, wondering why he hadn't had such a brandy-assisted conversation with his uncle before now. "I can take her on a drive without having to declare myself?"

"Of course you can, so long as you stay on public roads and it's an open carriage. You can take the gig." Uncle smiled somewhat indulgently. "And I would suggest you do it sooner rather than later. If she is not the woman to make you happy, then the sooner you know it the better for everyone."

"And no more letters?" Evan said, wondering how his glass had become empty.

"Only one more letter," Uncle said, returning to the sideboard to fill his glass yet again. "An invitation for a drive. Let it be the last letter . . . unless you do decide to court her." He paused, the bottle in his hand, and his expression softened. "Why, your aunt Lucy wrote to me during the few months she stayed with her aunt in Cheshire before we married. I still have those letters. The heart one puts on the page is a priceless gift." He paused and swallowed, then met Evan's eyes once again. "But letters alone are not enough. Drive out with her, see if she improves in your company. If she does not, I would consider whether she is the woman you want to base your entire future upon. Who you marry is the singularly most important decision you will ever make in your life, Evan. Do not take it lightly."

Chapter Twenty-Two

Cassie was descending the stairs with her easel under one arm and her box of paints and brushes in hand when she heard Mama and Lenora talking excitedly in the parlor. She paused, unsure what could cause such energetic conversation. The fact that Lenora wasn't playing the pianoforte was indication enough that something monumental had taken place. When Cassie reached the doorway, both Mama and Lenora turned toward her, their faces bright.

"Cassie, you'll never guess what's happened," Mama said, rushing over and taking the paints from her hand while Cassie set down the easel. A paper was thrust into her hand, but before she could read it herself, Mama told her what it said. "Mr. Glenside has invited Lenora for a drive this afternoon!"

Cassie's eyes went blurry a moment, then focused on those exact words written in a familiar hand on familiar paper.

> *It would be my greatest pleasure to escort you on a drive through the countryside where we might see the spring flowers and enjoy such a fine day. I shall call at 2:00 and return you in time for tea.*
>
> *Your friend,*
> *Evan*

Cassie's mouth went dry, and she had to force herself to breathe as the words marched before her eyes. The dinner party from two nights ago was thick in her mind—thick like honey or paste depending on what part she allowed control of her thoughts. The soft tenor of Evan's voice when they'd spoken at dinner was like the languid warmth on a summer's day, while watching him listen so attentively to Lenora's music was thick like glue, with bits of doubt and self-consciousness sticking to her.

She had thought much more about that evening at Glenside Manor than she had about what would follow. But *of course* Evan would ask Lenora on a drive. *Of course* he would want to improve his connection to her. Cassie hadn't dared write to him after the dinner party—her thoughts were so complicated—and part of her had hoped he would be put off by Lenora ignoring him and perhaps intrigued by Cassie's attentiveness. Only he hadn't been, apparently.

"Did this letter come to the front door?" Cassie asked, looking at her mother.

Mama pulled her eyebrows together. "Of course it came to the front door. Where else would it come?"

"Of course." Cassie looked back at the letter. They had both come to sign their letters with increasing familiarity. His last letter—which had come through the kitchen via Young—had been signed like this one, with only his first name. Apparently Mama and Lenora had not noticed the familiar detail. Cassie's heart began to race. A private drive. Just Evan and Lenora.

"Is it not wonderful, Cassie?" Lenora said, her face alight with happiness. "That he should show me such particular attention is beyond what I had hoped for." She paused and her forehead puckered slightly. "Only it does seem rather bold, Mama. We have had very little time in one another's company."

"It is quite bold," Cassie said quickly, seizing anything that might delay this. She was not ready to give Evan over to Lenora. What a terrible sister she was. She felt horrid.

"Mr. Glenside gets on well with your father and has been at church," Mama said, waving away any possible lack of etiquette. Could Cassie's argument from so many weeks ago about Lenora controlling Cassie's destiny be part of why Mama was so casual with the rules now? "And we have no objection to his attention. In fact, I think it shows great insight on his part, Lenora, as he has chosen an event for just the two of you. Perhaps he has taken note of how difficult it is for you to withstand a crowd."

"I am still quite nervous, Mama," Lenora said, her voice rising a note higher. She began to wring her hands. "I have never been on a drive with a gentleman."

"Now don't go getting yourself in a fit about it." Mama's former light tone now held a reprimand. She fixed Lenora with a serious look. "This is a great compliment to you and a remarkable opportunity. You are not getting any younger, my dear, and your father and I have prayed earnestly for a man to see your character and seek a connection with you." She took both of Lenora's hands in hers and softened her expression, but her voice remained intent. "Focus on your strengths and do not overwhelm yourself, but you *must* make the most of this opportunity, Lenora. I don't know how to impress upon you the importance of this drive, except to say that this may promise salvation from a future that, with every passing year, shall become dimmer until you may very well find yourself without the home and family we have all so longed for you to have."

Cassie's mouth had fallen open. Her mother had *never* spoken to Lenora this way. To Cassie, yes, Mama was frank on any number of subjects, but the family treated Lenora carefully, as though she could break at the slightest jostle of her tender feelings. The carefulness was something Cassie had resented on many occasions, and yet something she'd understood. Lenora *was* fragile, and she had been broken enough times that the family protected her like a fine vase. Cassie had never anticipated what it would be like to watch her mother strip away that protection and essentially tell Lenora that she was running out of chances.

Lenora's eyes were wide, and her countenance open, absorbing every word. Cassie could feel her sister's determination to please their mother. Lenora wanted to do well. She wanted to succeed. This drive with Evan was Lenora's chance to prove herself.

What have I done? Cassie screamed inside her own head.

Mama continued. "I shall have Young set out your blue muslin. It is just the thing for a fine day as this. Mr. Glenside will not be able to ignore your loveliness."

Mama left the room, and Cassie reached out and took hold of Lenora's elbow. Cassie closed her eyes and prayed for the strength to do what must be done.

"Cassie?" Lenora asked, a sharp crease in her forehead. She attempted to pull her arm away, but Cassie did not release it. She had to do the right thing, but, oh, she did not want to!

"What is wrong?" Lenora asked.

Cassie felt numb to her toes. This moment had been unavoidable, yet she had hoped. She blinked at her sister, her mouth dry, and then forced the words out. "I must tell you something." She licked her lips and took a deep breath. "I must confess what I have done before you go on that drive." A drive. Alone with Evan. Cassie's stomach turned over.

Lenora's eyebrows rose. "Confess?"

Cassie forced each word out like air from a bellows. "And before I tell you what I've done I must beg your forgiveness. I promise I only meant to help—to do for you what you had not the confidence to do for yourself. I never meant for it to be deceptive, though it was, and I never meant for it to go so long as it did." That it *had* gone on so long tied Cassie in knots. Evan was no longer a stranger, no longer an unknown person in the village like he'd been when she'd began her campaign. She knew him now, but the connection she'd forged with him did not change the facts, nor did it change Lenora looking at her as though she'd lost her mind.

"What do you need my forgiveness for?" Lenora asked, carefully and cautiously forming each word with her pretty, sweet, and innocent mouth.

Cassie knew Lenora would never guess the truth. She did not have the capacity to comprehend what Cassie had done.

She released Lenora's arm and turned toward the doorway. "Come with me. I've something to give you; something that should be yours." *The letters were meant for Lenora,* she told herself, and yet she didn't believe it anymore. It was Cassie who read the letters, Cassie who responded to them. It was Cassie who knew Evan better than anyone. But it didn't matter. Lenora had been the motivation behind Cassie's actions. The letters were hers because Evan thought they always had been.

Cassie's steps were shaky as she lifted her skirts to ascend the stairs, and she had to concentrate on breathing evenly. *This is what I'd always planned,* she told herself again and again. Only there was so much she *hadn't* planned, including the extreme regret she now felt. She should be glad to be done with the ruse, but she felt as though she were losing a friend.

Cassie led Lenora into her room and to her writing desk. She rested her hand on the knob of the drawer, and then took a breath and pulled it open, not allowing herself any more hesitation as she took hold of the letters. She turned and thrust the stack to Lenora, who took them and stared at them in her hand.

"Is this my ribbon?" she asked, fingering the purple satin ribbon that Cassie had used to tie the letters together.

"Yes." Cassie swallowed and had to clear her throat before she could continue. She had all but forgotten the small theft. "I took the ribbon from your vanity, to use for the letters."

Lenora glanced at Cassie before turning the packet over in her hands, as though only now realizing that the ribbon was not the focal point.

After inspecting the letters—but not releasing them from the ribbon—Lenora looked at Cassie, more confused than ever. "I don't understand. These letters are addressed to Young."

Cassie took a breath, which trembled slightly in her chest, and then told the whole story. Mr. Bunderson. The Dyers' ball. The letters sent through Young. And more letters sent back to Mr. Glenside.

It was impossible to keep her emotions at bay as she laid herself at her sister's feet. The waver in her voice was in part for the shameful confession, but the additional sense of loss was truly shattering.

Cassie finished with her eyes focused on the floor at her feet. There was the smallest sense of relief regarding her disclosure. She had fulfilled her original intention. Lenora would read the letters and know Evan as Cassie had always expected her to. Lenora could go on the drive with a full understanding of the man at her side. Cassie felt like hollow glass.

Hollow enough that the faintest hope rose up within that space inside.

Perhaps Lenora would be unwilling to be any part of the deception. Perhaps she would see that though Cassie had pretended to be Lenora, it was Cassie Evan had truly been writing to. If Lenora refused to go along with the deception, the false connection she had with Mr. Glenside would come to an end. Perhaps then Cassie and Evan could come to know one another in person, face to face. Somehow.

Lenora, after listening silently to all Cassie said, untied the bow and let the ends fall away, unbinding the letters in her hand. She picked up the first one, and Cassie tried to hide how desperately she wanted to take them back. They were *her* letters, not Lenora's. But "Dear Lenora" was written on every one of Evan's letters. Cassie's hands tightened into fists, and she held them behind her back so Lenora wouldn't see her whitened knuckles.

Lenora turned the letter in her hand before she looked up, her expression soft. "You wrote on my behalf?"

Cassie could not properly interpret the tone of voice. Was Lenora angry? Hurt? And she could not answer. The campaign had begun on Lenora's behalf, but it had not remained that way. Cassie simply nodded in reply.

"And he wrote back?"

"For weeks now," Cassie said, striving to remain calm. If Lenora knew how *Cassie* felt toward Evan, would she go on this drive? If she knew that Cassie's heart had become entangled, would she relinquish any claim? "I had only intended it as a way for you to be introduced to him. But the correspondence grew to more than that." She nodded toward the letters. "Mr. Glenside was remarkably candid in his responses, more than I expected he would be. He is a most interesting man, Lenora, and he came alive to me on these pages. Relocating to Leagrave and finding his place in the new society has been difficult. I had thought the letters would help *you*, but they were helpful for him too, and so I didn't stop as I planned to."

She watched Lenora's face as she looked between Cassie and the letters, but she could not interpret what her sister was feeling.

"I had always planned to tell you, when I felt you were ready to continue in my place—in person, not in ink—and I made copies of every letter I wrote to him so you would have everything we exchanged. Only now . . . with his invitation . . ."

She couldn't continue as the emotion rose up, and she blinked away the tears. She waved toward the letters and hoped Lenora would understand what Evan had come to mean to Cassie and that she would refuse the drive. Or perhaps send Cassie in her place. The fantasy was sweet, like sugar crystals on her tongue, and began to carry her away until Lenora wrapped her arms around Cassie's shoulders.

"Thank you," Lenora breathed, seemingly unaware of Cassie's stiff posture. She pulled back and smiled. "You have done for me what I could not do myself, and I will never forget this kindness." She held the letters—Cassie's letters—to her chest. "I shall read every one before he comes for me!" Her smile widened even more. "I will not let you down. I shall be as I ought and justify all you have done. You truly are the best of sisters."

Lenora hurried from the room, leaving Cassie to stare blankly at where her sister had stood.

Cassie looked at her hands. Empty. Traitorous.

What have I done?

Chapter Twenty-Three

After arriving at the vicarage, Evan was shown into the modest parlor where Mrs. Wilton awaited him. She welcomed him as if he were an old friend rather than a man she had only met twice. That Mr. and Mrs. Wilton had approved his invitation bolstered his confidence. He had never driven out with a woman—in London he had not had a carriage—however, Mrs. Wilton's charm and poise put him at ease.

When he heard footfalls on the stairs, he rose and turned to see Lenora in the doorway. She wore a blue dress the same shade as a summer sky and the darker blue bonnet he had seen her wear in town on another occasion. The color of the hat matched her eyes, presenting a view equal to that of a portrait, where an artist weighed each shade and matched it to the others to create the most striking image. Evan wondered if Cassandra might have helped Lenora choose what to wear today. Then he told himself not to think about Cassandra.

"Good afternoon, Miss Wilton," he said as he straightened from his bow. She had signed the last letter with only "Lenora," but he thought he should abide by the formal address in the company of her mother.

She opened her mouth to speak, then closed it, her cheeks turning pink. She looked at the ground, fidgeted with the string of her reticule, took another breath, and then raised her head without meeting his eye. She stared at the knot of his cravat instead. "G-good afternoon, Mr. Glenside." She let out a breath and licked her lips as though she had accomplished a great feat.

Evan tried to ignore his disappointment. He'd hoped the awkwardness he'd felt between them at the dinner party would be changed now. Determined to be optimistic, he hoped her nerves would be better remedied with their ride today.

"You look lovely, Lenora," Mrs. Wilton said from behind Evan. He stepped aside as Mrs. Wilton moved forward and took her daughter's hands. She gave them a squeeze, then leaned in and kissed her daughter's cheek, whispering something Evan felt sure he wasn't supposed to hear, but he did.

"He is everything Papa and I would wish for you. Carry yourself well."

Evan shifted his feet and looked away as the women parted, not wanting them to know he'd overheard. It was only a drive, was it not? But Uncle's warning about conducting a secret affair rang back to him. His intentions did not matter nearly as much as the interpretation of his actions did, and at the moment he felt very caught. He looked at Lenora, hoping her loveliness would help him overcome his increasing anxiety, but she looked as nervous as ever. Still, he knew from her letters that there was more to her than she showed the world.

"Now," Mrs. Wilton said, turning to look at him, "we shall have tea when you return; Mr. Wilton and Cassie will join us. Do enjoy the countryside this afternoon. It is a lovely day for a drive."

Evan thanked her, then followed Miss Wilton out the front door. At the side of the carriage, he put out his hand to help her up, and she looked at it a few seconds before tentatively putting her hand in his. It was the first time he had touched her, and he had hoped to feel some positive physical sensation. His mother had met his father at a dance, and she said that when he led her to the floor, her hand had tingled like her nose did after her first glass of wine. Perhaps it was the white glove Lenora wore that interfered. He would have to ask his mother if she'd been wearing gloves the night she met Father.

Evan's hand did not tingle when he lifted Miss Wilton into the carriage. His chest did not swell when she whispered her thanks, then ducked her chin sheepishly.

Surely not every couple has a physical sensation, he told himself as he crossed in front of the horse to the other side of the carriage and stepped up. He was grateful Uncle had taught him to drive the gig himself; it gave him something to do with his hands and eyes.

He flicked the reins, and the horse fairly jumped forward, causing both himself and Miss Wilton to fall back against the seat. He reached one hand out to steady her, and she flinched at his touch, prompting him to withdraw his hand quickly.

"Are you all right?"

"Yes," she said. Nothing more.

After a few seconds, he attempted additional conversation. "It is a fine day."

"Yes."

"Is May always so lovely in Bedfordshire?"

"Yes."

Another pause.

"The May Day social was a lovely event. Your family gave a great service to the community with all your effort."

"Thank you."

Another pause. Evan searched for something else to discuss.

"The piece you played at my uncle's the other night—what is it called?"

Miss Wilton straightened in her seat. "*La Pastorella* by Franz Schubert."

"I don't believe I have heard of Franz Schubert, but then you know I am not well versed in music."

"He is a new composer."

Evan smiled at her, but it was lost because she was staring at the tail of the horse in front of them. "Well, that makes me feel a little better at least."

"My aunt sent me three of his pieces a few weeks ago, but that is the only one I feel I have mastered."

Finally, some substance to work with. "That you have mastered any piece of music in so short a time is an impressive talent. I enjoyed hearing you play very much."

She shifted and ducked her chin again. "I did not mean to boast."

Boast? When had she boasted? "I only meant to compliment your abilities." Was he was out of place to speak to her so openly? Was there a rule about how to compliment a young lady?

"Thank you."

They drove in silence for several minutes, Evan wishing he knew how to fix this awkwardness. How could he court a woman who would not talk to him? Could he hope for improvement if he rode out with her a second time? Or would a second ride signal an increased level of intention in the eyes of other people? He began to sweat.

Miss Wilton cleared her throat, and he almost jumped in response.

"It seems Leagrave has improved upon you these last weeks."

Initiation of a topic—that was a good sign! "Yes, I believe it has." He offered her a smile in hopes it would encourage her to continue. "The people have been very kind."

She flushed pink and returned her gaze to the horse's tail.

Evan faced forward again, wondering if that were all he would receive from her.

After another minute passed, she cleared her throat again. "Are the renovations of the Dower House still in progress?"

"Yes, we hope it will be finished in August." He went on to tell her how excited her mother and sisters were to come, how they had been selling or donating the things they would not need in Leagrave. Lenora listened intently, and he thought she might ask a question to extend the topic, but when he finished she just smiled again.

Evan began counting through the silence and fifty-two seconds passed before she spoke once more. "Is your mother in good health?"

"Yes, she has always been very fit and energetic. I think she will enjoy the country very much."

Fifty-eight seconds later. "And your sisters? Are they in good health?"

"Yes, they take after my mother."

The conversation continued in fits and starts for the rest of the trip. Her asking simple questions every minute or so and him attempting to give an answer that would spark additional conversation but never seemed to. Several times he gave a lengthy answer, hoping it would prompt her to do the same, only to have it fall flat.

He commented on the wildflowers, the houses, the clouds, a bird, another carriage they passed on the road, London, her father's sermon the week before, and even the ruts in the road until finally, he turned the carriage around and headed back to the vicarage. Either she was miserable and he should return her home out of courtesy, or this was how she always was. Either option left him with a decision to make.

Chapter Twenty-Four

Cassie was lying on her bed with one arm flung over her eyes when there was a knock at her door. She didn't want anyone to come in, but before she could say so, she heard the door open without her invitation. She propped herself up on her elbows as her mother entered.

"Oh," she said, sitting up completely and getting off the bed. She attempted to put an easy smile on her face and clasped her hands behind her back. "I thought you were Young."

"Are you ill, Cassie?" Mama regarded her daughter with her head cocked to the side.

"I am fine. Only tired, I suppose."

"That's not like you. You're usually outrunning the lot of us."

"Perhaps such exertion has caught up with me, then." It was far too true a sentiment.

"That is unfortunate as I was hoping you would join us for tea."

Cassie's head came up quickly, and her muscles tensed. "Lenora is back from her drive?"

"Yes, they just returned. Your father is in the parlor already, but Lenora is not making much conversation. We would appreciate your company, if you feel up to it, of course."

Don't make me go, she begged in her mind, but some traitorous part of herself wanted to see Evan. "I am well enough. Only give me a few moments to freshen up."

Mama smiled gratefully. "Thank you. I feel we have good reason to hope that Lenora may make a match, but she will continue to need our help a while longer, I think, until she and Mr. Glenside are more comfortable with one another."

Cassie nodded, unable to trust herself to speak. Once Mama left, Cassie let her eyes fall shut as she stood in the middle of the room. Before she completely fell victim to her regrets, she forced her feet to move to the washbasin, where she splashed tepid water on her face and then patted it dry. She pinched her cheeks to bring out the color and pressed her lips together so hard they hurt, gratified by both the pain and the rosy bloom that accompanied the release. She stared at her reflection and lifted her chin, convincing herself that she did not appear to be pining.

The resolve she built up lasted until she stepped into the parlor and met Evan's eyes across the room. Her feet stopped and her heart rate increased. What was wrong with her?

Papa was telling Mr. Glenside about the ruins located south of the village, so Cassie forced her eyes away and took a seat beside Mama on the settee. Lenora sat in a chair beside Evan with a nervous but satisfied expression on her face that pricked Cassie's heart. Anyone who knew Lenora could see the pride in her eyes and contentment in her smile. What had Evan thought of their time together? Was he as satisfied as Lenora?

"Cassie has made several drawings of the ruins," Papa said, bringing her into the conversation. "Where is your sketchbook?"

"Uh, I left it upstairs." She began to stand, grateful for the chance of escape. "Would you like me to get it?" She could take her time and say she hadn't found it right away. It wouldn't be difficult to spend several minutes on her pretend hunt for the book, thus reducing the time she would have to spend in Evan's company.

Papa waved her back to her seat. "No matter, perhaps next time."

"Or perhaps you and Lenora might ride out to the ruins and see it for yourself, Mr. Glenside," Mama said with a sweet smile. "Lenora is an excellent horsewoman."

Lenora ducked her chin like a child who was to be seen and not heard. Cassie was embarrassed for Lenora's sake that she couldn't talk with this man. She wondered again what the drive had been like.

"Lenora *is* an excellent horsewoman," Cassie confirmed, trying to spur her sister into conversation. She felt Evan's eyes move to her, but she kept her own gaze on Lenora. "Tell him of our favorite trail, Lenora."

Lenora looked confused, her eyebrows pulled together as though she didn't know what Cassie was talking about.

"The one through Brewster Wood," Cassie prompted.

"Oh, yes!" Lenora smiled, but then lifted her cup and took a sip of tea.

"Brewster Wood?" Evan repeated.

Cassie waited for Lenora to speak, but she didn't. Instead she cast an imploring look at Cassie, who had no choice but to make up for the silence. She looked at Evan, who was watching her intently, and felt his gaze like a breeze.

"Brewster Wood is located on the western edge of the village, and spans nearly four miles. There is a lovely footpath that follows the riverside, and there are places where the river is shallow and still enough that the horses will walk right up the center of it. The only thing you can hear is the chime of the water and splash of the hooves and you feel as though you are the only person in all the world. On a warm summer day, the coolness of the water meets the heat of the day with a perfect temperature that feels like cream against your skin."

A silence followed her words. Evan did not blink. He stared at her and she could not look away from him.

"What a poetic description," he finally said.

"Yes," Mama echoed, watching Cassie with an unreadable expression. "Poetic indeed."

Cassie turned her attention to her cup and followed Lenora's example by taking a sip of the tea, which was too hot. She gasped slightly. Evan was still watching her, and she looked up to meet his worried expression. She gave him a slight smile to let him know she was all right, and he smiled back.

"Cassie is the most artistic of our girls," Papa said. "Drawing and painting mostly, though she has always had a way with words, as demonstrated, a bit dramatically perhaps, but it is a lovely pathway through Brewster Wood all the same."

Cassie felt her cheeks turn hot at Papa minimizing her artistic qualities.

"Lenora's gifts are with music," Mama interjected. "But then you have heard her play."

"Indeed," Evan said. "She is marvelous."

Cassie felt the green vapor of envy rise up in her at such a high compliment. No one diminished *Lenora's* accomplishments. Cassie took another sip of the too-hot tea, wishing it would injure her enough that she might have reason to leave.

Mama straightened as though the praise had been for her. "Marvelous is a very apt description of our Lenora's talent. Are you musical, Mr. Glenside?"

"I'm afraid not," he said, a note of caution in his voice that Cassie felt sure only she could hear. Cassie knew from his letters he was insecure about his upbringing. So did Lenora, yet she showed no sign of coming to Evan's rescue.

"You will make a wonderful student, then," Cassie said. "Lenora is not only a talented musician but she also teaches music lessons and pianoforte. If you've ever wanted to learn more of the subject, you could not have a better tutor than Lenora."

Evan met her eyes. Cassie found herself sinking into their blue depths again. He did not blink. She forced her gaze away, and after a moment Papa asked after Evan's uncle, expressing how much he had enjoyed their dinner party together.

Cassie focused on her breathing and took a bite of shortbread. In her head she counted slowly to keep herself calm. When she got to seventy-five, she turned to Mama. "I am sorry to be poor company," she said, "but might I be excused? I'm afraid I feel a bit peaked." She avoided Evan's eyes though she could feel them on her.

Mama did not argue. "Then you must lie down with a cloth over your eyes. Call for Young. I shall look in on you later."

Cassie nodded, fearing that the reason Mama was allowing her to leave was because she sensed the connection between her and Evan. When Cassie stood, Evan and Papa did as well. She gave a quick curtsy and then hurried up the stairs to her room.

She closed the door behind her, pressing her back against the wood and raising both hands to her face as though she could hide from the world. Apparently Lenora had enjoyed her drive with Evan, but that did not make it any easier for Cassie to push aside her feelings for him. The ache she felt to converse with him, *just* with him, was sharp as pins. It was not right for her to feel this way; he was Lenora's . . . beau. The term caused her to clench her jaw. Cassie had done this for Lenora and must stay *that* course, not indulge in the fantasy that had begun to overcome her.

After taking adequate time to compose herself, Cassie took a breath, dropped her hands, and stared unseeingly out the window. If she truly hoped to rid herself of the attraction she felt for Evan—Mr. Glenside from now on—there were only two remedies: distance and time. She sighed and began to think of how she could build equal measure of both.

Chapter Twenty-Five

"You're committed," Bunderson said with a nod and a wry grin from the other side of the table. "Your uncle's exactly right about that. You have entertained Miss Lenora's affections and—given your status and hers—I don't see any way 'round it."

Evan slumped against the wood-backed chair of the pub. He had just come from tea at the vicarage. It was too early for drinks, and yet he had needed advice desperately enough to send a card around to his only friend in Leagrave. When they met at the pub, Evan confessed the whole of the "affair" for the second time in as many days and received an even worse reaction than he'd had from his uncle, which only depressed him further.

"It was a handful of letters and a single country drive," he argued. "Surely that is not enough to base a lifetime upon."

"My brother married a woman he danced with one time too many," Bunderson said, nodding his commiseration as he turned his glass of ale on the table. "She was the niece of Mr. Crackage, visiting for the summer and pretty as they come. James was smitten with her enough that he asked her to the floor three times in a single evening. By the time the church bells rang the next morning, the town gossips had spread word that they were engaged."

Evan stared at Bunderson with a slack jaw. "And he *married* her?"

Bunderson shrugged. "She *was* pretty and of a good family, and things turned out well enough. They seem as happy as any other married couple. He took a commission, you know, but he doesn't seem to regret those three dances, or the three sons they've made together since then." He winked.

"I can't imagine my life married to a woman who cannot speak to me," Evan said.

"She spoke to you," Bunderson said, waving away Evan's concern. "You said she asked you a dozen or more questions on your drive."

"But she didn't *care* about the answers," Evan said, trying to describe how he'd felt as he'd sat beside Lenora. She had felt like a stranger to him. "She didn't ask for clarification or offer her own experience on a topic. It was as though she had a list of questions to ask but no idea what to do with the answers. When I asked *her* questions in return, she would answer with a smile or a nod or a simple yes or no. If I'm to pull no punches in my description, the drive was torturous. I don't know when I have been more uncomfortable, and that is saying something since I have found myself in one uncomfortable place after another ever since I arrived in Leagrave." He doubted his relationship with Bunderson warranted the burden he was placing on his new friend's shoulders, but he couldn't seem to help but unload his troubles. And he had spoken the truth.

"But she *did* answer the questions," Bunderson pointed out. "And you said you were taken with the love notes the two of you have been sharing. There's hope in that connection for the future—more hope than three dances at a country ball, I wager."

"A future I *must* share with her?" The edge in Evan's voice was sharp as a knife. He felt tricked and betrayed, and yet was it reasonable for him to feel that way? He had been a participant, not coerced into the connection he'd made. And the woman on the page *was* intriguing. Only . . .

"I don't make the rules, Glenside," Bunderson said, leaning back in his chair. "But we all dance to the tune of them. You're no different than any of the rest of us any longer."

Except that I didn't fully understand the rules of the game, Evan thought to himself. Protests would get him nowhere, however. "There really is no way around it?" Uncle had made it seem that Evan could ride out with Miss Lenora and use that visit as a point of measure. But Mr. and Mrs. Wilton's obvious expectations had created more insecurity in Evan. Enough that he needed a second opinion, which was not what he'd hoped it would be.

"Well, you *could* stand down—you've made no *official* declaration. But you risk your reputation, to say nothing of hers, and the village will not look kindly on your behavior, especially if they learn the foundation you set with those letters."

"I can't afford to alienate the entire village," Evan mused aloud. He thought about what he'd heard Mrs. Wilton tell her daughter before the drive, about how pleased they were about the match. It didn't appear that Miss Wilton had many opportunities to choose from. "And I would hate to damage Miss Wilton in any way. I bear her no ill will."

"Then you must be the hero and do right by her," Bunderson said as easily as he would order another round of drinks. "And do try to have confidence in the match." He leaned forward, his expression more serious. "My mother has always told us that a good marriage is equal parts *choosing* a good partner and *being* a good partner. Simplistic, I know, but you have both aspects in your favor. Miss Lenora is a good enough woman and you're a good enough man to make a success of this thing. That she doesn't send your heart racing or astound you with diverting conversation *now* does not mean she won't do so later."

It was surprisingly heavy wisdom from a young man whom Evan suspected did not often think all that deeply about anything. Which made

Evan wonder why he had asked Bunderson's advice in the first place. Yet who else could he have asked? The fact that Bunderson echoed what Uncle had said, and then some, could not be ignored. Evan couldn't disregard the opinion of two men from two different perspectives and situations. But their answers did not sit well with him. He did not *feel* the rightness of this course.

Evan closed his eyes and allowed the regret to bury him alive for exactly four seconds. Then he began to dig himself out, one fistful at a time. He had always been a practical sort of man, not steeped in emotion or romantic notion. For many years he had wondered if he would ever marry; his mother and sisters were so dependent upon him that he doubted his ability to care for them and a family of his own. But his situation had changed now. He *could* marry, and, from a logical point of view, Miss Lenora was a fine woman who would make a fine wife. She was not a gifted conversationalist and her anxiety was extreme, but there was more to her than that—he knew it from her letters. And she came from a good family who was accepting of him. Many men would wish for his place.

The face and figure of Cassie Wilton came unbidden to Evan's mind, and he shifted awkwardly in his chair. He enjoyed her company very much, and her skill at conversation and . . . Well, it was not hard to list Cassie's good qualities. But thinking of her at all made him a cad. Hopefully once Lenora was more comfortable around him, she would behave more like her sister—with ease and humor. But the drive had not proved such a thing, and seemed to have sealed his fate rather than provided an opportunity for a more informed choice.

But this was not his uncle's fault for advising him, or Bunderson's for confirming Uncle's concerns. Evan had replied to that first letter of his own will, and though some part of him wanted to feel as though Miss Wilton had trapped him, it only took picturing her guileless face to know that was unfair. He believed that she had acted in a way she felt was best, with sincere intent. She was simply as ignorant as he was in how it would be perceived by others. Certainly she'd be embarrassed if she knew the predicament her innocent letters had put him in, and he cared enough about her to want to protect her from any shame she would feel.

"Have I convinced you?"

Evan looked at Bunderson with a tinge of misgiving. Bunderson spoke as though he had something to gain from Evan seeing things his way, but he was smiling with such an easy look on his face that Evan ignored his misgiving. It was the circumstance that had him confused and contrary. Nothing more. Honestly, so much thought and consideration was exhausting. Maybe it was better to be done with the pursuit of a wife before he got any further in. If one woman could cause so much trouble, what would exploring a second or third option do to his befuddled mind?

"I suppose you have convinced me of my own folly and reminded me of my duty," Evan said. "And that I could certainly do worse."

Bunderson lifted his glass. "Indeed you could," he said with a laugh, then raised his glass an inch higher. "To you, Glenside. May you find a lifetime of happiness with Miss Lenora Wilton so that one day we shall share another drink and laugh at the reluctance you felt today."

Evan lifted his glass and tapped it against Bunderson's, resolved to make the toast a prophecy. Regret for what could have been had never served him in the past and certainly would not serve him now. Instead of allowing this to weigh him down, he would embrace what was and what would be.

"Here, here," he said, then finished his drink in a single swallow that would have made his uncle proud.

Chapter Twenty-Six

The evening of Lenora's ride with Evan, Cassie stood outside the parlor door and took a calming breath. She had not joined the family for dinner, claiming a headache. Lenora was playing one of the Schubert pieces Aunt Gwen had sent two weeks ago; the sound filled the house entirely. Cassie knew that Papa would be reviewing Sunday's sermon in the parlor while Mama knitted or sewed. It was how they spent every evening at home, and though Cassie had often found the quiet evenings rather dull, she hoped she would miss them soon enough.

Bletchley was only twenty miles away, after all, and it was her idea to leave. Cassie entered the parlor and stood just inside the doorway as all three sets of eyes came to rest upon her. Lenora stopped playing.

"Cassie," Mama said, setting down her sewing and rising from her place. "Are you feeling better?"

"Yes."

Mama crossed to her and placed her cool fingers against Cassie's forehead, then her cheek. Cassie was grateful for the sincere sympathy she saw in her mother's eyes and allowed it to fuel her motivation. Perhaps Mama did not suspect anything untoward after all. That made leaving an even sweeter prospect for Cassie, as then she could protect her mother from learning the truth of her deception. Cassie smiled at Lenora.

"Do not let me interrupt. The piece is sounding very well," she said with complete sincerity.

Lenora smiled and went back to playing the same line she'd been practicing when Cassie stood outside the door. She would often play the same line over and over, experimenting with different emphasis and pacing. The family was used to the redundancy, and tonight Cassie was grateful for it as Lenora's focus would afford her some privacy.

She looked at Mama, then glanced at her father. "I would like to speak with you and Papa, if you have a moment."

"Certainly," Mama said, ushering Cassie to the settee. She sat beside Cassie, then lifted her eyebrows expectantly.

"I wonder if I might visit with Mary for a time, now that the social is finished. I haven't seen her in ages, and what with a new baby on the way, she could surely use an extra set of hands about the place to make ready."

"Is she ill?" Papa asked, glancing up from his papers to look at Mama. "Has she asked for help?"

Mama shook her head. "Not that I'm aware. Mary is particularly hardy with her confinements. Has she asked you to come, Cassie?"

"Not exactly," Cassie admitted slowly. "She did tell me at Christmas that I was welcome for a visit whenever it suited me, though that was before she was in the family way again."

"I'm not sure where you would stay," Mama said, her brow puckered. "The rooms are full of children, and she is not due until November."

"I shall find a place, and I am not worried for my comfort. I can share a room with the girls if needs be." Mary had four children, and her home was already barely controlled chaos in too small a space. But it would be preferable to here. Cassie needed time and distance, and Mary could give her both. She had considered asking to visit Aunt Gwen in Bath instead, her widowed aunt was always eager for company, but Cassie feared there would not be enough there to distract her. She knew that would not be the case at Mary's.

"Perhaps you would be of greater use once the baby actually arrives. Rose will need assistance before Mary will."

Cassie refrained from showing her frustration. Why could they not simply give their consent? Why must everything be an inquisition? She took a breath, reminding herself that her parents did not deserve blame. "I simply feel it would be good to have a change of scenery. That is all."

Mama looked at her with greater intent, similar to that which she'd had at tea this afternoon. "Perhaps you are right."

The words were pointed, and Cassie looked into her lap.

"No more than a fortnight," Papa said, distracted and yet not really. "You've responsibilities here too."

"A fortnight?" Cassie repeated. "I had hoped for a month, perhaps even two."

"A fortnight is all we can spare." Papa looked over his spectacles. "It would be unfair to leave the household to your mother and Lenora alone as well as expecting Mary to put you up for much longer than that."

Cassie nearly asked what they would do when there were no daughters left to help manage the household, but that only led her to think about Mr. Glenside and Lenora . . . getting married . . . setting up a household of their own. He would be Cassie's *brother*.

She had to get away from Leagrave, even if it were only for a fortnight. With some distance she could better convince herself of her foolishness and be spared watching Mr. Glenside court Lenora. She nodded her consent. "May I write to Mary and ask if I might come?"

"You have my blessing," Papa said, then returned to his paper.

"It is a credit to your character that you feel such compassion for your sister," Mama said.

Cassie met her eye, wondering which sister Mama was referring to but not daring to ask for clarification. It would tell too much that must not be told.

"Being sisters is a particularly important relationship," Mama continued, holding Cassie's eye. "It requires sacrifice and patience at times, especially when sisters are close in age and situation. More than any other people in the world, your sisters are bound to you and you to them. You should always be mindful of their needs and opportunities and do what you can to support and extend such things, even if it is sometimes difficult."

"So true, my dear," Papa said as he crossed out a line on his paper. "Sisterly affection is one of God's greatest gifts, and what a lucky girl you are, Cassandra, to have five such gifts from your Creator."

Cassie could feel the heat in her neck and face, caused by both Mama's warning and Papa's patronization. There was no need for argument, however, and so she simply nodded.

Lenora continued to play the same musical line over and over again.

"If you write to Mary tonight," Mama said, picking up her sewing, "I shall see that it's posted first thing tomorrow. Tell her we'll send a food basket."

Cassie stood quickly. "Thank you, Mama, Papa." She hurried from the room. "Two days for the post to reach Mary," she said under her breath as she lifted her skirts and fairly flew up the stairs. "Then two days to hear back, three at most." Cassie could be on a coach for Bletchley in a week's time. "Not soon enough."

What she wouldn't do to go back in time and never have sent that first letter. Then she wouldn't know Mr. Glenside enough to want to know him better. Then she would not be standing on the precipice of coveting her sister's husband.

Chapter Twenty-Seven

Mary's response to Cassie's request for a visit was—blessedly—received Friday afternoon. Mary would be more than happy to have Cassie come for a visit and would have a bed made up for her in the room her two daughters shared, if Cassie didn't mind. Cassie didn't mind. She would sleep on the kitchen floor if it meant she could get away from Leagrave. Away from Mr. Glenside. Away from what she'd done.

Mr. Glenside came to the house on Saturday evening to escort Lenora to a dinner party. For once, Cassie was *glad* she wasn't attending a party. The idea of seeing Lenora on Mr. Glenside's arm all evening would be more than Cassie could handle, she was sure. Instead, Cassie stayed home all evening, packing her trunk in order to leave for Bletchley first thing Monday morning.

Sunday dawned bright and beautiful, and although Cassie considered feigning illness to get out of going to church, the concern it would trigger in her parents—especially her father—did not seem worth the risk. They might change their mind about letting her visit Mary. So Cassie went to church and forced herself not to look behind her to see if Mr. Glenside was there, though she was certain he was. He'd been attending church every Sunday since the May Day celebration. *To see Lenora?* she wondered. Envy rose up like steam from an open pit.

After services, Cassie struck up a conversation with Miss Parell, a spinster always eager to talk of her four canaries. Cassie hoped that by the time she exited the chapel, Mr. Glenside would be gone from the church-yard. She and Miss Parell were the last two out of the chapel—other than Lenora, who was still at the organ, and Mama, who was gathering up the hymnals—but they had not taken enough time. Mr. Glenside was talking with Mr. Bunderson and a few other young men beneath the shade of an elm tree beside the path leading to the vicarage.

Mr. Bunderson caught her eye and said something to his companions before crossing the yard to her. She put a welcoming smile upon her lips and raised her chin while waiting for him to join her. Flirting was exactly what she needed to distract herself.

"Good afternoon, Miss Cassandra," Mr. Bunderson said with an elab-orate bow. "Your father's sermon was particularly moving today."

"You are an abominable liar, Mr. Bunderson." Cassie cocked her head and narrowed her eyes playfully, glad she could so fully cover her other-wise mournful mood. "I'm quite sure I heard your snores. I happen to know you only come to church because your mother sulks if you do not."

"Not true." Mr. Bunderson put a hand to his chest as though of-fended. "I come to church because the view"—he paused and looked her over with completely improper boldness—"is always so delightful. I love to see the ladies turned out in their Sunday best."

Cassie didn't even blush. Why did she not blush? Mr. Bunderson had never said anything so bold to her—no one had. And yet she did not blush a single shade. Trying to cover her lack of reaction, she lifted her chin higher. "You are a cad, Mr. Bunderson."

He moved his hand from his chest to his forehead. "Ah, you wound me."

Taking the chance for escape, Cassie began moving forward. "Which is no less than you deserve."

Mr. Bunderson stepped in front of her, blocking her way. She stifled her irritation. "I'm afraid the only remedy—for both my caddish ways and your insulting accusation—is that you allow me to walk you home by way of the canal road."

Cassie felt her polite smile falter. She had no interest in being walked home by Mr. Bunderson. In fact, she felt a mild irritation with everything he said to her, though she felt sure a few weeks ago she'd have been aflutter from his attention.

"I don't believe my father would allow it," she said as an excuse. "I am not out in society, you know. Perhaps you should walk Lenora home instead." *And fall in love with her and propose marriage before Evan can and then he and I can be together!*

Mr. Bunderson wrinkled his nose, which made Cassie feel defensive of Lenora even though she was as irritated with Lenora as she was with Mr. Bunderson. Yet neither of them deserved her annoyance. She was so out of sorts.

"Well, you might not be officially out," Mr. Bunderson said, leaning toward her slightly, "but I hear it on good authority that the situation will be shortly remedied, and, as I am a bit of a gambling man, I am willing to play the odds now so as to be the first man to walk arm in arm with you. Once word spreads that the prettiest of the Wilton girls is on the market, so to speak, I am quite sure I shall have to stand in line."

Cassie swallowed, his extreme compliment lost on her. It was not easy to keep her tone casual, but she did her best. "What do you mean my situation is to be shortly remedied? Are you a fortune teller, sir?"

Mr. Bunderson lifted one eyebrow. "In fact I am." He leaned even closer. She could smell the musk of his cologne. Such nearness would have sent her swooning—at least on the inside—not long ago. "And I have divined a very happy turn for your family and, more specifically, for your dear sister."

He looked over his shoulder, and Cassie couldn't help but follow his gaze to where Mr. Glenside stood beneath the elm tree. The other gentlemen were gone, and Mr. Glenside seemed to be waiting, either for Mr. Bunderson or, perhaps, for Lenora, who was not yet in the yard.

Mr. Glenside caught Cassie's eye and smiled, making her cheeks heat up in an instant. What traitors! Not blushing when Mr. Bunderson said brazen things but turning on like lamps when Mr. Glenside did nothing but look her direction.

Cassie forced her eyes from Mr. Glenside's blue ones to Mr. Bunderson's brown ones. Such boring eyes. Nondescript. Ordinary. She refocused on their conversation, though she wished to all the stars in heaven she were *not* talking of this at all. "You are making reference to Mr. Glenside?" she asked.

"The very man," Mr. Bunderson said with pride. "His relocation to Leagrave could not have come at a better time, do you not agree? With a few more well-placed—and well-meant—bits of advice from his newest friend—" He put a hand to his chest and bowed slightly. "—I feel sure the banns shall be read in just a few weeks' time."

Cassie sorted through Mr. Bunderson's words, moving them around until she thought she knew what he was implying. She did her best to keep her expression free of judgment. "*You* have encouraged Mr. Glenside's attention toward Lenora?"

Mr. Bunderson's smile grew slightly, and he shrugged his shoulders with mock humility. "Perhaps."

"How so, exactly? Do you mean that Mr. Glenside's attention is not sincere on its own?"

"I certainly don't mean that." The fact that Mr. Bunderson's tone lost some of its teasing lilt seemed to emphasize the truth behind the words. "I only encouraged him to do right by her, that is all."

"Do right by her?" Cassie's stomach tightened.

"I mean the letters, of course," Mr. Bunderson said, his eyebrows coming together slightly. "Mr. Glenside told me you were aware of them."

He's spoken of me. He's told his friend that I know about the letters! What would Mr. Bunderson say regarding Mr. Glenside "doing right" if he knew *Cassie* had written the letters?

Cassie forced a nod, swallowing to relieve the increasing dryness of her mouth.

"I told Mr. Glenside that no gentleman could toy with a woman's heart that way, not in Bedfordshire and certainly not with one of the Wilton girls. Poor chap doesn't really know the way of things, you understand, so I explained that the exchange of letters was as good as an understanding." He winked and smiled.

Cassie put a hand to her stomach in hopes it might put off the burning.

"So Mr. Glenside is not truly interested in Lenora's hand." It was the same thing she'd said before, only worded differently. How horrid she was for wishing for Mr. Bunderson's confirmation.

"Oh, no, he thinks very highly of her," Mr. Bunderson hurried to amend. "Only he seems concerned by the contrast between the woman on paper and the woman in person." He shrugged again. "But I have relieved *all* his concerns, and he is moving forward as best *we* could hope."

"We?" Cassie said, noting his emphasis.

"Why, yes." Mr. Bunderson turned and put out his arm, apparently ready to walk her home even though she had not agreed to it. Cassie hesitated but did not know how to deny him, especially when she needed to hear exactly what he meant by *we*. Once her arm was through his, he put his hand over hers and gave her fingers a quick squeeze. "When Lenora marries, you will be free to make a match of your own, will you not?"

The idea made her muscles stiffen. "Well, I would need to be presented first."

"A formality, to be sure." He leaned close so that his breath tickled her ear. She shuddered with poorly suppressed irritation, not delight. "And once those formalities are out of the way, perhaps you can thank me for making it happen. Why, I do believe you might very well owe me the greatest favor of your life, but we can talk of repayment at a later date."

She looked over in time to catch his wink, then faced forward and told herself to breathe and smile and try to feel complimented. What more *could* she do? "I'm afraid Papa would never allow me to walk along the canal road," Cassie said. "But if you would like to walk me through the churchyard, you may. I am leaving to visit my sister in the morning, and there is a great deal to do before I go."

"Well, it is not nearly the time I hoped to spend with you, but I suppose I can be patient a bit longer. Know that you will be greatly missed while you are gone."

"Thank you, Mr. Bunderson." *However, I am so very eager to go.*

Chapter Twenty-Eight

Evan came in from what would soon be his woodworking room—not a *shop*—and undid the knot of his cravat, letting the ends hang loose down his shirtfront, damp with sweat. He was hot and dirty and starving, since he hadn't come in for lunch, but he'd enjoyed working with his hands again. There was something about the straining of muscle and sharp intake of air that felt rebellious considering his current situation and status. Now that the storage room was emptied and the items once stored there properly contained elsewhere, he could determine the best setup for the interior structures. With a bit of time and effort, he might have his shop complete in just a few more weeks.

Evan took the back stairs to his room two at a time. Though he'd enjoyed the work, he was eager to clean up now that he was finished for the day. Once he was presentable in fresh linens and clean boots, he went to his study. He sat down at the desk and shuffled through a collection of old newspapers and the stack of mail on the corner of his desk—it must have come while he was working. When he caught sight of his mother's familiar, flowing script, he smiled and moved her envelope to the top. She wrote him once a week and he was always glad to hear from her, but he was particularly interested in *this* letter.

Last week, after both his uncle and Mr. Bunderson explained Evan's obligation to Miss Lenora, Evan had written his mother. Though he trusted both men, he had remained unsettled to the point where he had not sought out Miss Lenora's company since Sunday, when he'd accompanied her home from church and watched Mr. Bunderson flirt with Cassandra. He'd walked with Lenora's arm through his and not cared that she didn't say a word to him. His eyes were on Cassandra. He wanted to hear what she was saying; he wanted to be the one walking with her. Was it because he believed Lenora was like her, only not yet comfortable enough to show it? Because he had conversed with Cassandra more easily at his uncle's dinner party than he had ever spoken with Lenora?

Evan shook his head and pushed the confusing thoughts away for the hundredth time so as to focus on the letter he held in his hands. It was his final attempt at making sense of his situation. Unlike Uncle and Bunderson, Evan had not only trust in his mother, but history.

Dearest Evan,

I am grateful that you confided your circumstance with me, and I have done all I could to find reliable information. I spoke with Mr. and Mrs. Mundy and they have confirmed that while you are certainly not obligated to pursue the match—and if you have a strong objection to it you should not—the correspondence has put you in a bit of a spot. You are new to Leagrave and therefore your character is unknown. Should you withdraw your attention and the letters become public, you could face some recrimination. Yet the young woman would be foolish to broadcast the correspondence, especially where she was the one who began the exchange. She would be the one inflicting damage on her own reputation in that regard, and Mr. and Mrs. Mundy felt it a slim chance she would do so, especially considering her shy nature.

That said, I must confess that it is the greatest wish of my heart for you to find a good woman with whom you can have a family and a future. For so long you have put the comfort of your sisters and myself ahead of your own, and now you have the chance to pursue happiness and contentment for your own sake. I have told you before that my marriage to your father was arranged by our parents. He was little more than a stranger to me when his family returned from India, and we were introduced just weeks before the wedding. It was during those early years of marriage that my heart truly opened to him, and I have always been grateful that I did not allow only my heart to guide me prior to our vows. I would have missed the greatest joy of my life.

Miss Wilton sounds like a fine woman who does not give her trust easily, yet she has trusted you. I would never presume to tell you what to do, but I would be a poor mother if I did not encourage you to consider carefully before you withdraw your connection. A good woman from a good family is a very fine start to years of happiness, and as she is not so young as the typical debutant, you may find in her a more steadying element.

Please know that I would welcome a new daughter such as you have described with open arms and an open heart. What a gift she would be for our family and, most importantly, for you. She sounds loyal and good-hearted. I could wish for little more.

I long to see you again and look forward to joining you in Leagrave as soon as the Dower House is ready. Mr. Carswold has informed me that you may have your father's equipment collected any time after the first of the month. He is having it packed in crates for safe transport before then and appreciated your generosity in allowing him to use the tools without charge this last year—the money he has saved has allowed him to buy enough of his own equipment. I am so pleased to know you will

continue your father's legacy in woodworking. That Grace has
smiled on us with such brightness fairly dazzles me.

Your loving mother,

Carolyn Glenside

Evan leaned back in his chair and looked over the elegant hand—too elegant for the wife of a carpenter. He had known his parents' marriage had been arranged, but he had not thought much of it since all his memories and experience were of two people who loved each other very much. Thinking on that relationship now, he wondered if his earlier determination not to marry was partly due to the fear that he could never recreate what his parents shared. And yet according to this letter, their love had come in time, not all at once.

He reread the part where Mama had said that Miss Wilton did not seem to trust easily and yet she had trusted him. He hadn't considered that before, but it was true. Lenora had revealed herself to him in her letters and that was no small thing. And she *was* a fine woman. A fine woman who would be hurt if he withdrew from her. He did not want to hurt her. Only, he still felt hesitation, an impulse to proceed with caution. Was that because for the last twelve years he had *had* to be so cautious? Was it because he had not considered marriage with any seriousness until recently, and therefore it was the institution that had him feeling such reticence?

How he wished Lenora could be as open in person as she had been in her letters. He missed the connection he felt through her words. Cassandra entered his thoughts again. Why could Lenora not be as comfortable with him as her younger sister seemed to be? He chased the thoughts away. There was no space for such speculation. He could not allow it.

Evan folded his mother's letter, pondering the primary question that plagued him. Was asking Lenora Wilton to be his wife the right thing to do? Bunderson thought so, and now his mother. Two different perspectives and yet both came to the same point. How could he continue to argue what needed to be done?

The fatigue he had felt over this situation compounded in his mind, like stones held fast with setting mortar. He was tired of questioning himself, and he had no one else to go to for advice. There was one path to take; it was foolish of him to think otherwise.

Evan pulled a clean sheet of paper from the shelf on the side of his desk and trimmed his quill. He took a breath, then dipped his pen and began a letter to Mr. Wilton requesting a private audience tomorrow afternoon. Perhaps if he had better understood the way of things he'd have gone about things differently, but who was he to say things weren't exactly how they were supposed to be?

He stared at the blank sheet, quill poised over the paper, and forced down any further misgivings. He thought of how happy his parents had been in their arranged marriage, and how much Uncle Hastings had loved Aunt Lucy. Bunderson had relayed his mother's advice that a good marriage was equal parts choosing a good partner and being a good partner. Evan knew he was capable of his part, and he had no reason to doubt Lenora would not be a good partner too. Evan's own mother had said that Grace had smiled upon their family. He would be ungrateful not to embrace every good thing that had come his way and face his future with eager resolve to make the most of it.

He put the point of the quill to the paper and began writing. There would be no turning back.

Chapter Twenty-Nine

Cassie smiled as the familiar spire of the church tower came into view through the carriage window. When she'd left Leagrave a fortnight ago, she didn't think she'd be happy to come back, but two weeks away from the poor choices she'd made, and, most importantly, away from Mr. Glenside, had been the right course. She was sure of it. She had run through orchards with her nieces and nephews, helped make new curtains for Mary's parlor, baked, cleaned, and filled several pages of her sketchbook with drawings and paintings. The activities had pushed Mr. Glenside from her mind just as she'd hoped they would.

She felt some lingering anticipation regarding how she might react when she saw him again, but she was convinced that her feelings for Mr. Glenside were nothing more than a misplaced reaction to her frustration at having had to wait on Lenora for so long. But no more! Now she was eager to have Lenora and Mr. Glenside further their connection—excited even. If they married, she could pursue her own attachments, as had been her original plan.

Perhaps without the distraction of Mr. Glenside, her opinion of Mr. Bunderson would improve. And if not, well, there were other young men to consider, and there would be even more once the London season ended and those who had gone to town returned home. Cassie would have new dresses and shoes next spring, baubles—to a point—and a reason to wear that pearl-studded tiara she'd loaned to Lenora the fateful night of the Dyers' ball. That Lenora would be Mrs. Glenside by then would barely warrant Cassie's notice once she found the right man for herself. She had grown through this hardship, matured and improved, and therefore it was not a waste. Rather, it was for her good. She was content.

The carriage slowed, and Cassie waited for the driver to open the door for her. By the time she stood on the cobbles, the driver was wrestling her trunk from the rack. Once it was down, she explained that a servant would come for it within the hour.

"Very good, miss," the man said before working on the next trunk.

Cassie turned toward home and had just let herself through the gate when the front door opened and Mama came out to greet her.

Genuinely glad to see her, Cassie embraced her mother when they met on the pathway.

"You look very well, Cassie," Mama said when she pulled back. "A bit browner, perhaps, but I expected as much."

Cassie wrinkled her nose. "The weather was so fine these last two weeks, it was difficult to stay indoors. My nieces and nephews do love to run about."

"I am sure Mary enjoyed you being there to distract them."

"She seemed to, though she never seems to tire. I'm not sure I helped her much."

"I'm sure you were a great help." Mama put her arm through Cassie's and turned her toward the house. "I'll send Reginald out for your trunks, but you are just in time."

"In time for tea, I hope. I finished the bread Mary sent with me hours ago." Mary was a practical cook, and Cassie was looking forward to indulging in some of Cook's fine tarts and light breads now that she was home. They reached the front door and Cassie undid the bow beneath her chin before removing the pin that held her bonnet in place. She smoothed the sides of her hair. She'd been in the coach for hours and feared she looked a fright.

Mama turned to her and smiled. "We are celebrating."

Cassie was touched. "My return?"

Mama's smile fell just a little. "That too, but, we are also celebrating your sister. Mr. Glenside has asked for her hand, and she has accepted him."

Cassie froze, one hand in midair as she stared at her mother.

"Is it not excellent news?" Mama said, her smile returning to full form. "Lenora is fairly over the moon about it, and your father and I could not be more pleased. We shall have a family dinner on Sunday to celebrate, but we have not yet told the rest of the family. We knew you would be home today so we saved the happy news for you to hear first."

Cassie was still frozen in place, all the discomfort from before she'd left Leagrave sliding right back into place.

"Are you not happy?" Mama asked, finally seeming to note Cassie's lack of reaction. "I would think you would be as happy about her match as anyone, seeing as how she controls your destiny."

Mama was trying to make a joke, but Cassie could not respond. What had she expected? Hadn't she left Leagrave so as not to interfere with the courtship? Hadn't she convinced herself during her time at Mary's that she had been indulging in a silly fancy without any true foundation in her heart?

Mama's smile began to slip and her eyebrows pulled down, prompting Cassie to force a response. "I am happy for her, of course. Only surprised."

"I hope you don't mean that unkindly." Mama's tone held a reprimand. "Did I not tell you that your sister would find a man who could see through her insecurities to her good and pure heart?"

Cassie smiled, though it was hard to do. "You did," she said evenly. "I should not have doubted you."

Mama lifted her chin. "No, you should not have, but all is well." She took hold of Cassie's arm. "Come to the parlor. You can be the first to congratulate the happy couple."

Couple? Mr. Glenside was there too? Could her timing have been any worse?

If not for Mama taking her arm, Cassie was sure her feet would not have moved of their own accord, but they obediently followed her mother up the front steps, through the open doorway, and into the parlor. She locked eyes with Mr. Glenside immediately and found it difficult to breathe. He put down his teacup and rose from his chair. Papa stood as well, but Cassie was not looking at him. She was looking into the blue eyes she had felt sure would not affect her this way. Eyes of a man who would be her brother.

"Ah, Cassie," Papa said. She looked at him as he crossed to her and kissed her on the cheek. "I'm so glad you've come in time to celebrate with us. Your mother told you the news, no doubt."

"Y-yes," Cassie stuttered, moving to an empty chair as far from Mr. Glenside as possible. She looked at Lenora and forced her smile brighter. "I am so happy for you, Lenora."

"Thank you, Cassie," Lenora said with a calm and confidence Cassie did not recognize. Mr. Glenside was right here in the room with them and Lenora had not stumbled over her words. She had not simpered or ducked her head. While Cassie watched, Lenora turned and made eye contact with Mr. Glenside, who smiled at her. "I am so very blessed."

Cassie's heart sank another inch deeper into her chest. Lenora was in love with him. He had asked her to be his wife. Would more time in Bletchley have helped her heart forget Mr. Glenside better than two weeks had? Without meaning to, she met Mr. Glenside's gaze again.

"I wish you both very happy." She spoke as though reading from a script.

"Thank you," he said, his words seeping into her, wrapping around her, filling her up and emptying her at the same time.

This is ridiculous, she said to herself, mentally shaking herself back to sanity. The voice inside her head became a shout: *You can't want this for her and still want him for yourself!* She took a breath—a deep, empowering breath of acceptance for what was done and what would be. That the feelings she thought had faded had not done so did not mean that they wouldn't over time. They had to. Especially now.

She would find another man to fall in love with. Mr. Glenside would find happiness with Lenora, and Lenora . . .

Lenora was sitting up straight with a contented smile on her face as she looked at her fiancé—a man she hadn't been able to look in the eye at the church social five weeks ago. Lenora was happy. Happier than Cassie had ever seen her before.

This is right, Cassie told herself. *This is good.*

Then she looked at Mr. Glenside again. He, too, sat up straight in his chair and though he was smiling, there was a tension about it. He looked anxious and ill at ease and yet trying very hard to cover that fact. He met her eyes from across the room, and she had the briefest mental image of a bird in a cage, beautiful and cared for, but trapped all the same. He looked away, and she stared into her lap. She had often felt like that bird, but it didn't make sense that Mr. Glenside would. He had *asked* for Lenora's hand. Likely it was her own suffocation of feeling attributing such an image to him. She should be ashamed of herself. For so many things.

The conversation moved around her, and she was able to occupy herself with treacle tarts she could not taste and tea she did not want. The wedding would take place in August, after Mr. Glenside's mother and sisters had relocated. Papa would conduct the service. The newlyweds would live on the Glenside estate.

Cassie answered simply when required but otherwise did not assert herself into the conversation. Was it her imagination that Mr. Glenside was behaving the same way? She tried not to be attentive to him. She tried not to engage with him directly. She tried not to look at him. She tried not to let his voice move through her. The longer she sat, however, the harder it was to withstand the effect of his presence. The space in the room seemed to shrink with every passing minute.

During a lull in the conversation, she spoke up. "I hope it is not rude, but I have been traveling all day and would like to freshen up." She turned to her father. "Might I be excused, Father?"

"Certainly," Papa said, waving her toward the door. "We're having Mr. Glenside to dinner tonight, along with his uncle, so we shall see you then." He stood, as did Mr. Glenside—but Cassie did not look at him.

Once free of the room and those hypnotic blue eyes, Cassie hurried up the stairs, tears threatening with every step. She rushed into her room, then jumped when Young turned around—equally startled. She was unpacking Cassie's trunk, laying the dresses over the foot of the bed.

"I need to be alone," Cassie said too sharply.

Young raised her eyebrows. "I was just—"

"Please," Cassie said, choking on her emotion and closing her eyes. She willed the tears to stay back for a few seconds longer. She pressed a fist into her stomach. "Please, Young. I shall b-be fine to unpack my own trunk, but I must be alone."

Young nodded, put down the dress she was holding, and left.

Cassie pushed the door closed behind the maid and rested her forehead against the wood. There was no reason to hold back the tears any longer and so she let them come, covering her mouth with her hand.

She was *in love* with Mr. Glenside—the man Lenora was to marry.

Such love should send her heart to fluttering and make her smile. Instead her heart felt like stone.

She loved him.

So did Lenora.

How would she withstand a life of seeing them together? If two weeks away had not cured her, what would?

Chapter Thirty

P lease share our congratulations with your sister," Mrs. Grieves said as she handed Cassie the parcel of fabric across the counter. "It is happy news indeed."

Cassie kept her smile in place despite the fact that every time someone shared their congratulations for Lenora and Mr. Glenside she felt as though she might cry. Only she didn't cry; not since that first night in her bedchamber, when she let loose her emotions until she could not breathe. She'd had to pull herself together to manage dinner, but she'd cried herself to sleep that night.

The next day she awaked with determination to act well the part she'd been given—that of sister of the bride. In the two weeks that followed, while wedding clothes were ordered and the wedding day planned, she had become adept at keeping her expression devoid of anything taking place within her heart.

"I shall certainly share your compliments, Mrs. Grieves," Cassie said graciously, then turned and left the store.

A member of Papa's congregation called to her, and she was forced to smile her way through another round of congratulations. She agreed it was a lovely thing for Lenora, and that Mr. Glenside was indeed a most eligible man.

Once she took her leave, however, Cassie felt like spitting out the pretty words. She couldn't bear to repeat them over and over again. Sometimes it was easier to feel anger than pain; how she wished she could feel nothing.

Rather than continuing down the main street of the village, Cassie took the road north out of town, then along the canal road that led to the back of the vicarage. She often walked this way to extend her time out of doors, but today it was an escape. Time to give in to her regret, time to wish she'd done things differently, time to admit the horrible turn she had done to herself and to pray, once again, for deliverance. It seemed her prayers were going nowhere, however. Neither circumstances or her heart had changed. The first reading of the banns would take place on Sunday. The reading of the banns was both an announcement and a chance for anyone who felt the marriage should not take place to state their objection. Would that she could object somehow, but that was only a fantasy. Would she publicly admit she was in love with Mr. Glenside? Would she tell the entire parish what she'd done?

Of course not. On Sunday, she would sit in the congregation and breathe and smile her way through the reading of the banns and be one step closer to the wedding day. Yesterday Cassie had suggested her going to Bath and attending to Aunt Gwen. She'd felt desperate for escape and assured her mother she'd return in time for the wedding. Mama had not even considered it, claiming there was too much work to be done at home.

Rose's pregnancy was becoming troublesome, and she'd begun to rest every afternoon even though she wasn't due to deliver for nearly three months. Mama was dividing her time between all her daughters, and Cassie was needed to assist with parish responsibilities and household tasks. Cassie had not argued, but it was the closest she'd come to crying since the day of the engagement. She was trapped, and it was stifling.

The sound of hoofbeats approaching from behind broke Cassie from her ugly thoughts, and she stepped to the side of the lane before looking to see who was coming. When she saw Mr. Glenside looking rugged and handsome on the back of a beautiful butter-colored gelding, she felt sure her lungs had stopped working even as her heart thrilled in her chest. He pulled up alongside of her, then pranced his horse in a circle before jumping down from his saddle. He seemed to have improved in his riding, but she didn't dare compliment him.

"I thought it was you, Cassie," he said as he came to stand before her, his bright blue eyes sparkling in the summer sun. He had started calling her Cassie last week and had said it eighteen times since then. She'd tried not to count but couldn't help herself. Now it was nineteen times he'd used the nickname reserved for those closest to her. "Might I walk you the rest of the way home? I am to take tea with your family today."

If Cassie had known of his invitation to tea, she would have avoided being home in time to join. Or would she? She felt warm and comfortable in his presence, and she could not avoid him forever, though she had tried her best during the last two weeks. "You may certainly walk me the rest of the way home, Mr. Glenside."

He held her eyes—was it a moment longer than was required of such a meeting? She faced forward and took a breath to calm herself.

"You have been to a shop?" he asked, nodding toward the parcel she held by the string. "May I carry it for you?"

She smiled and handed over the parcel, which he tucked beneath his arm. He had not offered his other arm to Cassie, and she was glad for that, even though part of her wished he had. What would it feel like to walk so close to him? Oh, she was wicked for wanting it and moved to the side so there was even more distance between them.

"Mama is making herself a new dress for the wedding—that parcel is the silk she will use. She is a talented seamstress, and as the other wedding clothes have been hired out, she can focus on her own."

"I've no doubt she is very talented," Mr. Glenside said. "I have heard much of the Wilton girls' talents during my time in Leagrave, and I have been able to see for myself the extent of their charms." He glanced at her, and her cheeks filled with fire. That her reaction caused him to smile too set her quickly at ease. How was it possible for her to feel both so bad and so good in his proximity?

"You have a lovely horse," Cassie said, needing to change the subject but hoping he would keep talking. The compliment made his smile even wider and revealed a dimple on one side of his mouth. Why must he be so handsome?

"It was a gift from my uncle," Mr. Glenside said, looking over his shoulder at the animal with obvious pride. "He keeps a very fine stable and, once I completed the training he set for me, let me have my choice."

"Training?" Cassie asked.

Mr. Glenside explained about his uncle's bargain: riding lessons in exchange for a woodworking room. "I admit I was avoiding the saddle before then, but I find it quite comfortable now. Not that I'm up for a race or anything like that." He smiled at her, the dimple deepening. "I never thought I would own a horse. Do you ride?"

"I adore riding," Cassie said. "Especially in the rain."

Mr. Glenside laughed, and she wished she could capture the sound of it. "I have not yet ridden in the rain. It seems very uncomfortable."

"It is not." Cassie glanced his way to see that he was interested in what she had to say. "For one thing, you will find yourself quite alone as most people don't go out, but there's a crispness to the air and a feeling of escape, I suppose. I've never actually tried to explain it, so perhaps that does not make sense."

"It makes enough sense for me to be intrigued. Perhaps I shall have to give it a try."

She wanted to invite herself to join him the next time the skies opened, but of course she could not. It was time for another change in the subject. "You said you are building a shop for your carpentry?"

"Wood-work-ing-room," Mr. Glenside said, enunciating each syllable. "My uncle gets very uncomfortable when I call it a shop."

Cassie laughed. "And you'll use your father's equipment?"

He looked at her in surprise, and she realized belatedly that he'd never spoken of his father's equipment, only written about it in his letters. Letters he knew she had been privy to because of her dishonest ways. Bringing up the letters made her feel conspicuous. She looked away, and they walked in silence a few steps before he spoke again. "I'll pick up the items next time I go to London. I'm eager to improve my skills."

"What do you hope to build?" Cassie watched the ground so as not to look at him too much or too often.

"Well, in the past I have created more functional things, like chairs and racks. Now, I suppose I can explore the art of it. Carving, perhaps, and artistic things like picture frames. I may need some lessons from an artist, however, for the design portions."

Cassie's cheeks colored again from both the compliment and the idea of spending private time with Mr. Glenside. Yet such a dream could never happen. She merely smiled, unable to give any other reaction.

"That reminds me," he said. "I still have never seen your work."

"I'm sure there is no way you could avoid it much longer." She meant it as a joke, but it soured on her lips. As Lenora's husband, Mr. Glenside would most certainly see her artwork and any admiration he might have of it would be as that of her new brother-in-law. The thought depressed her, and she let out a heavy breath. The house was in view, and within it was his intended. Cassie's sister.

"Might your work be on display at the vicarage?" he asked.

She could feel her steps slowing and noted that his were slowing as well. Finally they seemed to stop of one accord, though they were still some distance from the back door. She could feel him watching her, and the sensation was like drinking a cool glass of lemonade on a hot and humid day.

"There are none which are properly framed," she said. "Only pinned to the wall of my bedchamber." What a child that made her seem. "But perhaps one day I might choose some of my finest works and show them to you." The idea was temping, but also intimate. No one paid much mind to her artwork, not that she made a point of including anyone in her accomplishments, and the idea of showing Mr. Glenside her work and perhaps having him compliment it would be far too much.

"I hope that you do." He watched her intently. "And I wish that you would not discount your talent."

She breathed in his words, and though she knew the etiquette would be to duck her chin or brush off the compliment, she raised her chin instead. "Do you?" she said softly, in a tone as intent as his own. "I am not often singled out from my sisters."

His focus should make her feel unsettled—she needed distance—but instead she felt refreshed beneath his gaze. She could not help but wonder what he saw when he looked at her like that. The younger sister of his beloved? Or did he see a woman in her own right, with charm and character he could admire?

"Ah, I think you quite stand out." He started to smile and then seemed to catch himself. He took a step back and fidgeted with the reins he was holding. "Forgive me, Miss Cassandra. I . . . uh . . ."

She stepped toward him. "Please don't apologize," she said quickly, placing a hand on his arm. "I am quite flattered to hear it. Truly." She smiled so he would know she meant it, but her heart was racing.

He looked into her face, and she sensed he was struggling with some internal battle. Some balance that had shifted perhaps. She dared think that maybe his affections were not so certain as everyone thought. But that would only create more complications. She looked at her hand on his arm and removed it, though she did not—could not—step away.

"I admire you a great deal, Mr. Glenside," she said, almost in a whisper as she looked at the toes of his boots. Her chest became hot. With warning? With encouragement?

He was silent for a long moment. When she looked up, he opened his mouth to say something—perhaps something equally intimate and wholly inappropriate—when the creak of a hinge captured their attention. They both turned toward the door where Lenora stood on the back step.

"Evan," she said sweetly, coming into the yard while Cassie quickly stepped away from him. "You are early." Her gaze flitted to Cassie, but only for a moment. "Cassie would be happy to take your horse to the stable, I'm sure."

Cassie looked at the ground as the guilt of the conversation she'd just shared with her sister's fiancé descended. Had she truly wanted Mr. Glenside to share words of affection? What would that say of his character? What did it say of hers that she wanted something so much?

"Certainly," she said. She reached for the reins, and her hand brushed Mr. Glenside's as she took the leather straps from him. Their eyes met for the briefest of moments, and once again she sensed he was troubled. By her? The idea both thrilled and terrified her. "I shall see he is cared for," she said, then she dipped a quick curtsy and turned toward the stable.

Chapter Thirty-One

Cassie was at her dressing table, pinning up her hair and trying not to think of the time she'd spent with Mr. Glenside the day before. It had been such a simple thing, walking perhaps a quarter of a mile together toward the vicarage. But every word he'd spoken to her continued to float through her mind. Every smile she'd brought to his face and every glance she'd felt from him played over and over in her head. Her dreams had been full of him, except that her sleeping mind had not stayed confined to the facts of their exchange. Rather, her dreams had included her hand in his, his eyes gazing deeply into hers, his lips moving toward her own . . .

She shook her head as her cheeks filled with heat, and she reminded herself, again, that Mr. Glenside would soon be her *brother*, the husband of her sister. Such thoughts—such dreams—were of the very worst sort. Not only were they sinful, they left her feeling perfectly wretched as they merely amplified what she could not have. Mr. Glenside belonged to Lenora. How many times would she have to tell herself that before she believed it?

There was a tapping on her door and she bid the person to enter as she turned around. Young came in and closed the door behind her. The maid's eyes were wide as she hurried across the room with a letter in her hand.

"He delivered it to me himself, Miss. Right there in the yard."

Cassie took the note and saw her own name scrawled across the front in Mr. Glenside's beautiful script. Her name. His hand. She caught her breath and stared until Young waved toward the letter, reminding her of the urgency.

> *Miss Cassandra,*
>
> *I must speak to you right away. Please meet me in the glen behind the barn as soon as you can without alerting anyone to your errand.*

The note filled Cassie with a rush of excitement, and her fingers tingled where they touched the paper. Paper he had touched. Paper on which he had asked to see her. "He wants to speak with me." She rose from the dressing table, turning to look at herself once more in the mirror. She should have worn the green dress that matched her eyes.

"Alone, Miss?" Young asked.

Cassie nodded, then held Young's eyes, unable and unwilling to discuss the impropriety of it. She had no expectation of what Mr. Glenside might need to speak with her about—she dared not consider the possibilities—but she would not refuse his request. Could not. She strode past Young and then turned back with her hand on the door handle. "Please make excuses for me if anyone is to ask."

Young paused, but then nodded, visibly concerned. Cassie didn't care. Her heart hummed in her chest, and her breathing quickened.

Cassie ensured the hallway was empty before she made her way to the servants' staircase that led her to the back of the house. Once in the yard, she looked around again to ensure she remained undiscovered, then lifted her skirts and fairly ran to the side of the barn hidden from the back windows. What could Evan want to speak with her about? A warning pulsed in her head, but appealing to her better judgment would override the need she felt to see him. And she *needed* to see him.

The path on the west side of the barn was shielded by the yew trees that flanked the lane to the house. Once free of the yard, she took the path that rounded the back corner of the corral. She saw a flash of blue in the trees that surrounded the meadow where she had once left a basket of toffee for Mr. Glenside and felt her heart race even faster.

Cassie took a deep breath and tried to slow her step as she approached. He was pacing across the grass and did not see her until she reached the tree line. He looked up at her and, though she'd hoped for a smile or softening of his eyes, his expression was stoic.

She could not move beneath the weight of his stare, but felt heat rising in her chest. They were alone, just the two of them.

"I must know the truth," Evan said without preamble.

His words unfastened her feet from the ground, and she stepped forward quickly. For concealment, she told herself, though she wanted to be closer to him. It was not until she noticed a coldness in his eyes that she stopped and his words registered. He wanted to know the *truth*? The heat in her neck and face cooled and some measure of the good sense she'd been trying to ignore pushed through like a seedling from the soil. *No!*

He reached into his jacket and extracted a stack of letters she recognized immediately. "You wrote these letters, didn't you?"

Cassie swallowed, but a spring of hope bubbled up within her. Perhaps his heart was more invested in the words they had written back and forth than in the time he'd spent with Lenora. Maybe he was as tortured as she was and this moment would be the relief they both ached for. A dozen cautions knocked and hollered at her to pause, consider, restrain, but she ignored every one of them once again. "Yes," she said simply, the single word breaking free.

He took a step back. She took a step toward him but he retreated again. The cautions rose up, louder this time, demanding that she consider what was at stake. But she longed for him to know the truth. She longed for him to know all of her, not ascribe the aspects of her letters to Lenora for another moment. He looked confused, frightened, and so she took a breath and gave him what he'd asked for—the truth. She felt sure in this moment she would give him anything he asked for, and he would be as glad to receive it as she was to give it.

"In the beginning, I had meant for the letters to be from Lenora, to help encourage your attention to her." She was surprisingly relieved to be telling the truth even as she questioned if it was the right thing to do. But what was *right*, now? Continuing a deception? Not admitting what she'd done when he'd already discovered it?

"But they were *not* from Lenora." He looked from the letters in his hand to her face. "They were not the thoughts of *her* heart—they were your own."

"Yes. As I said, they began as letters on her behalf, but the more I learned of your innermost thoughts, the more my heart felt them, embraced them, and was filled." She smiled at him, pleadingly. She needed validation, understanding. Surely he understood now, didn't he? Surely everything was coming together in his mind just as it had in hers.

"Do you know what you have done?"

Cassie startled, both at his words and the level of regret in his voice. He continued before she could answer.

"I thought I fell in love with Lenora because of these letters." He held the bundle of papers up as evidence. "I opened my heart to her. I gave all my secret thoughts to her."

"To me," Cassie said, putting a hand to her chest to remind him. "You were writing to me all along, not Lenora."

"But I *thought* I was writing to Lenora. It was her company I sought out because of these letters, her hand that—"

"The *words* of those letters are mine, and if they are what you fell in love with, if they are what made the greater impression . . ." Her voice trailed off. She watched him intently, waiting for his expression to reflect his understanding. He wanted the truth and here it was: she loved him and she felt to her bones that he loved her, too. Otherwise he wouldn't be here.

Evan's expression remained hard. "You do not understand what you have done," he said again, shaking his head and closing his eyes.

"I pray your forgiveness," Cassie said, still hopeful. They could repair this. They could make things right. "I never meant anyone harm, and I never expected to create such a connection with you of my own. Now that you know the truth—"

Mr. Glenside opened his eyes and his gaze pierced her straight through—cutting through the fantasy she had been forming since receiving his letter. His look made it clear that he was closed to her. She could feel a distance growing where moments ago she felt sure they were closer than ever. What was happening?

"You think your intention is enough? You think that your apology, or my forgiveness for that matter, is *enough*? You cannot make this right, Cassie. You cannot fix it. I am *engaged* to your *sister*."

"But you do not love her." Desperation rose in her heart and spilled into her tone.

"I do not know what I feel," he said with a shake of his head. He pushed his hand through his hair and looked at the ground.

You are in love with me, Cassie wanted to shout. *Say it. Say it out loud so I might gather up the words and hold them in my heart for the rest of my days!*

He did not say anything. He stood with his shoulders stooped and a staggering tension forming a wall around him. The moments ticked by, and his silence resounded through Cassie's ears.

The words of the letters were Cassie's, but he had believed they belonged to Lenora. He had believed it was Lenora's heart on the page. It was not Cassie he had gone riding with; it was not Cassie he had escorted about town. Had he fallen in love with *her* words, and *Lenora's* person? Had he become invested in them both? If so, Cassie and Lenora had been a full woman in his mind and now that belief was broken into two parts. He would have to choose between them.

Cassie moved forward, soft and silently enough that she was mere inches from him before he looked up at her. She lifted a hand to his cheek, her heart pounding and blood rushing through her veins. The warmth of his skin against her hand made her whole body tremble, and when he placed his hand upon hers, her chest tightened. The intensity of his gaze confirmed to her that what they felt for one another would surpass anything he thought he felt for Lenora. It seemed so simple in her mind, yet the heaviness in his eyes testified of the burden he carried.

"I am sorry, Evan," she whispered. "We will fix it together."

Evan held her eyes another moment, then he removed her hand from his cheek, and stepped away from her.

"You do not understand," he said quietly, still holding her hand.

"I understand that you need to choose. And while I did not intend for any of this to happen, I cannot deny that I love you. My heart aches for the man I met through your letters, and you cannot tell me you don't feel the same draw I feel whenever we are together." She took a breath to infuse her already shocking boldness with more confidence. "You did not go to Lenora with your questions today—you came to me. Does that not convince you which of us holds your heart?"

He looked at their hands, still joined, and she squeezed his fingers.

"It is not so simple, Cassie." He looked up, and she saw his pain, a deep and mournful pain that made her want to take him in her arms. "I cannot simply move my attentions to you. I would be a man without honor to your parents, to your village, and Lenora would be broken by it. Your family could never welcome my attention to you; no one could pretend that what happened had not happened. Unless we were both willing to break all ties to our families and station, we could *never* be together. My position is precarious. I did not grow up in this world, and I cannot risk my honor or the honor of my mother and sisters."

Cassie blinked as the wholeness of their plight began to take form, a hideous, murky form that frightened her. "But surely there is some way . . . your uncle can—"

"There is no solution to this," Evan said, shaking his head. "Not if I have any decency. Not if I care for either of you at all." He dropped her hand and turned away.

She felt sure he would say something more, but he kept walking. When he was far enough away that she realized he was leaving, she ran after him.

"Wait, Evan. Please. I am so sorry," she said when she caught up, out of breath from both the exertion and the anxiety she felt in every corner of her heart. "But—"

He turned to face her. "As am I, Miss Cassandra." This time it was his hand that rested on her cheek, and she lifted both of her hands to hold it there, keep it there. She closed her eyes, savoring the closeness and trying to think of some way around the mess she'd made. Love was supposed to conquer all, was it not? She had tried to resist her feelings when she believed only she felt them, but he felt them too. Could that not be enough? There must be a way, even if it was not an easy course.

When Cassie opened her eyes, he was looking at her with such tender regret that she could not keep her tears from falling. He brushed his thumb over her cheek to catch a tear, then pulled his hand away. She held onto him, not able to let him go, until he pulled sharply from her grasp and stepped away. Her arms fell to her sides.

"I will not see you again," he said quietly, his expression closed.

She felt the hardness and resolution of his words so completely that she could not form a response.

Evan turned and took long strides away from her. He didn't look back. Not even once.

Chapter Thirty-Two

Cassie did not know how long she stood in the glen, looking into the trees, repeating Evan's words in her mind, and trying to understand them. The dew had soaked through her shoes before she finally returned home, where she hurried to her room and told Young to pass along the message that she was ill. She took off the dress she had put on only an hour before and climbed into bed. It was only a few minutes later that her mother checked on her, as Cassie knew she would. Cassie steeled the torrent of emotions in her chest, waiting until this inspection was over.

"It's not a fever," Mama said, the back of her hand held against Cassie's brow. "I shall have cook send up broth."

Her mother's tenderness only deepened the knife in Cassie's heart. If she knew . . .

Cassie nodded. "Thank you."

Mama planted a kiss on Cassie's forehead, nearly undoing her completely, and then left the room.

Finally, Cassie gave in to the agony she felt. For herself, for Lenora, for Evan. What kind of woman was she? How could she have allowed this to happen? How could she have believed when she'd received his note this morning that anything other than what had happened would be the result? How could she have been so cruel?

If Evan broke the engagement he would suffer greatly—they all would—but they would all suffer if he didn't. What had she done to him? What had she done to Lenora? Could it be fixed? Would he really never see her again?

It was afternoon when Cassie was roused from fitful sleep by a commotion downstairs. Loud voices. Crying? She pushed back the covers and grabbed her dressing gown, fearful of what had happened until she pulled open her bedchamber door. Lenora was crying on the main level. Lenora, who never showed such emotion. Lenora, who had never in all of Cassie's life lost her calm demeanor. Cassie's mouth went dry as she realized *why* Lenora was crying. Had Evan broken the engagement already? Did they know everything?

Unable to face the distress she had caused, Cassie stayed frozen in the doorway of her room. The hollow ache in her stomach reminded her that she could do nothing, that she had already done too much. The sound of feet on the stairs broke Cassie from her stupor, and a moment later Lenora, her face red, reached the landing and made eye contact with Cassie.

Shocked and frightened, Cassie stepped back into her room and tried to shut the door, but Lenora reached it first and pushed it open with all her strength. Cassie stumbled backward and caught herself on the bedpost while the door slammed into the wall.

"You have ruined everything," Lenora screamed. "You have shattered my chance at happiness!"

Cassie's parents entered the room behind Lenora, rushed and frantic. Cassie could barely breathe and wished that hell could swallow her up whole. Surely she deserved it. "I am sorry," she managed, her throat tight with building emotion. "I am so sorry, Lenora."

"Is it true, Cassie?" Papa asked, his features shocked. "Did you pose as your sister in letters to Mr. Glenside?"

Cassie covered her face with her hands as though they could protect her from the accusation, then nodded her accountability.

"Why would you do such a thing?" Mama asked, the disappointment in her voice cutting Cassie to shreds.

"Because she blamed me for her not being in society," Lenora said.

Cassie dropped her hands and looked Lenora in the eye. "I did not mean for any of this to happen," she said, her chin quivering. "You must believe that I only wrote those letters to help you."

"To humiliate me," Lenora said bitterly, tears streaming down her reddened cheeks. She was equal parts rage and heartbreak. "To make me into an utter fool! You had always meant to reveal me as pathetic so he would not want me."

"That was never my intent." Cassie turned her pleading eyes to her parents. "You must believe I would never have set out to cause such pain to the people I love." In her heart, Cassie included Evan in that group. She loved him. So help her she did, and she had hurt him too.

"You are hateful and cruel!" Lenora spat.

Cassie stared at the floor and wiped at her eyes. She had no foundation upon which to defend herself. The only argument she could make was based upon her *initial* intent—intent that had changed to fulfilling her own desires. That *was* hateful and cruel. She deserved every accusation hurled at her.

"Enough," Papa said, his voice calm and ecclesiastical. "Lenora, you shall come with me so we might discuss the particulars."

Cassie glanced up in time to see her parents share a look as Papa escorted Lenora from the room, his arm wrapped protectively around her back.

Mama closed the door behind them before she spoke to Cassie directly. "So you are not ill."

"Sick of heart," Cassie said, wishing there were some way to purge that type of illness from her soul. She wiped at her eyes again. "I did not set my cap for him, Mama. I truly wanted to help Lenora, not hurt her." She shook her head as more tears ran down her face. Her explanation sounded so pathetic and ridiculous. "I never expected to . . ."

"To what?" Mama asked, her voice careful. "To fall in love with him?"

Cassie moved to the bench beside the window and sat down, burying her face in her hands once again. She began to cry—unrestrained and unrelenting tears of regret and sharp sorrow.

Mama sat beside her and placed her hand upon her back. "Tell me the whole of it," she said softly, stroking Cassie's hair. The unexpected—and undeserved—tenderness undid Cassie even more. "What happened?"

Cassie took a deep breath and told the shameful tale. She left nothing out—what good would that do? She ended with her meeting with Evan just that morning and all that he had said.

"He is right, you know. There can be nothing between you."

Cassie could not respond, realizing that she still hoped, against all reason, that maybe . . . She met her mother's eyes. "Is it so certain? Perhaps in a year when feelings are not so sharp, when Lenora has found a different match."

Mama wiped away Cassie's tears, but she did not smile nor offer concession. "I feel badly that Mr. Glenside was an unwitting pawn in a game he did not know was being played out around him, but even with that, as Lenora's parents we could never welcome his attention toward you. We would never put one daughter against another in such a way. There is no course other than to forget him as completely as you can."

Cassie looked down, her lower lip trembling. Mama put her fingers under Cassie's chin and lifted it so she could not look away. "And he has not proclaimed affections for you, Cassie."

For a moment Cassie didn't understand. He *loved* her. She'd seen it. She'd felt it.

Mama continued. "He did not even afford us the respect of coming in person. He sent a letter stating that he was returning to London for a time, that he was very sorry for all the distress but that his new understanding of events had left him divided in his heart and mind and unable to keep any connection to our family."

Divided. "But Mama," Cassie said, "he loves *me*. I know that he does. I feel it when he is near and—"

"And what does that leave for Lenora?" Mama said, a sharpness in her tone. "You would have her know he had chosen you over her, even after their engagement was known? The banns were to have been read on Sunday, Cassie. Regardless of what Mr. Glenside *might* feel, he has made it clear that when he returns, which he is most certain to do, he will have no connection to our family. He broke the engagement in a *letter*, Cassie. His character and his manners are less than we could ever want for any of our daughters." Her tone had turned bitter.

Cassie's defenses rose. "He didn't know I was writing the letters, Mama."

"That is neither here nor there. He has shown himself well enough in the time since he learned. Meeting privately with you? Ending the engagement in a letter? Leaving town!" Mama shook her head, and her nostrils flared as she took a deep breath. "Lenora is the victim here, and her alone. It is her we will be considerate toward, not him—and not you, who caused this to happen in the first place. Honestly, Cassie, what were you thinking?"

Mama's judgment broke Cassie into pieces. Evan had not only lost the connection to the Wilton family, he would lose the acceptance he'd gained thus far in Leagrave. Mama would not forgive him. Papa would not forgive him. He really would never see her again, yet he would bear the scars of what she'd done. "I truly have ruined everything, haven't I?" Cassie breathed amid the emotions tumbling inside her.

Mama's expression turned sad, her cheeks drooping and the line between her eyebrows deepening. "Yes, I'm afraid you have. However, God is forgiving. You must hold to the hope that the pain you feel now can be swallowed up in the sacrifice of the Lord as you take accountability for what you have done."

"I know it was all my fault," Cassie said, wiping at her eyes but feeling numb. "I am so sorry. I did not mean for anyone to be hurt."

"There will be additional consequences to your regrets. You will not go to any events for four weeks' time, not even the parish dinners, and you are to read your Bible every night. We shall all hope that your part in this is never revealed—what a further blight that would be for all of us. It will be difficult enough to deal with Lenora's scorn alone without adding your scandalous behavior. With such actions and continual evaluation of what you've done, I believe we can heal your soul and preserve our family as best we can."

Cassie blinked and felt her chin begin to tremble, not because of the punishment but because of the truth her mother had spoken and the severity of the situation she had caused. Lenora and Evan would suffer publicly, while she would take no share of the pain she herself had caused.

"My greatest fear is for your sister," Mama continued, her frown deepening as she looked past Cassie. "She has a tender heart, and I do not know how she might recover from this betrayal."

Lenora. Cassie's thoughts moved to her sister.

Twenty-three years old, crippled with anxiety, and now jilted by Evan. Cassie's heart dropped further. How could such a simple act lead to so much pain for so many people? Was there anything—anything at all—that she could do to fix it?

The question went unanswered as the new reality grew wider and louder in her mind. The future was so bleak, and she had never felt so alone in all her life. She imagined Lenora was feeling the exact same way.

Chapter Thirty-Three

Evan rode hard for London, trying to outrun the women who haunted him: Lenora with her quiet disposition and serious eyes; Cassie with her striking confidence and engaging manner. Both of their images swirled through his mind, but it was Cassie's upon which his mind lingered, which only made him ride harder. Cassie had deceived him, and then Lenora had known and not confessed it. Neither could be trusted. Neither could be forgotten nor separated from the other.

It was late in the day when he arrived at Mile End, and by the time he'd found a public stall for his horse, the sun was setting, casting shadows into the doorways of the homes he had known all his life. The tightly packed tenements had always been so familiar to him, yet now he felt like a stranger. In his fine coat and new boots, he no longer belonged here, and he could feel it in the looks he received from the people he passed on the street. Did he belong anywhere anymore?

When he finally arrived at his mother's apartment, he was so overcome with a wave of nostalgia he could not move. In that moment he wished he were returning from the accounting office at the end of a long day, tired and worn, and in old scuffed shoes, but with his place sure.

There had been heavy burdens placed upon him back then, but they were familiar and somehow steadying compared to these new problems.

A woman gave him a suspicious look as she passed him on the street, and he remembered why he was standing there in the first place. He took off his hat and moved to the door set flat against the brick wall, as was every door on this block. He did not know whether or not to walk in as he had done when he lived here. Did the four-room apartment count as his home anymore?

He knocked and when the door opened to reveal his mother, her eyes went wide. He swallowed a sudden lump in his throat.

"Evan?" she said, as though she couldn't believe it was him. A moment later she threw her arms around his neck, kissing him on the cheek. "Oh, my dear boy."

He reached his arms around her and felt some of his tension drain from him. For the first time in months, Evan knew he was exactly where he was supposed to be.

"Where are my sisters?" Evan asked. He sat at the table as his mother bustled back and forth, fixing him a plate. He had offered to help, but she would have none of it, insisting he take off his boots and rest his back, which, if he was being truthful, was sore after traveling so many miles in one day. In fact every part of him ached from spending so much time in the saddle, and from carrying so much burden in his heart and mind.

"Mrs. Dorister had her baby this morning," Mama said as she removed the lid from a pot on the stove. She used a fork to serve a portion of pork roast from the pot—meat they could enjoy on a weeknight only because of Evan's rise in circumstance. It was a humbling reminder of the good that had come from his new position. He needed that reminder very much. "That makes four little ones now, and all of them under five years of age. The girls have been there all day catching up the washing and the mending." Mama shook her head. "Children are a gift from God, you'll never hear me say otherwise, but I fear Mrs. Dorister will need strength beyond her own to endure the blessings she's received."

"Are the Doristers still in the house on the corner?" He remembered it having oilcloth stretched over one broken window and crumbling brick in the back. The Doristers would never be able to afford to fix the house on their own, but a very small portion of his quarterly allowance could make a difference.

Mama gave him a sympathetic look. "The very same. Three rooms and a leaky roof. I don't know how she'll manage another winter."

"And Mr. Dorister?" Evan asked, thinking self-consciously of the thirty-two rooms at Glenside Manor, most of them unused.

"Employed at the docks again, thank the Lord." She turned with the plate in hand and smiled, obviously pleased to be able to give her son a good meal. She set the food before him and then retrieved the kettle from the stove to pour herself a cup of tea. "Well, tuck in," she said, using a country accent she knew would make him smile.

Evan grinned and enjoyed every bite of the plain food. There was something to be said for a simple meal of meat, potatoes, and boiled carrots all served on one plate.

"Now," Mama said, "what brings you home unannounced?"

He glanced up at her, his mouth full of food, and she hurried to amend the question. "Not that I'm complaining, mind you, only I know my son and he is not the type to make a hasty journey. I hope you have not had a falling-out with your uncle."

"No," Evan said once he'd swallowed. He thought of the letter he'd left on Uncle's desk before he'd made his escape. A cowardly escape, but it was all he could manage amid the swirling realizations of what he must do and what it would mean for the people involved. "At least I hope I have not."

Mama pulled her eyebrows together, and Evan hurried to explain. "I left in a hurry. He was not yet awake for the day so I left him a letter."

"A letter you feel will not be well received?"

Evan paused, wishing he knew how to go about this conversation. He had been the head of house since he was thirteen years of age. He made the decisions for the family, set boundaries for his sisters, and kept his mother on a budget. She never begrudged him the position, rather she seemed glad he had taken the lead. Due to the roles they had assumed, he did not often confide his concerns to his mother. The letter he had sent to her regarding Miss Wilton was the only time he remembered asking for her advice on a personal matter. Perhaps that was why he had taken her encouragement so seriously. But once again, he was in need of a solace he had never needed before and found the change of position between them an awkward one to manage.

Evan pushed a bit of potatoes across his plate. "I have broken my engagement to Miss Wilton." He waited for a gasp or some other reaction but when none came, he looked at his mother again.

"You must have had good reason," she said simply, evenly, without judgment. Her response melted some of the fear lodged in his gut like a rock.

"I believe I did." Evan felt encouraged to tell her the whole of it. "The letters I believed to be sent by Lenora were actually written by her sister on Lenora's behalf, without Lenora's knowledge initially. Yesterday I chanced to meet with Cassandra and walked her home. There was something familiar about our conversation, something I could not identify. I thought at first it was because we had spoken at dinner some weeks ago, but once I got home, I opened a letter Lenora had sent when her sister was out of town a few weeks ago, confirming that I could escort her to a dinner party. The handwriting was very similar, but the signature was different. Also, it was signed 'Miss Lenora Wilton,' while her earlier letters had disposed of that formality. I read through all the letters again and noted other differences, including a reserve in this latest letter that did not exist in the earlier. I realized other things too, like the way Miss Cassandra tried to avoid me, but then I would find her watching me. And the strange reaction she had to our engagement. She went quite pale and kept her hands clenched in her lap, though the words she said were exactly right. I sent her a note asking that she meet me, and when I accused her, she admitted her deception."

The relief he felt at being able to express his thoughts was surprising. Evan was used to being a solitary man and keeping his own counsel. He'd have never guessed that verbalizing his burden would feel so good.

"And so why did you break the engagement?" Mama asked.

Evan pulled his eyebrows together. Had he not spoken clearly? "Lenora did not write the letters, Mama."

"But you and Miss Wilton had more than just those letters between you. Have you not spent a great deal of time in her company these last weeks?"

Evan considered her question, and the answer came to his mind with clarity and truth.

"Evan?" Mama prompted after several seconds had passed.

He pulled his unseeing gaze from the window, where it had become caught, to his mother's face. "It was the letters that touched me and gave me hope that more time with Lenora would soften the awkwardness I felt in her company. My interest was in what the letters held."

His mother smiled sadly and reached across the table to place her hand over his. "It is Miss Cassandra you fell in love with, then."

Evan closed his eyes but did not deny the simple truth of his mother's words. Words he himself had not been able to admit on his own. At least not completely. "I do not *dislike* Miss Lenora Wilton," he said, slowly. "But it was the woman in the letters that drew my interest, who prompted me to make Miss Wilton an offer. My expectation was that the woman in the letters would be revealed as the woman I was with."

"And the advice of your mother pushed you toward making that offer," Mama said with regret.

"You hold no blame here. I bear no ill will toward you for helping me navigate the situation as I understood it to be. Which," he said sadly, "was not what I thought it was."

"What a horrible trick for them to play."

Yes, he did feel tricked. Only . . . "I do not believe it was intended that way." He thought back to Cassie's explanations in the glen that morning. "I think Cassie was genuinely trying to help her sister when she began."

Mama seemed skeptical, and Evan wondered why he felt the need to defend Cassie. His mind went back to the confession she'd made that her own heart had become entangled. She was left with a very different outcome than she'd expected. Enough that she'd confessed her feelings to him, enough that she had hoped in a way he never could that somehow they would be together. He let out a heavy breath and brought a hand to his forehead.

Cassie. With those snapping eyes, her easy conversation, and her genuine interest in what interested him. Even during their short time together, she'd had an ability to make him feel sure of himself, to lift him up. And when he was wrestling with his decision regarding Lenora, had his mind not wished she were more like Cassie? It was freeing to identify the fullness of his attraction to her. He was unsure he could call what he felt *love*, but the pull he felt toward Cassie was more than he felt for Lenora, especially now that he knew the letters had been Cassie's doing. Cassie had said she loved him. *Loved* him.

"What are you thinking of, Evan?" Mama asked.

Evan looked at her. "Cassie cares for me, Mama." He could not tell her the extent of Cassie's confession. It felt too sacred, but he could say this much. "She said as much this morning, and I had to explain to her why it could never be. Her parents would never accept my attention to her even if society would, which it will not. By the time I return to Leagrave, the broken engagement will be known. I do not know how I shall stand it. I do not know what to do."

Mama's brow furrowed, and she squeezed his hand. She opened her mouth to speak just as the familiar chatter of voices sounded from outside. A moment later the door opened and Natalie entered, followed by Camilla. They both stopped in the doorway, their eyes widening as they looked in surprise upon their brother.

"Evan!" Natalie said, rushing to cross the room and throw her arms around his neck. Camilla was only a step behind, and soon Evan's arms were full of his giggling sisters, and his ears were ringing with their inquisition.

"Why are you here?"

"Is our house finished?"

"Did you bring Miss Wilton?"

"How did you get here?"

"Did Uncle Hastings come?"

"Did you bring us anything?"

"Girls," Mama finally said, "you must allow your brother some breath."

She pulled them both back so Evan could sit up straight in his chair again. Was it possible they had grown taller in the months he'd been gone? Camilla was seventeen, but Natalie had had a birthday and was now sixteen years old. He felt the sweet burden of their care. His eyes moved to his mother's face and that sweetness only compounded. It was only in this moment that he could admit having considered giving up the inheritance—walking away from it all—in order to pursue Cassie. But as he looked on the faces of his young sisters, he knew he would do whatever was required to ensure their future security.

"How are your classes going?" Evan asked.

"Very well," Natalie answered quickly.

Camilla hurried to be the next one to speak. "We have elocution classes every Monday, dance on Tuesdays, and general etiquette on Thursday afternoons." She furrowed her brow. "Honestly it's exhausting, Evan."

"But exciting," Natalie cut in. "We are learning ever so many things. For instance, did you know that a young woman is *never* to scratch her nose in company? Not for any reason at all."

Evan smiled. "Yes, I imagine there are a hundred such details just like that. I'm glad you are enjoying the classes."

"I love them," Natalie said, then glanced at Camilla. "Camilla simply tolerates them."

"That is not true," Camilla said, glaring at her sister. "I'm glad to take them, Evan. I am simply less eager about the continual travel to Regent Park where Miss Ellington conducts the classes."

"How is the renovation?" Natalie said, her face bright with anticipation. "I cannot *wait* to see the cottage."

"I cannot wait to have my own room," Camilla said, narrowing her eyes at her sister.

"Camilla," Mama said, "do not be ungracious."

"The renovation is coming along well," Evan said, but his mind was spinning with an idea. It would be so much more comfortable to return to Leagrave with people who knew and loved him and who would not hold the broken engagement with Miss Wilton against him. He would have allies—three, at least—and, if he were entirely honest, distraction. "It should be finished by August, as we expected." It was supposed to have been done in time for the wedding. His stomach sank. How could he tell his sisters the wedding was no longer happening?

"I wish we could go now," Natalie said with a wistful tone.

When Evan had first gone to Bedfordshire, he wouldn't have dreamed of requesting his family come to Leagrave early and live in the big house. It wasn't his place to ask Uncle to share his home, but in light of his stronger relationship with his uncle, and Evan's need to feel the support of his family around him, he had little hesitation now. Truth be told, having his family with him might be the only way he could make himself return. After so many years of being needed *by* them, he now needed them for himself. Whatever happened upon his return to Leagrave, he would not be alone if they came with him. It felt like salvation. It felt like hope.

Chapter Thirty-Four

The air at the vicarage was so laden with tension and regret following the broken engagement that it became difficult for Cassie to breathe. She kept to her room, coming down only for mealtimes, which were awkward and silent, and then escaping to her self-imposed prison as quickly as she could. The house was silent during the day. Lenora did not speak in Cassie's presence nor did she play her beloved pianoforte. She seemed folded in on herself, broken and shrinking.

They were both prisoners in their own way, and Cassie prayed morning and night for reprieve, some way to make restitution, some way to free them all from the chains she had bound them with. There was no answer, just the suffocating silence.

Friday morning, Cassie went down to breakfast, hoping that she would have the meal to herself, as had been the case the day before. The clatter of a fork against plate made her stop just outside the room. What if Lenora was inside? Cassie turned quietly and had taken a single step toward the stairs when she heard Mama's voice.

"Are you certain, Lenora?" Her voice held such compassion that Cassie envied the recipient. While her mother had not harangued Cassie or been cruel, neither had she softened or reached out with kindness.

Not that Cassie deserved kindness. The censure from her parents was well earned, and yet she longed for the comfort she knew she would not receive.

"I cannot face him, let alone the entire parish, Mama."

"Your absence might be misinterpreted as some kind of admission. You have done nothing wrong. He was the one to cry off."

"I can't stay here."

Cassie had been shocked by Lenora's strength of feeling immediately following the broken engagement when she'd confronted Cassie in a rage. Cassie had never seen her sister in such high emotion, but since then Lenora had shriveled back into her unobtrusive self. Her voice now was resolute rather than pleading, though there was still a pitiable quality to it. Cassie moved closer to the door, careful not to reveal herself.

"Lenora," Mama said softly, and Cassie could imagine that she extended her hand to her daughter. "I feel it would be best for you to stay. If anyone should go it should be Cassie."

Go? Go where?

"So that I might be left with the household duties? So that I must make the parish visits and pretend my heart is not broken within my chest?" She sniffled, and Cassie clutched at her stomach. "I would rather go to Bath and serve as Aunt Gwen's companion for the summer. Let Cassie be the one to suffer here in Leagrave."

"The request I sent was for Cassie to be her attendant, and it was an imposition to do even that much. To change daughters after overstepping my bounds already—"

"When have I ever asked for anything, Mama?" Lenora said with startling ferocity. "I cannot stay here. In Bath, I shall have an occupation and the distance I need to recover myself, which I don't believe I ever shall if I remain here." She lowered her voice. "I am the subject of gossip and accusation, Mama, and it cuts through me like a knife. Cassie's deception is *completely* unknown. I bear the sharp eyes and sharper tongues alone."

"Oh, my dear girl," Mama said, her words muffled in what Cassie assumed was an embrace. She clenched her eyes tight. This was the first Cassie had heard of a request being sent to Aunt Gwen, but knowing she might have the chance for escape filled her with longing, even as it was being taken from her. Had Lenora insisted Cassie be removed and now changed her mind, or was it their parents' decision to send Cassie to Bath? Could Lenora not stand the sight of her sister even twice a day at family meals? Had Cassie managed to ruin every bit of sisterly love and friendship they had ever shared?

Cassie did not stay to hear the end of the discussion but returned to her bedchamber. She closed the door softly behind her before making way to her writing desk. She did not know if she would be informed of Lenora's departure and felt the need to speak her heart before they were separated.

She removed a piece of paper and tried not to think of all the other times she had written letters at this desk. Letters to Evan. How had she ever believed that such a thing would end any differently than it had? Why had she believed the deception would be purified somehow?

The Bible did not say, "Thou shalt not lie—unless you believe it will improve your situation." She had justified herself all along and tread unfairly upon the hearts of people she loved. She ached to make it right, and yet such hope seemed impossibly out of reach. Cassie had never understood the true nature of repentance before and now felt as though she could not partake of the offering due to her own failings. But she had to try. Surely the sweet nature of her sister would prevail, and Cassie would at least know that Lenora did not hate her for what she'd done.

> *Dearest Lenora,*
>
> *It is difficult to find the words to express what is in my heart, but that difficulty must stem from the fact that I have*

never in my life felt such regret and remorse for something I have done. I was wrong to write those letters in your place, and if I could go back I would instead encourage you to have done it. It interfered with what might have grown between you and Mr. Glenside naturally. And I did not stop even when I realized my heart was becoming involved. I am so sorry. I know I cannot make it right and undo your suffering. I know I deserve your anger and scorn. I am so sorry.

I can only hope that one day our sisterly affections can return to what they once were—before I so arrogantly presumed to force Providence upon you. Please forgive me, Lenora. From the bottom of my heart—amid all the pain and regret I feel—it is your forgiveness that I pray for, long for, and need so very much, though I know I am undeserving. I beg of you to ease my heart and forgive me my selfishness that hurt you so severely. I am glad you are able to go to Bath and escape the situation I have created here in Leagrave. Know that my love and support goes with you, and that I wish you every good thing.

Love always,

Cassie

Cassie felt raw as she reread the letter, as though she had bled across the page. Expressing such vulnerability was not something she was used to. And yet she meant every word and prayed that Lenora would feel her sincerity. When she finished, she sealed the letter with wax as she would a letter she'd planned to send by post. She opened her bedroom door, ensured the hallway was empty, and then walked across to Lenora's room. She slid the letter beneath the door and then hurried back to the security of her own room, wishing she could watch her sister read it. Surely Lenora would be as affected by the words when she read them as Cassie had been when she wrote them.

At dinner that evening, Papa announced that Lenora was leaving for Bath on the morning coach and would serve as Aunt Gwen's companion through the summer. *That soon?* Cassie thought.

"I hope you have a lovely trip," Cassie said.

Lenora said nothing and did not look up. She cut a bite of her chicken as though Cassie had not spoken at all. The meal returned to silence.

The next morning, Cassie offered to help as Mama and Young rushed back and forth to gather this item and that. Mama shook her head and asked that Cassie remain out of the way until she was called to say good-bye to Lenora.

Cassie was sitting at the window seat in her room, waiting to be called, when a sound outside her door caught her attention. She turned to see a white square resting on the floorboards a few feet into the room. Cassie's heart jumped. Lenora must have read her note and written a response!

She hurried to snatch the note from the floor, only to pull her eyebrows together. It was the same note she had put beneath Lenora's door yesterday. Lenora's name was written across the front in Cassie's own hand. She turned the letter over, thinking perhaps Lenora had written her response on the same paper, but the seal had not been broken. Lenora had not even read it.

Hot tears came to Cassie's eyes, and though she tried to blink them away, they would not be held back. Lenora would not forgive her, Evan would not have her, and her parents would not comfort her. She had lost everything.

Chapter Thirty-Five

Cassie was at her dressing table Sunday morning when Mama came to stand in the doorway. "We shall leave in ten minutes," she said.

"Yes, Mama," Cassie said obediently, though she wanted to protest. She had kept to the vicarage all week where she encountered no one outside of her family and therefore did not have to pretend all was well. By now, the news of the broken engagement would be all through the parish. Would people pull her aside at church and ask her questions? She would have to act the role of sister of the scorned, but hide her part in it. The ability to meet the expectations placed upon her felt impossible.

After Lenora's departure yesterday morning, Mama had outlined Cassie's responsibilities. She could not play the organ in Lenora's place at services, but she was to take over Lenora's other Sabbath chores such as laying out the hymnals, polishing the organ keys and pedals, and making sure Mr. Peterson—Lenora's replacement—had everything he needed. This was in addition to Cassie's usual responsibility of preparing the pulpit, which she had done for several years.

On Mondays, Cassie would accompany her mother to visit the parishioners who did not attend services. Tuesdays, she would help Rose. On Wednesdays, she was to go to Victoria's house and oversee her niece's lessons. Mama determined that Cassie's rudimentary skill at the pianoforte was a better option than skipping lessons until Lenora returned. She would also head up the children's Bible class in the afternoon. On Thursdays, Cassie would help with the wash and attend the parish dinner. Friday would be more visits, and Saturday was always full of Sabbath preparations.

Cassie was to tell no one about the letters and was to defend her sister at all costs. It was exhausting to think of keeping such a schedule while she nursed her secret pain, but she agreed without argument, knowing she had earned the punishment. She hoped that meeting her mother's expectations would amend her wrongdoing.

Overshadowing all of the foreseeable difficulties, however, was the possibility that she would see Evan at church today. If he came. How would she react? Perhaps her broken and embarrassed heart would not reach for him after all that had happened, but she had thought of him every day, and she worried about him. Was he back from London? Would he attend services if he were? Did he hate her for what she had done?

Cassie dressed in her plain lavender gown without any embellishments and went downstairs so that she would be ready when her mother appeared. Mama did not compliment Cassie's punctuality but instead repeated Cassie's Sabbath duties as they crossed the yard between the vicarage and the church.

When they entered Father's office, Cassie gathered Papa's sermon from where he always left it on his desk, then went to the chapel and put the sermon on the pulpit. She retrieved the crate of hymnals and set them out on the pews. When that was done, she returned to the pulpit and laid out the pencil and ruler Papa insisted be at the ready for him each week. She filled a water glass and put it on the lower shelf and straightened the altar cloth that hung over the sides. There was nothing invigorating about the work, but it felt good to be doing something other than pining at her window, thinking of Evan, and wishing she could rewrite the last few months of her life.

When the parishioners began to arrive, Cassie sat in the second pew—
where her family always sat—and steeled herself for the uncomfortable
questions that were sure to find her. Within a minute, Rebecca Glanchard
slid into the empty space beside Cassie on the bench.

"Goodness, Cassie," she said, keeping her voice low as though every-
one didn't already know. "Whatever has gone on? I couldn't believe it when
I heard the news about Lenora and Mr. Glenside." She snorted in disgust.
"I knew from the moment I saw him he was unfit for our level of society.
And to think everyone was so excited to have him come to Leagrave."

Cassie's stomach tightened, but she bit back the sharp defense of Evan
that had so easily risen to her mind. She was to defend Lenora, and yet
it was not fair that Evan should bear the accusations. Could she defend
them both?

"It is not his fault," Cassie said, shaking her head for emphasis. "They
simply were not well suited."

"Not well suited?" Rebecca repeated. "He should have thought of that
before he made her an offer. I find what he's done completely reprehen-
sible. Why, Mama said she will not dine with him, and she told Aunt to
scratch him from the list of attendees for next month's ball."

"That seems rash," Cassie said, sick to her stomach at the continuing
consequences of Evan's actions.

"Rash?" Rebecca countered. "No *gentleman* would treat Lenora as he
has. Such action is not to be tolerated in Leagrave." She paused and narrowed her eyes at Cassie. "I am surprised you are not more upset about it,
Cassie. She is *your* sister, after all."

The continuing battle within herself left Cassie without a reply.

Rebecca remained a few seconds longer, obviously waiting for Cassie
to further abase Evan. "Oh, there is Aunt now," Rebecca said when
Cassie did not respond. "Please tell Lenora how sorry I am for all that's

happened. Perhaps it is best this way. Can you imagine being married to a man of such low manners? Happy Sunday, Cassie."

Cassie could only nod in response. She felt ill and looked at the clock near the pulpit, counting the minutes until she could escape. She'd no sooner thought it than someone slipped into the bench behind her and leaned forward.

"Cassie," Sarah Modfield said softly. "How is dear Lenora doing? Why I could hardly believe it when I heard the news. And now I hear she's left for Bath. My heart is truly broken for her." She patted Cassie on the shoulder before leaving.

Rose and her husband joined Cassie on the pew, and Cassie was grateful for the buffer of their support even though she knew Rose should have stayed home. She had several weeks left in her pregnancy but looked as big as a house. Victoria and her family arrived, filling in the bench behind them. Cassie felt protected in her place beside the wall. But even Victoria and Rose did not know Cassie's part. What would they think if they did? Once surrounded by her sisters and their families, Cassie did not have to deflect the comments herself, but she heard the whispers all the same. She was glad Lenora had gone to Bath so she did not have to endure this.

Finally, Father walked up to the front of the congregation. His face was drawn, leading Cassie to believe he had been fielding many of the same questions she had faced. He was supposed to have read the banns today.

There were a few minutes yet before Papa would begin his sermon, and everyone moved to their places.

Mama moved past Rose to take her seat beside Cassie. "This is torturous," she said under her breath.

Cassie nodded. She could not think of a better word.

"At least Mr. Glenside isn't here," Mama said.

Cassie was surprised by the chilly tone and turned to look in Mama's face, which was hard as she faced forward. The weight in her stomach became heavier still. What would happen when he did return?

Chapter Thirty-Six

Cassie's new responsibilities began the next morning, and though little of the work was enjoyable, she found satisfaction in being busy. On Monday, Cassie spent half the day on parish visits with Mama and the other half helping weed Widow Bott's garden, which was so horribly overgrown she couldn't even find the cucumber plants. On Tuesday, Cassie spent all day at Rose's, catching up the wash and tending the garden. They spoke little; Rose was too tired and Cassie too anxious. On Wednesday, Cassie ran through the C-major scales with Victoria's daughter in the morning and was on her way back home to prepare for the children's Bible class when Rebecca Glanchard waved at her from the other side of the street.

Cassie's heart plummeted in her chest, but she put on a polite smile—the best she could muster—and waited as Rebecca ran across the dirt road, one hand holding her bonnet on her head. Cassie had no choice but to wait for her friend, though she did not relish the idea of conversation. She had little doubt what Rebecca wanted to say. Lenora was all anyone talked about these days, and each conversation added new weight to the wretched state of Cassie's soul.

"I thought it was you," Rebecca said when she reached Cassie, her cheeks flushed from exertion. "How are you? Have you heard how Lenora is in Bath?"

"Mama received a letter yesterday. Lenora made it safely to Bath and is enjoying the society there."

Rebecca frowned. "Poor Lenora," she said, shaking her head. "Every time I think of what that horrid man did to her I want to . . . Well, I don't know what, but it's not very Christian."

Cassie kept her smile in place, but only just. Were this any other family and any other man, she would take an equally strong position against the gentleman's poor behavior.

Rebecca continued. "And soon we will have to tolerate his mother and sisters too. It's downright vulgar, if you ask me—them prancing into town, pretty as you please." She let out a huff of air. "I hope not a single drawing room is open to them once they arrive. I know we shan't call upon them."

Cassie took a breath to steady herself. "I expect our family shall call."

Rebecca's face screwed up in sympathy. "I'm sure your parents shall have to do so, being clergy and all, but what a horrible irony that they should have to. I expect they shall be the only ones, however, and everyone will know it was out of duty. I hope you shall not have to attend them. Mr. Glenside's sisters are surely pock-faced and shabby."

"I see no reason to think so," Cassie defended, though she fiddled with the string of her reticule as she spoke. "And I certainly am not deciding now to dislike them simply because of this unfortunate occurrence."

"What?" Rebecca said, genuinely surprised. "After his treatment of Lenora, I would think—"

"He did not treat her poorly, Rebecca," Cassie said, feeling fire building in her chest. She held the other woman's eyes. "They were ill-suited, that is all."

"Well," Rebecca huffed, pulling her eyebrows together. "I certainly know where I shan't go for comfort should anyone treat me as base as he's treated Lenora."

"I feel badly for Lenora as well. It is a terrible situation for everyone."

"At *his* hand. His mother and sisters shall bear the shame of it just as any of the rest of us would if someone in our family behaved so badly. Oh, I dread seeing them at church on Sunday. I'm sure that will be our first occasion to get a good look at the bunch."

Cassie felt her eyebrows lift. "Church on Sunday? *This* Sunday?"

"Yes. I mean, I am only assuming they shall be there because Mr. Glenside was attending services before he left, but I do hope they think better of it. Church is for the God-fearing."

"Wait," Cassie said, sure she'd misunderstood. "Mr. Glenside's family does not come until August when the Dower House is fully ready." Cassie had thought of their coming many times but took comfort in the fact that their arrival was two months away. By then the scandal would at least be lukewarm, and she hoped some portion of the town's natural kindness would be back in place.

"You have not heard?" Rebecca said, leaning in. "They are coming to Leagrave tomorrow."

"*Tomorrow?*" Cassie said as her stomach plummeted to her toes. "That can't be." Why would they come so much earlier than expected? Why would Evan allow them to come when the branding irons were still red-hot?

"My maid is sweet on a footman at Glenside Manor, and he told her that the lot of them will live in the big house until the cottage is done. The footman said they are adding three more staff, and they are bringing in more workers to finish the renovation quicker. I feel for the elder Mr. Glenside, having to put up with such a parade of common folk in his own house. I feel he's already been generous beyond his character."

"What do you know of his character, Rebecca?" Cassie snapped, filled to the brim with the mean-spirited gossip. "You've never spoken to the man in all your life, and yet you're as quick to pass judgment on him as you are on three innocent women who have done nothing to deserve the censure you are so very eager to bestow upon them."

Rebecca's eyes went wide as she stared at Cassie, the silence drawing long between them. Long enough for Cassie to regret her sharpness. But she did not regret her words, and so she did not offer the apology that Rebecca was surely waiting for.

The young women stared at one another until Rebecca lifted her chin and offered a tight smile. "Good day, Cassandra." She turned and crossed the street.

Cassie began walking toward home, albeit slowly, and imagining the reception the Glensides would receive when they arrived in Leagrave if Rebecca's attitude reflected that of the rest of the town. Perhaps because Evan had not been raised amid the gentry, he did not understand how tightly they could pull together when they felt threatened. Perhaps he did not fully understand the prejudice they held toward the lower classes.

Cassie herself understood she was accepted in higher circles only because of her father's position in the church; he was still a workingman. That his work was God's allowed him to maintain gentle society. Cassie knew the rules; Evan did not. His mother and sisters were entering a lion's den, and Cassie was not certain that even God could close the mouths of such beasts.

Chapter Thirty-Seven

The Wilton family always had stew for an early dinner on Wednesday night due to choir practice starting at seven o'clock. Often they invited fellow parishioners to join them, especially other members of the choir. Tonight, however, they had no energy to offer companionship to each other, let alone anyone else.

This must be what hell is like, Cassie thought as she spooned up a bite of potato. *Surrounded by people you love and yet still alone.*

She pondered on redemption and forgiveness. Not for herself, as that seemed a long distance off. Since the confrontation with Rebecca, she could not stop thinking about Evan and his family. He was taking the fall for what had happened even though he was the least to blame. And his mother and sisters would soon join him in the undeserved disgrace.

Cassie knew from his letters that he felt great responsibility for them. It was one of the many things she admired about him. He had already been concerned about their finding a place in a higher level of society. Their arrival would give rise to more gossip and mean-spirited comments. Cassie would have to continue to defend Lenora and cast Evan in the role of villain by default. Who deserved her loyalty? Who should she protect? Why did she have to choose?

She thought back to her father's sermon on Sunday, which had been centered on putting God first in our lives and neighbors second. Evan was their neighbor. He was a member of her father's parish, as his family would be now that they were coming to live here. She thought of her last moments with Evan, of his hand on her face and the pain in his eyes. What would she see in his eyes when next they saw one another?

After a few more minutes of agonizing silence, Cassie cleared her throat and looked at her mother. "Did you know that Mrs. Glenside and her daughters are coming to Leagrave?"

Mama stopped chewing for a moment and cast a look at Papa, who quickly returned to his bowl of stew. They knew. "I heard something of it, yes," Mama said.

Cassie went back to her dinner, unsure how to have this conversation without antagonizing her parents. Silence filled the room again until Cassie put down her spoon and placed her hands in her lap. "I am responsible for the cold reception they will likely receive when they arrive. I want to make it better, only I don't know how."

"You are not responsible," Papa said, running his bread along the bottom of the bowl. "And people will not be unkind."

"Will we visit them on Monday when we make the other parish visits, Mama?" Cassie asked. Her parents shared another look. Cassie looked at her father. "Will you welcome them to the parish?"

"I only recently called on Mr. Glenside," Papa said. "I don't feel I should make another call unless I am invited."

Cassie turned to her mother. "Will *you* call on them then, Mama?"

"Not socially, no," Mama said, finally meeting Cassie's eyes. "It would be inappropriate, considering the circumstance."

"A circumstance of my actions, not theirs."

"Mr. Glenside plays a part," Mama reminded her.

"Unwittingly," Cassie reminded them. "He did not know the letters were from me, and as soon as he did know, he verified the information. Once he knew the truth, he could not in good conscience pursue the match. I feel that makes him honorable."

"Your definition of honorable and mine are very different, then," Papa said, straightening in his chair. "He made a declaration to Lenora. He had a moral obligation to see that through, and he broke his word. That is not honorable."

"Would you have rather he followed through when he knew he did not love her as he should?" She did not point out that his feelings for Cassie were what prevented him from following through. That truth was nothing more than salt in the wound. Evan was lost to her, and she knew it. He should not be punished further for what had already hurt him.

Mama fixed Cassie with a tired look, as though they had had this conversation a dozen times before. "Love grows over time and through committed promise. What happened was unfair to him, I agree, but *he* made the choice that ended the engagement, and there are consequences for such things."

Cassie stared at her mother for several seconds, then turned her eyes to her father. "You would truly have preferred him to follow through with the marriage even when his heart was not in it?" She hoped such bluntness would help them hear themselves. "You would prefer that Lenora have a life with a man who did not love her rather than feel the embarrassment of a broken engagement?"

"It is not about embarrassment," Papa said, his eyes flashing. "It is about honor."

"Whose honor? Yours?"

Father clenched his jaw and narrowed his eyes. "You are in no position to advise us on this matter. We need not remind you of your part in this."

"No, you do not need to remind me," Cassie said, as soft and humble as she could manage. "I am well aware of my part, and so very sorry for having done what I did. To protect me, and our family, we are choosing not to tell my part, which is putting the whole of responsibility on Mr. Glenside, and I do not think that is fair. He is the only innocent in this, and yet he is to suffer the greatest for it. And now his mother and sisters shall share in his undeserved shame."

Her parents were silent, and then Mama spoke. "You say Mr. Glenside was the only innocent—but what of Lenora? Was she not a victim here? You seem much more concerned for his comfort than for your own sister's, and I find that distressing."

"Lenora is a victim too," Cassie said with a nod. "But she at least knew I'd written the letters. Mr. Glenside did not."

"What?" Papa said, staring at Cassie across the table. "Lenora knew of the letters prior to the engagement being broken?"

Cassie looked at him, surprised at his surprise. She had rehearsed and reviewed the situation many times and never hidden any information once the deception was discovered. Surely she had mentioned this detail.

"When Mr. Glenside asked Lenora on the carriage ride, I knew he would likely bring up topics of discussion from the letters, and she would not know what he meant. I confessed the whole of it to her, thinking she would be angry or perhaps too embarrassed to continue with the drive, but she was not. She read the letters before he came for her."

Papa's brow came together, and he turned to Mama. "Were you aware of this?"

"I suppose it was told to me, though I'm not sure why it makes a difference. It changed nothing."

"I disagree," Papa said. "It means that Lenora was part of the deception too." He pushed away from the table, glaring at Cassie. "Have I no daughters with integrity?" Without another word, he stalked from the room.

Cassie and Mama sat in silence, neither of them speaking or touching the stew left in their bowls. Finally, Mama stood from the table, placed her napkin on her chair, and turned to leave.

"Mama," Cassie said in a pleading tone.

"I must see to your father."

She left the room. Cassie was left by herself, but she felt no less alone than when she had first sat down.

Chapter Thirty-Eight

By the time Sunday arrived, Cassie was as high-strung as a racehorse. She had thought of nothing but the arrival of the Glensides for days. She was kept so busy at home that she had little chance to pick up on any gossip, and she did not dare ask her parents. What had been coldness between them was frostier than ever after her attempts to talk to them Wednesday night. So she stopped talking. She stopped drawing. She had not lifted a paintbrush in weeks.

Cassie arrived at the church early and prepared the pulpit and the music before taking her place on the second pew. Rose was resting at home, but Victoria's family filled the third row again. Every muscle in Cassie's body felt tight, and though she tried to relax her shoulders, and then her jaw, by the time she succeeded in releasing tension from one part of her body, she would find it settled into another part. She kept looking toward the back of the chapel, anxious about the Glensides' arrival. When her father made his way to the front of the church, as he did every week, she wondered if perhaps they were not coming after all. It was a relief to imagine not having to confront the awkwardness, yet she was disappointed too.

The shifting of skirts and shushing of children as the parishioners found their places was familiar until it went oddly quiet. Cassie turned around as the silence grew.

Evan stood at the back of the church while an older woman and two younger ones took seats on the very last pew. The girls were not pock-marked nor shabby, as Rebecca had claimed, but their clothing wasn't to the level of the rest of the gentry gathered in the chapel, nor did they move to a forward pew as their station dictated. Instead they sat with the servants and merchants who filled the back half of the church.

It had been one thing for Evan—single and attending alone—to sit in the back as he had on previous Sundays. It was very different for a family to not claim their place in the church. The irony was not lost on Cassie; many of the parishioners likely thought the Glensides were sitting where they belonged.

Evan caught Cassie's eye for only a moment before he looked away, and she felt her face catch fire at the simple connection. She faced forward again, worried the other parishioners would misinterpret her reaction. Or perhaps guess it correctly. She swallowed in hopes of remedying her dry mouth. The appearance of the Glensides had obviously been the cause for the hush of the room, but now the twittering of voices might as well have been a trumpet.

"I am shocked he dares to show his face," a woman whispered to Mama.

"All are welcome in the church of God," Mama said, her smile tight as she faced stoically forward.

The woman grunted and turned away.

Cassie looked up at Papa. He was watching the newcomers, and Cassie hoped no one else could see the tightness in his shoulders and jaw. Her heart ached, and she wished she dared stand and tell the congregation it was not Evan's fault. It was *her* fault, and yet to say so was out of the question.

Tears came to her eyes, and she blinked rapidly. She could not fall apart here—that would never do—but her heart felt like tin in her chest. She should do something. But what?

Papa began to talk about the apostolic ministries outside of Judaea.

Cassie could not focus on his words. Instead, every one of her senses was attuned to Evan. She resisted looking over her shoulder and meeting his gaze. Had the days spent apart changed his feelings? She reminded herself it would do no good to think such a thing; she was to forget him. Forget how he made her feel. Forget his touch. She closed her eyes and relived the moments they'd spent together in the glen. Just thinking on their last conversation caused her face to tingle.

Mama took hold of Cassie's hand, causing her eyes to open. She gave her mother a sideways glance. Mama's jaw was tight, her eyes too intent to be truly focused on Papa.

"Do not appear affected," Mama said so quiet Cassie nearly did not hear her. "He is nothing to us. Pretend he is not there."

Impossible, Cassie thought. But she had no choice except to try to do exactly that. *He is everything to me.*

If Cassie were feeling high-strung when she arrived at church, she was wound as tight as a piano wire by the time services finished. As was his custom, her father made his way to the back doors so he might bid farewell to each individual member. Mama usually followed him, adding her sentiments to his. Today, she remained in her seat and engaged Victoria in conversation concerning Rose and how they might help her in the coming week.

Cassie's hands were already balled into fists, and she let out a breath. The parishioners would notice that the vicar's wife was not participating in today's farewell. They would read into it that the family was not welcoming the Glensides, and everyone would follow suit.

The congregation prepared to leave, and many began to visit in hushed tones. In a rush of energy, Cassie got to her feet. If Mama had been sitting on the outside of the pew, Cassie would not have been able to get past her. By the time Mama reached out, Cassie was out of range. She did not look back when Mama said her name under her breath.

Cassie hurried down the aisle, feeling sixty pairs of eyes upon her but not meeting any of them. Not even Evan's, though she longed to do so. Everyone was watching her, and she dared not risk anyone seeing more in the glance than she could afford them to see.

She took her mother's place beside her father and put a smile on her face when he gave her a questioning look. There was no time for more than that as the first parishioners reached them.

"Good to see you," Cassie said to Sir Keymont after her father thanked him for coming. She shook his hand and then those of his four children before moving on to the Richardsons. "Lovely to have you," she said to them and then proceeded to follow each farewell her father offered with a good-bye of her own.

The gentry faded into gentlemen farmers—including Victoria's family —and then to the merchants, tradesmen, and servant classes. By this time on a typical Sunday, Cassie was usually in the yard talking to her friends. She felt more and more conspicuous under the questioning looks of the departing parishioners.

Cassie felt her father tense, and she reached out to give Papa's wrist a squeeze. The Glensides were approaching. She understood how he felt, truly she did, but she also trusted in his compassion to handle this uncomfortable moment with grace. If he could be welcoming, the parishioners might follow his example.

"Welcome back, Mr. Glenside," her father said, his tone formal.

Cassie took a breath as the men shook hands. Did Evan sense the tightness of her father's demeanor? She prayed he did not.

"Thank you, Mr. Wilton," Evan said. "I would like to introduce you to my mother, Mrs. Carolyn Glenside, and my sisters, Camilla and Natalie."

"Pleased to meet you all," Father said, inclining his head. He did not hold their eyes, however, not even with Mrs. Glenside, who deserved his respect as a woman and a widow.

Cassie swallowed and felt heat rise in her cheeks. Did Mrs. Glenside know everything?

Evan would not look at Cassie, instead he stepped back, allowing his family to approach Papa. Cassie did not miss that the action prevented him from shaking her hand or exchanging a greeting. Her heart thudded in her chest.

Cassie looked back at his mother to find the woman's eyes on her. Cassie's mouth went dry again, and she felt as though her face was nothing more than a list of all her failings, which Mrs. Glenside was reading line by line.

Papa had already dropped Mrs. Glenside's hand and was looking past them to someone else. Cassie was embarrassed by his rudeness.

"Mrs. Glenside," she said softly, extending a hand. "I'm honored to meet you."

Mrs. Glenside furrowed her brows slightly, as though doubting Cassie's words, but she put out her hand all the same. "I'm glad to make your acquaintance, Miss Cassandra."

Cassie's face flamed even hotter. She had not introduced herself, which meant that Mrs. Glenside knew who she was due to her son's telling. Cassie withdrew her hand, wishing her skin did not feel like it was on fire.

"I'm Natalie."

The younger of the two girls stood before her, hand out and face beaming. Cassie took the girl's hand and gave it a squeeze. "Welcome to Leagrave."

"Oh, thank you," Natalie said, extracting her hand and tucking a strand of honey-blonde hair behind her ear. "We have been here only three days, and I love it to my toes." She bounced up and down on those toes, looking around her. "Our church in London smelled like a barn, but this church smells lovely. Like good soap. It is grand!"

Papa excused himself and moved deeper into the church, putting his arm across the back of one of the local farmers and steering him away from the exit as though seeking private conversation. Cassie felt sure he only wanted to get away from the Glensides.

The older sister stepped forward and put out her hand, recapturing Cassie's attention. "I am Camilla," she said. She did not have the exuberance of Natalie, but she did not have the knowing look of their mother either.

Cassie glanced at Evan for some sign as to what his sisters knew of the situation, but he was talking quietly with his mother and not looking her direction. She looked back at Camilla and brightened her expression, determined to do right by this girl who appeared to be only a few years younger than Cassie herself.

"Lovely to meet you, Camilla. Are you as pleased with Leagrave as Natalie is?"

"I like it," she said cautiously. "We haven't met anyone yet, though."

"We knew everyone in the Mile End," Natalie offered glibly. "Lived there all our lives, you know."

"It must be difficult to leave something so familiar." And how much harder to enter a place that had already made up its mind about you? Her heart went out to these girls, whose manners were not so rough as they were new. Evan had said they were taking etiquette classes in London, which was good as there was no such training easily available in Leagrave.

Would their charm and appealing natures count toward anything? Would anyone in the village give them a chance?

Out of the corner of her eye, Cassie could see her parents lingering in the aisle rather than passing the Glensides to exit. A quick look to the yard showed a number of people in pockets of conversation, casting cautious glances her way, likely whispering about what she was doing talking to *those* people.

The unfairness took hold of her, and Cassie turned to Evan and Mrs. Glenside conversing quietly a few feet away. "Mrs. Glenside," she said in a strong voice, pausing until she had the woman's attention. "Would your family do us the honor of joining us for dinner?"

Mrs. Glenside looked shocked, and a sharp gasp from her right told Cassie that Mama had approached in time to hear the invitation. Mrs. Glenside shared a look with her son. "Tonight?" she asked.

"Not tonight," Cassie said. But when? There was no time to properly prepare to host a dinner by Monday night, Wednesday was stew and choir, and Thursday was wash day plus the parish dinner, which had already been planned two months in advance. Friday and Saturday nights were reserved for entertainments. "Tuesday," she said, thinking quickly.

"Oh, well," Mrs. Glenside looked at Evan again, who gave her the smallest shrug Cassie had ever seen. Mrs. Glenside turned back to Cassie. "I suppose Tuesday would be fine."

"Very good," Cassie said, her heart nearly leaping out of her throat. She pointedly ignored her mother's gaze that was drilling holes through her. "We shall send round a note with the particulars."

Evan's eyes narrowed enough for her to know what he was thinking—he'd had his fill of her notes.

Cassie's smile faltered, so she looked at Natalie and Camilla. "We shall see you all on Tuesday, then."

"Wonderful!" Natalie said, clapping her hands as she hurried toward her mother to share her excitement.

"Thank you," Camilla said more appropriately, though her eyes danced.

They are fish out of water, Cassie thought, looking over the four of them as they exited the church. Her eyes lingered on Evan's back, and she swallowed. She would have an entire evening in his company, similar to the evenings he'd come to the vicarage when he was courting Lenora.

A tight grip on her arm caused her to start, and she turned to look into her mother's eyes that were flashing like sparks from a tinderbox.

"What on earth are you doing?" Mama said between clenched teeth.

"Being kind," Cassie said through her fear. She shook her arm free of her mother's grasp and stepped away from her, looking around to see if anyone had seen her mother's action. Everyone, it seemed, was watching the Glensides, who were making their way toward Glenside Hall. Not a single person offered them greeting.

"You have overstepped your bounds," Mama said in a dark whisper.

Cassie expected to feel anger at what she felt was an unchristian accusation, but instead she felt profound sorrow, regret, and exhaustion. Tears rose her eyes, and she felt her chin tremble. "I am trying to do right, Mama," she said in a shaky whisper. "It is not fair that they should be spurred for something that is my fault."

"You cannot have him," Mama snapped with irritation, seemingly unaffected by Cassie's emotion. "Ingratiating him to you through kindness to his family will change nothing."

Cassie turned away and wiped her eyes as discreetly as possible so that the parishioners would not see. "I am not trying to earn his affection. He would not even look at me."

"And if he had?"

"He didn't," Cassie whispered. It cut her to the quick to say it. She met her mother's eyes once more. "You have told me to forget him, and I am trying, but I cannot let his family carry the burden of what I have done. I have caused so much injury already."

Mama took a breath, her eyes still sharp, and looked past Cassie, presumably at the Glensides, who must still be in view. "Go to your father's office to recover yourself," she said. "We'll talk about this later."

Chapter Thirty-Nine

The next afternoon, Evan looked over the ivy-covered brick of the church and straightened his waistcoat. He had requested—and been granted—a conference with Mr. Wilton, which is why he and his uncle were now approaching the south door of the church. A quick glance over his shoulder showed him the vicarage, built from the same brick as the church. *Cassie is on the other side of those walls*, he thought to himself as he looked across the cemetery that separated the two buildings. Thoughts of Cassie should be buried like the dead; however, she was not so easily forgotten.

"Thank you for coming with me, Uncle," Evan said, embarrassed to verbalize his gratitude but needing to say the words.

Uncle stepped up beside Evan and gave a similar inspection to the church. "I haven't wanted to make a snort about it, but you and I should have spoken to Mr. Wilton in person when you broke the engagement in the first place." He gave Evan a sidelong look.

Heat ran up Evan's neck. "I was out of my element. I didn't know what to do."

Uncle Hastings put his hand on Evan's shoulder. "No offense, but you've been out of your element since you got here, my boy. Let's only hope we can find some mode of repair."

Evan looked at his boots. They had been polished that morning by a staff member whose job it was to polish Evan's boots. Before coming to Leagrave, Evan had never considered anyone but himself responsible for such a task. Before coming to Leagrave, he had never considered a great many things, including the proper way to break off an engagement.

When Uncle spoke again his voice was softer. "I'm here to help you, my boy, and I'm glad you asked me to come today. Despite my objections to God in general, I feel sure we can work things out with Mr. Wilton." He stepped forward and rapped three times on the door before stepping back. "Let's get to it."

When Mr. Wilton answered the door, Evan could only meet his eye briefly before looking back at his gleaming boots. The first time Evan had met the vicar, the encounter had been awkward but cordial. And the times Evan had seen him at church had been pleasant enough. But no longer. The vicar's face was clouded now, and his tension high. Evan was the man who had scorned and shamed his daughter—and on paper, no less. Even a clergyman, it seemed, could not forgive such an offense.

Evan was beyond grateful when Uncle took the lead. "Thank you for meeting with us, Mr. Wilton."

"Of course. Do come in. I'm afraid I haven't any refreshment to offer. Mrs. Wilton usually sends the maid from the house for such consideration, but under the circumstances, I felt it better to keep our meeting a private one."

"Understood," Uncle said as he stepped into the office.

Evan followed, removing his hat and looking around the rather cluttered office. There was a desk piled high with books and papers, as well as a large hutch behind it that seemed to be groaning under the weight of its contents. There was something comforting in the chaos of the place, a reminder that Mr. Wilton, at his core, was a man with strengths and weaknesses too.

"Please have a seat," Mr. Wilton said, indicating a settee and two mismatched chairs set before the fireplace, cold this time of year. This end of the room was not so cluttered as the desk, though there was a newspaper draped over one arm of the settee and one of the legs of the chair did not match the others.

Evan followed his uncle to the settee, where they sat in tandem, hats in hand. Mr. Wilton took the chair with the mismatched leg.

"We would like to settle the situation between us, Mr. Wilton," Uncle said. He nodded sideways to Evan. "My nephew regrets how he went about the matter. We want to make it right."

Evan swallowed under the vicar's penetrating gaze. "I should have come to you immediately when I realized I could not follow through with the engagement. I added insult to injury in the manner of my leaving. I am very sorry—so very sorry—for the embarrassment I caused through my actions." It was everything Evan could do to hold the man's eyes.

"As I said," Uncle continued as soon as Evan finished, "we would like to make things right, and I'm prepared to offer an additional settlement to make up for the expenses incurred—"

"I don't want your money," Mr. Wilton said, a snap to his words. He shifted in his chair, drew a breath through his nose, and then continued in a calmer tone. "While I appreciate your offer, Mr. Glenside, the offense caused to my family is not a financial one, and I pray you will not insult me again with the insinuation that there is a monetary resolution to the difficulty."

Evan felt his neck heat up again. What's more, he could feel his uncle tensing beside him. He remembered the conversation the three of them had shared some months earlier in the Glenside drawing room. For the first time, he feared Uncle's presence might make things worse. He couldn't have that, which meant he would have to take more initiative than he had expected.

"I am so sorry for the offense," Evan said in hurried words. "Hurting Lenora was the last thing I wanted to do." He paused and decided to simply speak his mind. Surely it could not damage his character any more than his other actions had. "My uncle has told me the proper thing to have done was follow through with the marriage, but I hope you can understand why I was unable to do that, why I felt the better course was to sever all ties."

"He is young and hot-blooded," Uncle cut in.

"No, I am not," Evan said, surprising all three of them with his boldness. He fixed his eyes on Mr. Wilton. "I am an even-tempered man inclined to give a great deal of thought and consideration to the choices I make. Lenora—or the woman I thought was Lenora—was not a dalliance, sir, nor was my offer made lightly." He swallowed in hopes it would alleviate the dryness in his mouth. It did not, so he continued. "The offer was made, however, under the belief that in time the woman I met through the letters we shared would be revealed in Lenora. When I knew that would not be, I could have no confidence in my decision. I hate that I have hurt Lenora, and Cassie as well, that I have caused embarrassment for both of our families and created such discord, but I am surprised that everyone feels I should have continued a course that could only bring additional difficulty to everyone involved."

"You overstep your place, Evan," Uncle fairly hissed. He came to his feet. "Forgive us, Mr. Wilton, but might I have a word with my nephew?"

Mr. Wilton, however, remained looking at Evan. After a moment he said, "Do sit down, Mr. Glenside,"

Uncle paused and then resumed his place on the settee.

Mr. Wilton folded his hands together. "You speak very plainly, Mr. Glenside."

"He was not raised with genteel manners," Uncle said.

"I do not need genteel manners to want what's right," Evan said, not appreciating that his uncle seemed determined to make him appear rash and immature. "I may not have been raised in this level of society, but I could not have pledged my life to one daughter while divided in my affections toward . . . her sister. Lenora deserves better than that. I did it as much for her as I did for anyone." Speaking so boldly increased the tension in the room, and Evan paused for a breath. "If there is any way I can make things right between us, I will do so."

"There is nothing you can do to make things right," Mr. Wilton said.

Evan dropped his eyes, frustrated that no one seemed to understand what he was saying. Was a man's character so singularly defined by his social reputation that his integrity held no merit?

"But I appreciate your candor."

Evan looked up again. Mr. Wilton's expression had not softened, but he seemed to be trying to look past Evan's failings—and perhaps his own fatherly protectiveness.

Mr. Wilton shifted in his chair to a more casual position. "I learned last night that Lenora was made aware of the letters prior to riding out with you."

The detail burned. Evan wanted to hear nothing of it while also aching for more information. So many pieces of the debacle had not been clarified in his exchange with Cassie in the glen—such as what Lenora knew and when she had known it—but such elements would satisfy nothing but his own curiosity, and there were a great many debtors ahead of *curiosity* that demanded satisfaction.

"You were treated very poorly by my daughters, Mr. Glenside, and I am ashamed of them both for their parts in the deception."

"I don't wish to dwell on such things," Evan said, though the vindication he felt at Mr. Wilton's words was immense. "Nor do I in any way wish to cause greater discomfort for anyone involved. I only want to make things right, sir, but I have no idea how to do such a thing."

"Nor do I," Mr. Wilton said, letting out a breath.

"A settlement on our part would at least alleviate any financial burden and help us feel as though we had done something by way of remedy," Uncle said.

"I told you not to offend me with such an offer," Mr. Wilton said, the edge in his voice back. As before, however, his tone softened when he next spoke. "There is no price for what's happened. And besides, it is not your responsibility to make things right when it was my daughters who were behind the deception."

All three men went silent, and Evan felt as though he could breathe freely for the first time since entering the room. Mr. Wilton had admitted that Evan was not entirely at fault for the situation they found themselves in, yet despite the progress that seemed to have been made, they remained at the starting point. Evan was reminded of what had truly drawn him here.

"My sisters know nothing of what's happened beyond the broken engagement, and they do not even understand the full weight of that. My mother knows, but she is as good and guileless a woman as God ever made. I do not want you to feel obligated to me or my family or perpetuate further discomfort." He paused for a breath. "That was the other reason for wanting to meet with you today, Mr. Wilton. I did not want to refuse the dinner invitation and give the impression I was holding a grudge, but I do not want you to feel pressured into accommodating us tomorrow evening."

"Cassie took us off guard with that invitation," Mr. Wilton said.

"Yes," Evan agreed. He had known she was not acting on her parents' instruction. If only he did not admire her initiative. While he was still angry and embarrassed, he knew Cassie's intent was admirable. Still, their families would not be friends. Even he knew that.

Mr. Wilton leaned back in his chair and let out a breath. "I cannot deny that I wanted to see Lenora settled. A part of me even now would like to see the two of you make a proper courting of one another."

Evan's stomach tightened. That was a restitution he could not make. He could not court Lenora, properly or otherwise, because Cassie remained the primary thought in his head. Had Mr. Wilton not heard that aspect? Did he not understand that Cassie appealed to him where Lenora did not?

"But I realize my hopes are more fairy tale than reality." Mr. Wilton laced his fingers together and rested his palms on his chest. "We here in Leagrave are unused to scandal or having to forgive it, so I cannot promise how others will react, but I have no desire to make this more painful than it has already been. If you feel you can trust me as your vicar, I promise I will do my utmost to fulfill the charge to embrace each member of your family as a member of this parish. Perhaps if my family paves the way for inclusion, the rest of the village will follow, and we can all rise above this."

Evan could hardly believe what he'd heard. "Thank you, sir," he said with a grateful nod.

Mr. Wilton looked at Uncle Hastings, who nodded his own agreement.

"And we shall be glad to have your family for dinner tomorrow night."

"To that point, Evan is to accompany me and my bailiff to an auction in Aylebury tomorrow," Uncle Hastings said. "It's not on a grand scale, being so late in the season, but it will be his first experience with the markets. If you prefer his presence at dinner, we would need to put it off a week or more. If it is acceptable, however, his mother and sisters could come without us."

"Perhaps that would be best," Mr. Wilton said, his eyes fixed on Evan.

"It brings to mind an additional detail that must be made very clear to you as we work to repair this situation."

"Yes, sir?"

"I believe, under the circumstances, that my family reaching out to yours is the right thing to do. However, I will not tolerate any of your attention directed toward Cassie."

"No, sir," Evan said though a thump of coldness reverberated in his chest at the finality.

"While I understand that certain . . . attachments were formed between the two of you, they cannot continue. I will *not* tolerate any connection. It would only increase the scandal and hurt Lenora. What we are doing flies in the face of tradition, and, in the eyes of some, propriety and manners. Society's expectations are there for a reason, and I would never accommodate this . . . deviation from what is required for noble societies to continue. Should you in any way seek an attachment to Cassie, I shall make no further considerations, and you will have no place here—not in my church and not in this village."

"I understand," Evan said, feeling the fervor behind the man's words. "I told her before I went to London that I would never see her again." In his mind the words sounded like a slamming door.

"No personal conversation," Mr. Wilton said, his eyes intent. "And absolutely no letters. Should she make any advances of her own, you are to tell me immediately."

Evan nodded and held the man's eyes as the turning of a lock finalized his commitment. To pursue Cassie would hurt Lenora and damage his family's acceptance. He could only hope that his feelings for Cassie would fade in time. "I will neither pursue nor encourage any connection to Cassie, sir, and will report to you any action on her part. You have my word."

Chapter Forty

Mama tried half a dozen different excuses to get out of Tuesday's dinner, but each one came down to the fact that she didn't want the Glensides to come. Cassie didn't want to argue, and she understood Mama's reasons, but she felt as though her head was going to explode with attempts to convince her mother without shouting.

In the drawing room after dinner on Monday night, Papa folded his paper and put the arguing to rest once and for all. "We will have the Glensides for dinner."

Mama and Cassie looked at him in surprise.

"And we will all apply ourselves to being genteel and welcoming to the family." Papa fixed his eyes on Cassie. "However, you are not to extend invitations again, is that clear?"

Cassie nodded, content with this singular victory.

"And you are to have no personal contact with Mr. Glenside. Not private conversation, not letters."

"I won't."

"Should he engage you in either, I expect you to tell me right away."

"Yes, Papa."

Papa turned to Mama. "We will be as gracious and kind as we would be to any new members of the congregation. We must try to repair what our daughters have created for the Glenside family. My hope is that our actions will inspire a better welcome than the Glensides have received thus far."

Mama nodded, but her jaw was tight.

Papa stood, a weary expression on his face. "I am going to bed."

Mama gave Cassie one last unhappy look and turned to follow him.

Cassie let out a breath and rubbed her eyes, which ached in their sockets. She waited until she knew her parents were no longer on the stairs before putting out the lamps and making her way to her room. She was glad to have won, and yet the steel bands pulling tighter and tighter on her insides begged her to consider what it was she was getting herself into. Evan at her dinner table. Evan so close, yet completely out of reach. Her parents did not understand that advocating for the Glensides was harder for her than it would be for her to do nothing.

Cassie heard the excited voices of Evan's sisters before they knocked on the door Tuesday evening because she had been standing in the foyer for quarter of an hour already. She smoothed her skirts and took a deep breath while Mama crossed from the parlor to the dining room, scowling slightly at Cassie. Cassie rolled her eyes and was about to open the door herself—they didn't have staff to provide that exact service—when Papa came in from the back of the house.

"Sorry I'm late," he said, hurrying past her to the door as he straightened his coat. She had not seen him since his pronouncement last night. "Lost track of time."

Cassie stepped behind him as he opened the door, and she forced her face to show none of the anxiety she felt.

Mrs. Glenside stood in the center, with a daughter on each side. Conspicuously absent was the face Cassie could not banish from her thoughts. She looked past them and to either side before meeting Mrs. Glenside's eyes. Cassie quickly looked at the ground, hoping that her interest had not been noted.

"Welcome, Mrs. Glenside," Papa said with a slight bow. "And is it Catherine and Emily?"

"Natalie and Camilla," Natalie answered, though she should have allowed her mother to answer. "Camilla's the oldest."

"My apologies," Papa said with a smile.

"Mr. Glenside and my son asked that I send their regrets," Mrs. Glenside said, a touch of nervousness to her voice. This must be so awkward for her. "They went to Aylebury for an auction this afternoon."

"Oh, well, that is unfortunate," Papa said with what sounded like falseness. Had he known the two Mr. Glensides were not coming? Had he arranged for it? Perhaps it was best that Evan was not there. Then she would not be distracted from her true goal, which was to welcome his family and help them find a place in Leagrave.

"Please come in," Papa said. "Cassie, take their shawls, please."

Cassie moved forward and gathered their shawls, fine silk ones she thought might have been recent purchases. She hung them on the rack near the parlor door while Papa waved them into the room.

Typically, Mama would have invited additional guests so as to further extend the acquaintance between families, but of course this situation was far from typical.

Mama didn't join them until the others had been seated for a few minutes, and Cassie could only hope that since Mrs. Glenside did not know Mama's usual grace, she would not find Mama's disposition too off-putting. Mama was polite once she joined the party, but to Cassie her tension was in place like armor.

The six of them made small talk for nearly ten minutes, and Mrs. Glenside seemed to relax. The girls—Natalie especially—quickly settled in as though they were all long-lost relatives. Natalie told them of their journey here—in a mail coach of all the wondrous things!—and of the estate and the fine countryside. If Mrs. Glenside was embarrassed by her daughter's prattling, she did not show it.

"Uncle Hastings says that the cottage might be ready for us by the end of this month," Natalie said, fairly bouncing on her seat cushion. The girl's charm made up for the lack of manners, and, quite frankly, her lightness was invigorating in a house where everyone continued to walk on eggshells. "I shall miss the big house, though," Natalie said with a frown. "I've never seen such a fine house let alone *lived* in one."

"The cottage will be just right for us," Mrs. Glenside said, giving her daughter a mildly reprimanding look. "For my part, I will enjoy a smaller space." She looked around the room. "I do love your house here. I so hope that the cottage will feel like this."

"Feel?" Papa asked, though Cassie had wanted to ask the same thing.

"Loved," Mrs. Glenside said, though she seemed embarrassed to be the center of attention. "Don't you think you can feel love when you enter a home?"

"I am greatly humbled to hear you say such a thing," Papa said. "Though there is friction in any family."

"Oh, of course," Mrs. Glenside said with a nod.

Papa continued. "But it has always been my hope that love would conquer those difficulties."

It certainly didn't feel like there had been a great deal of love these last few weeks in the vicarage, but *could* the love they had shared for so many years overcome that? Cassie hoped so, from the very core of her being. She could not help but think of Evan too. Could love, or perhaps *should* love, be able to conquer all? Even deception? Even broken engagements? But she did not ponder for long; she had promised not to even consider a connection between them. And she was trying.

Mama stood first. "I believe dinner is ready," she said, her smile warmer than it had been before. Cassie's parents exited the room first, and as the rest of the party made their way into the dining room, Cassie found herself beside Mrs. Glenside.

"I'm glad you invited us, Cassie," she said so softly Cassie almost didn't hear it.

She looked at the older woman, surprised at the open kindness she saw in the woman's face. Had she so easily forgiven Cassie for the damage done to her son?

Before she could continue, Mrs. Glenside spoke again. "Evan tells me you are an artist."

Cassie's skin prickled from head to toe. Evan had spoken of her? In a positive way no less. "Yes, ma'am."

"Pencil or paint?"

"Paint mostly, though I sketch as well." Only she had done neither for such a long time. Creation felt like an indulgence she did not deserve right now.

"I hope one day I might see your work. While not an artist in any true sense of the term, I have made a skill of my penmanship and printing—but I believe you know that already."

"Yes, Evan says you have a great talent." Cassie nearly complimented his hand as well but stopped herself just in time. She did not want to say or do anything that might be misconstrued where Evan was concerned. "I think that printing is every bit as artistic as drawing. Only, perhaps, with greater purpose."

Mrs. Glenside touched Cassie's arm as they crossed into the dining room. "I hope one day we might be friends enough that we can enjoy one another's work."

Cassie felt on the verge of tears for the forgiveness this woman was extending so easily. What would it be to feel such a thing from her own parents? From Lenora? From herself? "I would like that very much, Mrs. Glenside."

Mrs. Glenside smiled wider, the apples of her cheeks rounding. "Then we shall do it."

As Cassie took her place at the table, she felt lighter than she had in days.

Chapter Forty-One

Bunderson's man set up a variety of targets—broken household items mostly—on a log some distance across the field then ran to the side.

Evan lifted the pistol the way Bunderson had taught him and lined up the notch at the front of the barrel. If not for the fact that he had always wanted to learn to shoot, he would never have allowed Bunderson to take him out for practice. The man took far too much joy in Evan missing the mark. Evan pulled the trigger and hit the second bottle on the log, resulting in a satisfying explosion of glass.

"Well done," Bunderson said, taking the weapon and handing it to another servant to reload. "Your aim is getting better. Nearly half of your shots actually hit something."

In the two weeks since Evan had spoken to Mr. Wilton, things had improved in Leagrave. His mother and sisters had enjoyed a comfortable dinner at the vicarage—he had been careful not to ask any questions about Cassie directly—and since then had been visited by half a dozen ladies of the village. The Wiltons' welcome and forgiveness seemed to have had exactly the effect they had hoped for.

No longer as concerned over his family's acceptance, Evan was able to relax somewhat. Bunderson had advised learning pistols first, then moving on to rifle shooting. If Evan had realized that being Bunderson's student would also make him the butt of endless jokes, he might have reconsidered. Still, he needed instruction, and Bunderson sometimes felt like Evan's only real friend here in Leagrave. Especially now.

"Ho," Bunderson's man called after setting up a new selection of bottles on the log.

"You take this," Bunderson said, handing the pistol back to him, newly loaded. He held his second pistol at his side, awaiting his turn.

Evan lined up the shot and had just touched the trigger when a crack from the side made him jump. The bottle shattered, and Evan turned to see a smug look on Bunderson's face.

"Sorry, man, I couldn't let them all go to waste," Bunderson said, lowering his other pistol. It wasn't the first time Bunderson had taken a shot he'd said was for Evan.

Evan lowered his gun, pride getting the better of him. Surely he could talk to his uncle about finding a way to practice on his own. The gun was still loaded, however, so he quickly lined up his shot and fired. He missed. "Perhaps we've had a day of it," Evan said.

"Is this because of my impatience?" Bunderson asked. "I suppose I'm not much of a teacher."

Whether or not Bunderson had meant it as a slight, Evan heard the insult of not being a quick study at what was a gentleman's sport. He was *definitely* finished for the day.

"I've enjoyed myself," Evan said. It wasn't entirely a lie.

"Good," Bunderson said, rolling his own shoulders. The men turned back to their horses, tied some distance away so as not to be spooked. "Will you join me for a drink at Stoney's?"

Evan's first thought was that he'd had enough of the man's company, but that was unkind. Bunderson had been a good friend to Evan, and Evan needed to get used to spending time with gentlemen.

"That sounds like just the thing," Evan said before he could talk himself out of it.

They reached their horses, left the servants in charge of the equipment, and headed directly to the pub on High Street. Bunderson wanted to race, so they made short time of the distance to town. Evan lost, unsurprisingly, and so he paid for the drinks. He kept to himself that he was already low on this quarter's allowance, which would have to last him another month. Before he'd left London, he'd arranged through a friend for some repairs to be made to the Doristers' house. The generosity had left his pockets substantially lighter, but he would not ask for an advance from his uncle. He would simply have to be more careful not to pay for too many drinks in the future.

The men found an empty table and ordered brandy for Bunderson and a good mug of porter for Evan.

"Porter?" Bunderson said, leaning back in his chair and stretching his arms over his head before letting them flop to his sides.

Evan smiled, determined to remain good-natured. "What can I say? I'm a common man with common tastes."

"You are a gentleman now, Glenside, and should drink a gentleman's drink."

"Thank ya kindly, gov'nah," he said in his best Cockney. "But I'll burn my belly with whatever I've a mind to, thank ya very much."

Bunderson hooted and clapped at Evan's performance, and Evan inclined his head in a makeshift bow. They continued their banter, Evan softening after he'd finished his mug. He ordered another. Porter was not nearly as strong as liquor so he could enjoy two drinks to Bunderson's one without feeling wobbly-headed. Only after ordering did he remember his need to economize. He would need to be more attentive.

" . . . New coat should arrive by Thursday," Bunderson said after taking the final swallow of his drink. "I daresay it's the finest thing you've ever seen. Blue superfine, cut to perfection in the latest fashion."

Evan's first thought was what the coat cost. Uncle had said men paid upwards of a hundred pounds for a simple waistcoat by the famous tailor Weston. Evan could not fathom paying such a price for any article of clothing. As it was, what he would pay for today's drinks was nearly what his mother had spent on a week of foodstuffs in London.

"You are going, aren't you? To the Allens' ball?" Bunderson continued. "A number of townspeople will be returned from London by then so it ought to be a merry affair. I shall introduce you all around." He looped his hand above his head.

"I'm unsure if I received an invitation and am not acquainted with the Allens—at least I don't think I am." He still struggled to keep track of names and positions.

"Of course you received an invitation," Bunderson said, shaking his head. "Everyone is invited. Even former fiancé's of the local vicar's daughter, I'd wager."

Evan smiled politely. "Or perhaps not. It is no matter." He was determined to play this off correctly. His sisters had only attended a few dinner parties since they'd arrived. They would love to attend a proper ball, but there were plenty of people still wary of the Glenside family.

"Well, my mother is good friends with Mrs. Allen. I shall inquire about an invitation."

"I would not—"

"It is ridiculous for anyone to be so harsh towards a man crying off in this day and age," Bunderson continued. He blew out his lips and shook his head. "I never understood why you proposed to Miss Wilton in the first place."

"You told me to," Evan said with as much of a laugh as he could muster to cover his surprise. "You said I had all but offered for her already."

Bunderson seemed to consider that. "I suppose I did say that. And it's a shame, now that you bring it up. If you *had* married Lenora, Cassie would be on the market by now. You should have seen it through."

Evan was surprised by the fire of jealousy that flared in his chest knowing that Bunderson could look at Cassie and see what Evan saw. Could pursue what Evan could not. He forced himself to take a breath, wondering if his growing irritation toward this man these last weeks had anything to do with Bunderson's feelings for Cassie. It was not a topic they discussed, but Bunderson had never hidden his interest in her.

"Do you know Miss Cassandra very well?" Certainly Bunderson didn't know her as well as Evan did. The letters she'd sent resided in a drawer in Evan's study. He had not looked at them since showing them to his mother, but he had not destroyed them either.

"Not nearly as well as I'd like to," Bunderson said, lifting his eyebrows. "My cousin married a vicar's girl, you know. Said all that holiness was just a cover for some real passion. Wasn't sure I could believe it until I saw Cassie after I returned to Leagrave last year." He shrugged one shoulder and his smile fell. "But unless Lenora gets swept off her feet by some widower in Bath, Cassie may very well turn to dust before anyone's allowed to find out how hot her passions burn."

Evan's jaw clenched, and he had to force himself to relax his grip on the handle of his mug. He took another long drink and wished he had ordered something stronger after all.

Bunderson leaned in as though inviting a private conversation. "I do have a question I've been meaning to ask you, Glenside."

"About Cassie?" Evan was not about to encourage the topic.

Bunderson laughed and shook his head. "Cassie is thoughts for another day. Next week, however, I'm meeting my cousin in London. He's newly released from the shackles of Cambridge, you know."

Evan had dreamed of having such *shackles* of education.

Bunderson continued. "I'm looking to get him a bit of fun . . . of the female variety. I've always had good luck at Covent Garden, but I've heard there are some delightful establishments hidden away from the greater part of London that offer more . . . customized fun, if you know what I mean."

Evan bit back a sharp retort, looked at the table between them, and turned his mug around in his hand. Going from a conversation about Cassie to one about light skirts was too sharp a transition for him to make in a moment. "I'm sure I'm not the man to ask. I've never been in the petticoat line."

"But you *are* from London, and not from the sanitized portion of the city. Surely you know a good house, tucked away in some corner somewhere, that could cater to a few men eager to cat about with the darker bits of society."

Evan wished he dared speak his mind plainly. Those darker bits of society existed because of unbridled appetites that created an industry that held souls hostage. Evan knew of a few women, widows or women married to drunks, who had turned to that employ when they had no other choice to keep their children fed. It destroyed them. "As I said, I'm not the man to give that direction. Wasn't a side of life I ever cared to look at."

"Ah, well," Bunderson said, shrugging. "You might have missed the best part of living in the slums, then."

Evan bristled and this time did not try to hide it. "I did not live in the slums, Bunderson, and most of the people who do are trying to make an honest living."

Bunderson put up both hands and shook his head. "Sorry, Glenside— too much drink in the afternoon. Forgive me?"

Evan could do little more than incline his head before making his excuses on why he needed to return to the manor. If Bunderson made the connection between his bawdy talk and Evan's exit, he gave no indication.

All the way home, Evan argued with himself not to cast judgment too harshly, but he could not get over the disgust he felt toward Bunderson's casualness regarding "a bit of fun." While Evan was determined to find his place in society, there had to be room for his own values too. And there had to be gentlemen somewhere who could provide better friendship than Ronald Bunderson.

Chapter Forty-Two

Cassie was getting faster at doing the wash. She and Mrs. Ashby, the laundress, had found a rhythm so that by three o'clock on Thursday, only a few items remained on the line. Mrs. Ashby returned home since Cassie was capable of finishing the rest. It was a warm day, and Cassie could feel the grit of dried sweat on her face. Her chemise was surely soaked through beneath her dress. But finishing early meant she could take a bath before dinner at the Wells' home that evening.

"Cassie."

She looked over her shoulder to see Mama approaching. She smiled, more honestly than she would have a few weeks ago. As Mama had come to accept Cassie's determination to help Evan's mother and sisters find a place in the village, and as Cassie had continued fulfilling all the responsibilities left in her charge, the edge between them had faded. Cassie was certain the truce was in large part because Cassie and Evan all but ignored one another, which allowed Mama's fears to cool. That a thrill still rushed through Cassie when her eyes met his was something she kept very much to herself.

"I'm almost finished," Cassie said, unpinning a sheet on the line so she could fold it. Young would take responsibility for putting the clean sheets back on the beds.

"I can speak with you while we finish," Mama said, falling in beside Cassie. She unpinned the next sheet on the line. "I received the invitation from the Allens for their ball Saturday next."

Cassie nodded, wondering why her mother was talking about the event since she would not be attending. Perhaps she would paint that evening. She could set up her easel in the orchard after her parents left and paint the sunset. It had been such a long time since she'd indulged in her art. She was beginning to miss it and felt like she might be ready to find a place for it again. Her mind was clearer and her thoughts not as dark as they had been.

"Would you like to go?"

Cassie snapped her head to the side. "Me?"

Mama did not meet her eye, still focused on the sheet. "Lenora is in Bath, and it feels awkward for your father and me to attend alone. We haven't attended without at least one child for, well, years. Victoria will be visiting in London that day, and Rose is confined to the house."

Evan might be there. Cassie quickly pushed away the thought. "I would very much like to go," she said carefully, as though Mama might be testing her and would snatch back the offer if Cassie proved too eager.

"Do you feel that one of your sister's dresses would serve for the occasion? I could help with the fitting."

"Certainly," Cassie said, still feeling cautious.

"I have two concerns."

Cassie braced herself and forced her hands to keep moving, folding the sheet.

"The Glensides will be there."

"I believe they were left off the guest list," Cassie said, remembering the conversation she'd had with Rebecca just after the engagement was broken. Mrs. Allen was Rebecca's aunt.

"Mrs. Allen brought me the invitation herself so she might explain the circumstance. Mr. Glenside *had* been removed, but with the arrival of his mother and sisters, and the increasing acceptance of them in the community . . ." She glanced at Cassie, offering her a small smile that acknowledged her role for those changing opinions. "She felt excluding them would be unkind, but she was equally worried about awkwardness on our part."

"It will not be awkward for me," Cassie said. She imagined seeing Evan dressed for a ball with a high collar and a fitted waistcoat, candlelight reflecting off his short, blond hair.

"If he were to ask you to dance it would be inappropriate for you to accept."

"He won't ask me," she said, the momentarily warm thoughts returning to cool reality. "He knows it would not be welcome."

"He knows it would not be welcome by *you* or by *us*?"

Cassie looked at her mother. "He will not ask me to dance, Mama. Surely you have noted the wide berth we give one another. He will not change his habits, and I will not encourage him."

Mama looked at her as though searching for confirmation.

Cassie thought back to when Evan had said he would never see her again. Though they were sometimes in one another's company, he had made good on his promise and never sought her out. "I promised Papa I would have no connection to Mr. Glenside. Is your fear of me going back on my word your only concern?"

Mama turned back to the laundry. "I am also concerned about how Lenora will feel if you go into society before she has made an arrangement."

Cassie had written her sister twice in the four weeks since Lenora had gone to Bath, but Lenora had not responded. Cassie was trying to forget Evan, and hoped in time she would truly be able to do so, but Lenora would always be her sister and she never wanted to hurt her again. As it was, she feared their relationship would never be repaired.

"If it will hurt Lenora, I would rather not attend," she said.

"I appreciate that sentiment, which is why your father and I wonder, with Lenora being in Bath, if some things ought to change. We can't afford to have you turned out properly now, and at this time of year it would be a silly investment, but we have been impressed with your behavior these last weeks and feel that if you can maintain the expectations we have set for you, that perhaps you could begin attending some of the social functions."

Cassie pulled the sheet in her hands and held it to her chest. "Do you mean it, Mama?" she asked quietly. Her mother's words from months ago rang back to her: *It is the meek and the mild who will inherit.*

"Yes." Mama smiled more fully on her youngest daughter than she had in a very long time. She took a step toward her and put a hand against Cassie's cheek. "I have seen the sacrifices you have made to put aside your own interests and help the Glensides. It is a hard thing to do what is better for someone else than what feels best for yourself." She lowered her hand.

Cassie had to look away. "Do not make me sound heroic."

"Do you know how to tell when you are forgiven for a wrong you have done?"

Cassie shook her head, but she ached to know it, to feel it, to own that mercy.

"When you can look at what you've done and know you are better for it. Only then can you truly understand God's grace, which was put in place so that we might learn to be like Him."

Tears rose in Cassie's eyes. "I want that relief, but I do not feel it yet."

Mama's eyes filled as well. "Take some time today to sit, quiet and still, though I know it does not come easily to you."

Cassie smiled.

Mama continued. "Think over what you have done. Look for the ways in which you turned straw to gold and be glad for the grace of our Lord, who saves us from ourselves."

"I'll do that, Mama," Cassie said, eager for such reflection.

"And I shall tell Mrs. Allen that there will be three Wiltons at her ball, and we have no objection to having the Glensides invited, too."

Mama took the basket of folded sheets into the house while Cassie wound up the line and stored the pins. She felt warm and soft as a result of her mother's words, and eager to take the advice. To sit and ponder on grace, forgiveness, and what she'd learned through this experience was inviting. But there was still a hollow place within her she did not believe would be filled, a longing for Evan that remained acute. Did it make her sinful to still want him? Did it mean she was not truly repentant? Or was that *wanting* part of the penance she would continue to pay?

A gambler could not regain his fortune simply because he repented of his folly any more than a man convicted for stealing could forgo incarceration. A girl who had deceived her family and the man she loved could not expect society—or her family, or him—to change its expectations because she changed her ways. Perhaps that hollow place would remain. But if the rest of her heart were right with God, perhaps that would ease the ache.

Chapter Forty-Three

Cassie stood before her mother's full-length looking glass and wondered if she'd have felt like this if she'd been allowed to go to the Dyers' ball three months ago. Back then she'd have been giddy and arrogant. Today, she was excited and . . . humble? Had she changed so much in the last few months? No, more like the last few weeks. Six weeks to be exact. Was she better for what had happened since then?

She'd followed Mama's advice to evaluate the situation and find the ways in which she had grown. She certainly had a better understanding of consequences and a greater empathy for people who behaved badly but wanted to improve themselves. She felt she had grown closer to God and had a better perspective on the process of repentance. Mercy could not rob justice, and yet mercy was such a sweet balm even when justice got its due. Only she wished she did not still feel so incomplete.

Mama had said all sorrow could be swallowed up in Christ, but Cassie felt as though there were pieces missing for her. She did not feel whole, even if she did feel wiser. Perhaps that incompleteness meant she was not yet forgiven, but she did not feel that God was angry with her. Rather, she felt that He understood and He was hoping for her . . . what? Success? And if so, successful . . . what? The answer seemed out of reach, yet she believed He had something in mind for her. When she was quiet and still and mindful of Him, she believed there was beauty ahead. She could not see what it was, but she could feel it waiting for her. Sometimes it was exciting; sometimes it made her nervous. If she thought about it too much, she simply felt confused and frustrated by her inability to understand.

Instead of allowing her thoughts to overwhelm her, she busied herself with household tasks. What had been meant as a punishment had become her solace. She had even returned to her art and sketched the view of the church from her bedroom window.

Cassie had visited with Mrs. Glenside and her daughters a few times and took comfort in their improved welcome in the village. They were over the moon with excitement about tonight's ball; they had never been to one before. Cassie had said she would look for them and answer any questions. She'd become a sort of tutor, filling in the gaps of their social education. She found them delightful.

Evan.

He was never far from her thoughts, but tonight she was increasingly aware that would be at the ball. He would not ask her to dance nor engage her in conversation, but he would *be* there. He would see *her*. How she wished she could talk to him. She would like to tell him all she'd learned from what had happened and how sorry she was for what she'd done. She wished she could tell him that her feelings for him weren't a passing fancy. Sometimes she would imagine just such a conversation. Sometimes he would forgive her and tell her he loved her too, but sometimes he turned and walked away.

She shook her head. "Enough," she said to her reflection. She looked over the lemon-colored dress from Rose's season. Mama had added a lace edge to the sweetheart neckline and changed the sleeve from three-quarters to a puffed cap. The sash had been white, but Cassie had found a wide ribbon the color of a robin's egg that contrasted the yellow. She'd used the same ribbon to make a fabric flower for her hair. Silver shoes completed the ensemble. Mama did not like such unconventional style, but she did not refuse Cassie the chance to make the dress her own.

Young had done Cassie's hair in a series of braids that looped and wove around one another at the back of her head, a few soft tendrils brushing her shoulders and framing her face. Her eyes looked bright green against the colors, and the rose of her cheeks complemented the picture. If it would not be considered the height of vanity, she would consider painting a self-portrait. The thought made her smile, and she gathered it close, like the first flowers of spring. She closed her eyes and imagined herself inhaling the scent of such happiness, of carefree joy and ease. If she could fill her lungs and her head and her heart with such sweetness, surely she could keep it with her all night.

"Cassie," Mama called from the hall. "The carriage is ready."

"Coming, Mama." Cassie took one last look at herself in the glass before she spun away and hurried to the foyer, grabbing her silver shawl on the way.

Chapter Forty-Four

Evan stood on the outside of a chattering circle of women that included his mother and sisters and told himself he wasn't watching for Cassie to arrive.

The reason he kept glancing toward the door, he assured himself, was because he knew so few people and every familiar face that arrived brought increased security. But when Cassie *did* arrive in the doorway, he finally admitted the truth to himself.

There were any number of well-dressed women in every color and with every imaginable adornment. Yet despite the array, Cassie stood out. She wore a yellow dress with a blue sash, and her shoes sparkled. Her hair was off her shoulders and shone under the lights as though it had been polished for the occasion. She was an absolute picture as she greeted the hosts and then whispered with her mother while her father engaged in conversation with another man. Her eyes were casual as they scanned the room, stopping now and then and lighting up with her smile when she nodded at a familiar face from across the room.

And then her eyes met his. Evan braced himself, ready to see her smile fall or her glance dart away. Instead, she held his eyes, and the pink of her cheeks got a little bit pinker. She was here, in the same room with him, but completely inaccessible. He no longer held her character in question despite what she'd done; instead, he felt as though he had come to understand it. Everything she'd done had been exactly as she'd explained it—she wanted to help Lenora make a match and had instead fallen in love with Evan herself.

She loves me, he said in his mind, and from the look on her face and the longing in her eyes, he could believe she loved him still.

The lump that rose in his throat took him off guard, and only then did he notice that it was not Cassie's eyes alone that watched him. Mrs. Wilton watched him too, her mouth tight and her eyes keen as though reading his very thoughts, which were not keeping to the promise he'd made to Mr. Wilton in the church a month and a half ago. He forced his gaze to the floor and turned away. Surely there was a card game somewhere he could join. The price of peace of mind was worth losing a few pounds. He hadn't spent a farthing since the drinks with Bunderson some weeks ago.

There were cards. And wine. And soon enough Evan's thoughts were easier to keep away from Miss Cassandra Wilton. He resisted returning to the ballroom until he feared he would lose more money than he could afford. Dancing, at least, did not involve a wager, and he felt the energy of the music calling to him. He finally rose from the table and made his way to the ballroom.

His mother was seated beside Mrs. Quiggins, an older widow who had taken a shine to the newcomers. He asked his mother how she was enjoying the evening, and she nodded, though she seemed overwhelmed.

"Would you like me to call for the carriage?" Evan asked when Mrs. Quiggins turned to discuss something with another matron on her other side.

"Goodness, no," Mama said, fanning herself with a painted fan Evan had bought her for Christmas. She'd exclaimed at how beautiful it was, then said she couldn't imagine ever attending an event so fine as to need such an item. How things had changed for all of them. "Your sisters are having a delightful time, and I am making so many new acquaintances."

Evan leaned close and spoke softly. "Your smile seems forced."

"Well, we shall hope only you think so." She closed her fan and patted his hand with it as though she'd done it a hundred times. "I am glad to be here, Evan, and determined to see it through."

While Evan wouldn't have minded an excuse to leave, he liked seeing her determination. He had hoped the new life they had in Leagrave would awaken the woman she was before Father had passed. So far, it seemed as though she was making progress.

Evan scanned the dance floor in search of his sisters, whom he quickly found partnered for a cotillion. He could see they were not as polished as the other dancers, but what they lacked in experience they made up for in other ways. Natalie was grinning from ear to ear, bobbing up and down like a rabbit. Camilla had a determined set to her brow and seemed to be carefully counting out every beat, but she would look up now and again at the gangly young man who was her partner and smile, her blue eyes dancing. It did Evan's heart good to see them in the thick of the entertainment, enjoying things they would never have otherwise.

A flash of yellow caught his eye, and Evan's gaze snapped to Cassie on the crowded floor. She seemed to be enjoying herself, and if not for the fact that another man was on the receiving end of her charms, Evan would have been perfectly satisfied to watch her. But there *was* another man, and his envy reared up, making the vision of seeing her so full of life entirely bittersweet.

He rehearsed everything he had already convinced himself of about Cassie and had nearly talked himself out of watching any longer when he caught sight of her partner.

Bunderson.

The formation brought the dancers face to face again, and for the space of a breath, Evan could think of nothing except the fact that Bunderson would have returned from his pleasure trip to London just a day or so earlier. Bunderson reached out his hand to Cassie as part of the dance, and Evan ground his teeth. How many women had Bunderson touched before tonight? Bits of fun. Perhaps the seedier type he was so intrigued by. Yet Bunderson was an acceptable match for Cassie and Evan was not.

Evan popped up from his chair so quickly that his mother startled beside him. "Evan?" she asked. "Is everything all right?"

"Everything is fine," he said, but his hands were clenched at his sides. "I-I need some air is all."

He turned on his heel and walked away from the dance floor. There had to be a back door somewhere. It took every bit of willpower he possessed to keep from looking over his shoulder. Bunderson had made it clear that he wanted to get Lenora out of the way so Cassie could be presented to society. Was her being here tonight a sign that she was *out*? That she was now able to be courted despite her family's tradition?

Evan found his way to the balcony and put his hands on the cool stone. Evening was past and night was settling in. He took a deep breath. Two. As his thoughts calmed, he found himself remembering the advice Bunderson had given him regarding the letters with Lenora and what sort of obligation that put on Evan. Bunderson hadn't said anything different from what Uncle and Mama had said, but was his motivation different? Had he purposely steered Evan toward Lenora so Cassie might become available for him? Available for when he was not busy with light skirts, that is.

Evan's hands clenched at the railing, and he had to consciously relax them. It was none of his business if Bunderson had serious designs on Cassie or if she enjoyed his attention. He should wish her happiness, and though he was not overly impressed by Bunderson's character, there were surely worse men Cassie could find herself shackled to for the rest of her life.

If only that knowledge made him feel better.

Chapter Forty-Five

Thank you for the help, Cassie." Rose sat back in her chair, her hand on her rounded belly. "I do not know how I would have gotten on without your help these last weeks."

Cassie smiled and continued folding the sheets she'd taken from the line. Rose was finishing her seventh month but seemed ready to have this baby at any time. Or, rather, babies. The midwife could not be certain, but she suspected Rose's first delivery would make her a mother of two, assuming all went well with the labor. Cassie had been helping with household tasks on Tuesdays, but was now coming three days a week. Mama was coming another two. Rose needed to rest so her body would carry the babies as long as possible. Her ankles were swelling, and she struggled to catch her breath when she walked any distance.

Cassie acknowledged Rose's gratitude and handed her one end of the sheet. She could help that much, and it made the folding easier. "I really am happy to help," Cassie said, bringing the corners together. "And excited for another niece or nephew, or both, or two of either."

Rose mirrored Cassie's actions so they could fold the sheet correctly. "I am trying hard not to be terrified."

"You will be fine." Cassie made the first fold once the width was correct. She began to fold end over end until there was a tidy square of fabric. "With so many people hovering about you, the work of bringing these babies into the world might be done by everyone else."

Rose laughed while Cassie turned to the next sheet on the line.

"Have you heard from Lenora?" Rose asked.

"No," Cassie said, surprised. Rose and Lenora had always been close, and Cassie assumed that Rose would be the first to know if Lenora were ready to talk to Cassie again. "I have written her a few times, but she has not responded."

Rose smiled sadly but said nothing. Together, they folded another sheet.

"H-have *you* heard from Lenora?" Cassie asked.

Rose frowned apologetically. "She writes me every week."

Cassie began the end-over-end folding, keeping the edges crisp. "Then she's certainly told you she's not writing me." As soon as she said it, Cassie winced. Her family did not know the sisters were at odds with one another. Or at least, they weren't supposed to.

"It's strange to me that she hasn't said anything about you one way or another," Rose said, watching Cassie closely. "Even when I've asked her directly if things are all right between the two of you."

Cassie's heart felt heavy in her chest, but she could not *make* Lenora forgive her. Another consequence. She attempted to sidestep Rose's obvious curiosity. "Is she enjoying Bath?"

"Quite a lot."

Cassie was surprised for a second time. Lenora was not one to enjoy many things. "*Quite* a lot?"

Rose nodded. "She goes with Aunt Gwen for the waters every day, but you know it is as much a promenade as it is a health restorative. Everyone attends."

Cassie held the folded sheet to her chest. "And Lenora *likes* it?"

Rose nodded, a soft smile on her face.

"And isn't too nervous?"

Rose shook her head.

"I'm glad to hear that." Cassie put the sheet in the basket. "I have feared she would feel as though she was in exile, cut off from the people she loves and the places where she was once comfortable."

"Perhaps it is just as it needed to be," Rose said.

Cassie unpinned the row of dishtowels on the line, disturbed by Rose's comment. She sat in a chair across from Rose and handed her half of the towels, which Rose could fold sitting down.

"I heard that Mr. Bunderson danced with you twice at the Allen ball on Friday night."

Cassie was glad for the change of subject. "He did," she said, thinking back to the evening. It had been fun to get lost in the buoyancy of the evening, and Mr. Bunderson had been quite attentive. Only it was not what she'd expected her first ball to be.

"And did you enjoy his attention?"

"Of course." Who wouldn't enjoy the attention of a handsome and eligible man?

"He is very handsome," Rose said. She balanced a folded towel on her swollen belly, making Cassie smile. "Do you not agree?"

"Of course he is," Cassie said, trying very hard to keep her thoughts to herself. She narrowed her eyes playfully at her sister. "A married woman should not notice such things, however. Papa would never approve, to say nothing of Mr. Capenshaw."

Rose laughed. "When you are a married woman, then you can tell me if you no longer notice handsome men. Of course, no man can hold a candle to my Wayne, but Mr. Bunderson comes close."

Cassie laughed to see this playful side of Rose.

"Do you like Mr. Bunderson?"

"I don't know." Cassie exaggerated the fluster she felt in hopes it would deter the conversation. "He is fun and lighthearted and, of course, handsome."

"But . . ." Rose prompted.

"But I do not know him very well." It was true. She had known Ronald Bunderson all her life, he was a good friend of her brother Christopher, but she didn't really *know* him. Deeply. Not the way she knew Evan. The pit in her stomach gaped wider. Why must every thought go back to him?

"Would you like to know him better?"

Why was Rose being so inquisitive? "I am not even officially out, Rose." Cassie finished folding the dishtowel and picked up another. "Mama said I'll get a new wardrobe next spring and then have my presentation."

"Suddenly you are so hesitant," Rose commented. "After pushing so hard to have your debut."

Cassie felt heat creep up her neck. What *did* Rose know?

"Don't be embarrassed," Rose said in her gentle way. "I've been worried about you and simply asked Mama some questions."

"Worried about me?"

"Did you love him, though, do you think? Or was it a simple fancy?"

Cassie locked her eyes on the fabric in her lap, overwhelmed by the rush of emotion brought on by Rose's question. Though Rose hadn't said Evan's name, Cassie still heard it. She couldn't talk about this. Not to anyone. That Rose knew Cassie's part in the situation was humiliating, and the vulnerability she felt made her want to run for the vicarage. Cassie kept her eyes on the ground. "Mama told you?"

"It took me weeks to get it from her. I understand she wanted to protect the situation, but I should have been told. I should know what is happening between my sisters."

Cassie said nothing.

"I am not asking after your feelings so that I might store up gossip," Rose said. She hefted herself forward in her chair enough to put a hand on Cassie's wrist. The gentle weight of it brought a lump to Cassie's throat. "But while it seems you have gained . . . a foundation these last weeks, you have lost some of your light as well. Is it because of him?"

"It is because of *me*," Cassie said softly, not daring to risk eye contact.

"But Lenora is happy, and you have put such effort into helping the Glensides find their place in Leagrave. You should be glad for those things."

Rose knew about that too? How much talking went on behind Cassie's back? Why did Mama insist on secrecy and then tell the whole of it to Rose? "I'm glad for both Lenora's and the Glensides' contentment. It brings me a great deal of comfort."

"But?"

Did she dare reveal herself? Even as she wondered, however, the words began piling up in her mind and in her throat. "But Lenora has not forgiven me, and the Glensides would not have needed my help if I had left well enough alone. Never mind that had I never written that first letter, I would never have . . ." She couldn't finish. Whatever words had wanted to be said had run for cover. Perhaps they sensed the danger of exposure.

"You would never have fallen in love with Mr. Glenside?" Rose supplied.

Cassie nodded.

"And you still feel the same?"

Cassie closed her eyes. She could only nod. She knew she should add that after what she'd done there was no chance for her to be with Evan—not ever—but her wicked heart could not give him up.

Cassie felt Rose's arms come around her, offering solace and comfort, and Cassie could not hold back the tears any longer.

"Oh, my dear sister," Rose said, smoothing her hair.

They sat that way for a handful of minutes, until Cassie finally pulled back. "There is . . . nothing to be done for it," Cassie said.

"Perhaps Mr. Bunderson can replace the emptiness you feel."

Cassie wiped at her eyes, embarrassed by her reaction and disappointed by Rose's advice, though she couldn't expect anything more. "I know that seems a reasonable remedy. Only I don't see how."

"Well," Rose said, tottering back to her chair. She sat down with a loud exhale of breath. "I don't know that there is a rule book for this sort of thing." She smiled at her attempt at a joke, and Cassie tried to smile back, but she was sure Rose knew she didn't mean it. "I think the first step would be getting to know him better. He may very well be as good a man as Mr. Glenside. He is more comfortable in our class, that is certain, and there would be no complications to a connection with his family."

"That's true," Cassie said, though agreeing felt like betrayal. She focused on folding dishtowels again.

"He has an appealing nature."

Cassie just nodded. Everything about Mr. Bunderson recommended him—everything except the fact that he was not Evan Glenside.

"Cassie," Rose said, "you must look forward, not back. Mr. Glenside is a piece of your past, one through which you have learned a great deal. Take that knowledge and move on with your life. You will find no solace in your regrets."

Rose was right. Living with regret would not change anything. And wasn't Mr. Bunderson the very reason Cassie had forged those letters in the first place? Perhaps she should not dismiss him so quickly. If she could stop comparing Mr. Bunderson to Evan, maybe his own charms would shine more brightly.

"I will try," Cassie finally said.

Rose smiled and patted Cassie's hand. "There is joy yet left for you, Cassie. Do not miss it simply because you cannot see past what cannot be."

Chapter Forty-Six

W hat a beautiful set of horses." Cassie sat next to Mr. Bunderson in his curricle. The seat was narrow, forcing her to hold on to his arm with one hand and the seat with the other. It was a handsome carriage—one of the finest she had ever ridden in—but the seat was very high, and he drove very fast and she felt very, very conspicuous so high above the ground. She'd had to use a ladder to get into the seat.

"I shall purchase a new pair at Tattersalls when I next go to London," Mr. Bunderson said.

"And when will you next go to London?" Cassie asked, hoping her nervousness didn't show in her tone. Perhaps if she told him she didn't want to go so fast he would slow down. She feared he would simply find her discomfort amusing. He was so easily amused, and she didn't want to encourage him.

Cassie had told Rose she would give Mr. Bunderson a chance, and he had visited her twice now at the vicarage before asking her on this ride. Any other girl would be glad for the attention. How she wished she were one of those girls. Instead, the more time she spent with him, the more her former irritation grew. In fact, she worried there was little more to him than a pretty face and pretty manners, and she found those two things less and less appealing all the time.

"Next month, I think." He finally began to slow down as they approached the center of town. "I like to go every month or so."

Cassie eased her grip on both his arm and the seat. She had pointed out a shortcut to the vicarage that bypassed the heart of the village, but he had wanted to take her down Main Street. Of course he did.

"What do you do in London?" Cassie asked. "I've only been when my sisters were buying wedding clothes." Lenora's engagement had been called off before they'd shopped for her trousseau. At least the money they had saved was one thing Cassie *didn't* feel guilty about.

"Oh, I'm certain nothing I do would be of interest to you. Mostly I have . . . business to attend to. Lots and lots of business."

"We went to church at St. Dunston's the last time we went to London," Cassie said. "Such a grand church. It put our little village chapel to shame."

"Oh, yes," Mr. Bunderson said. "St. Dunston's is remarkable. I am always sure to go to church when I'm in Town." He offered her a teasing grin and a wink. She wasn't sure what he meant by the gesture. He nodded ahead of them. "Ah, look, there's Glenside."

Cassie's heart flipped in her chest as her eyes met Evan's blue ones. Evan had been leaning against the wall of a shop, apparently watching them from beneath the brim of a black hat. He straightened as Mr. Bunderson maneuvered the carriage toward him. Was it her imagination that his gaze lingered on her? She had better convince herself of the opposite. What good was it to think he might have interest? It only made everything harder.

"Ho there, Glenside," Mr. Bunderson called out.

Cassie swallowed and busied herself with the strings of her reticule.

"Bunderson," she heard Evan say. "Miss Cassandra."

She couldn't ignore him. Surely Papa would understand the need to uphold her polite manners. She glanced at him quickly and inclined her head before looking back into her lap like some simpering green girl. She felt ridiculous.

"I hope they are paying you well for holding up that wall," Mr. Bunderson said, nodding toward the storefront behind Mr. Glenside.

"Quite the opposite," Evan said easily. "My sisters are doing a very fine job of buying out the stock of this fine shop so that they might make over every bonnet they own."

Mr. Bunderson shuddered dramatically. "Sounds like horrible sport. For my part, I have been gallivanting through the countryside with Miss Cassandra and telling her about London."

Evan tensed, drawing Cassie's attention. "Have you now," he said with what Cassie thought was forced calm. Was he angry? Jealous? What did it mean if he were?

"I'll be going again next month. My cousin and I would love for you to show us around *your* part of town, if you've reconsidered."

"Thank you, no," Mr. Glenside said, again with that forced calm.

Cassie watched him from beneath the brim of her bonnet. What was she missing in this exchange? Why would Mr. Bunderson want to go to East London? She had never heard anything particularly remarkable about that part of the city, but then she didn't know London well.

"I'm afraid I haven't plans to go to London any time soon, Mr. Bunderson, and there's nothing in *my* part of town that would factor in if I were. Now, if you'll excuse me." He finally smiled, and it softened when he looked at Cassie. She held his eyes a delicious few moments, and then looked away as she should. "I had better see that my sisters don't truly buy out the shop."

He nodded to them both and then disappeared inside.

"Odd fellow, Glenside," Mr. Bunderson said, snapping the reins to get the horses moving. "Don't know that he'll ever find his place in the world of gentlemen. Do you know he's fashioned himself a wood shop in his uncle's barn? Really, I would think his uncle would steer him better."

Cassie's defenses rose. "I think he seems to have found his way rather well."

"Aside from his blunder with Lenora, you mean."

"It was not his fault. They were ill suited." She wished she didn't have to hold on to Mr. Bunderson's arm to keep her seat. "But I am glad that he seems to have risen above it."

"If you ask me, he may have bungled his best chance to make a match here in Leagrave."

Cassie looked at his profile. "Why is that?"

He gave her a sidelong look, with that same teasing grin. "He's common—never mind his inheritance. And he's terribly dull. He can't shoot, only barely manages a horse, and doesn't . . . Well, he's just not a gentleman. Not really."

"I thought he was your friend." Did Evan know that Mr. Bunderson thought these things of him?

"He *is* my friend," Mr. Bunderson said with a shrug. "But enough about him. Will you be attending the Sorenson party next week? I wonder if I might sneak you away on a walk through their garden—overgrown trellises, lots of corners where we can *talk* privately. What do you think of that?"

Chapter Forty-Seven

Evan strode quickly to the side door of the church, stopped, turned, strode away and then stopped again. He shook his head and then looked over his shoulder toward the vicarage. Maybe Cassie wasn't even planning to ride out with Bunderson again. But if she did, would today be the day she'd fall in love with the cur? Evan turned back to the door and reset his determination. Before he could second-guess himself—or rather, third-guess himself—he lifted his hand and rapped three times.

He stepped back and took a deep breath he hoped would calm his heart rate. Meanwhile the shouting in his head got louder.

What are you doing here?

This is none of your business.

Things are bad enough as they are, must you stir up trouble?

Just as he'd begun to turn away, thinking that Mr. Wilton was not in his office and perhaps that was a sign that his visit was a mistake, the door opened.

"Mr. Glenside." The vicar quickly hid his surprise. "Did we have an appointment?"

"No, sir, but I wondered if I might speak with you."

"Uh, well, certainly." Mr. Wilton moved aside, and Evan entered, removing his hat. The room looked exactly as it had when he'd been here—had it been two months ago? In the course of those two months, Evan had kept his word and had no private communication with Cassie in any form. Yet his awareness of her had grown more acute in direct proportion with Bunderson's increased attention toward her.

Mr. Wilton shut the door. "Please have a seat," he said, waving toward the chair and settee.

"I'm sorry to have not made an appointment," Evan said. "I thought about it—sending a note or whatnot. I'm sure I am operating in a most ill-mannered way."

"That you chose against those courses must mean your reason for calling is rather urgent."

"Yes," Evan said, then thought about it. "Or perhaps no. I simply cannot get it out of my mind and concluded that I could have no peace until I had spoken with you, sir."

"Very well," Mr. Wilton said. "It is fortunate that I have the time, then. What can I help you with?"

Evan had organized the words in his mind at some point—he had been very concerned with how he should approach such a delicate topic on his way over here—but he could find no recollection of articulation now that he needed it.

"My uncle says that gentlemen do not . . . gossip about one another."

"Gossip, I have found, means that the information being imparted about someone is intended to harm them or their reputation. Is what you have to say detrimental to someone's reputation?"

Was it? Evan couldn't decide. What he had to say would harm Bunderson's reputation, but he didn't feel that was a bad thing. "I am here for Cassie."

Mr. Wilton's eyebrows jumped up his forehead, prompting Evan to review what he'd said and realize how it sounded.

"Not *for* Cassie," he fumbled. "For her *sake* . . . her well-being."

Mr. Wilton was on his guard.

Of course Evan would make a shambles of this. But he was too far in to back out now. "I have noticed that Mr. Ronald Bunderson is paying Cassie a great deal of attention."

"Yes, Mr. Bunderson is an especially good friend of the family. I have no objection to his interest and, I daresay, neither does Cassie."

There was a challenge in his voice, and Evan swallowed hard, feeling his neck heat up with embarrassment. Of course this would sound as though he were defaming Bunderson in hopes of increasing his own merit, but he wasn't. And that reminder helped calm him. He was not here to hurt anyone, not even Bunderson, only to spare Cassie potential pain. His motivation was pure; he must take confidence in that.

"Mr. Bunderson is a very amiable man," Evan said, his voice calmer, his motivation clear. "And I consider him a friend, which makes this meeting difficult." He paused for a breath and then told Mr. Wilton of Bunderson's request for information regarding the more questionable areas of London, as well as a summary of the conversation they had had while Cassie had sat beside Bunderson in his curricle. She wouldn't understand the references Bunderson made to Mile End, but it was vulgar all the same. Evan looked at his hat while he spoke, not wanting to see the vicar's expressions as he unburdened himself. "I hope I have not acted so out of place that I lose whatever respect you might have left for me. I assure you that I would have said nothing if not for concern for Cassie." The brim of his hat was bent completely out of shape.

After a few seconds, Mr. Wilton cleared his throat. "I assume I have only your word to take for this account."

Evan looked up and felt his shoulders drop. He hadn't considered that Cassie's father would need more than his word. Would his warning be ignored? Had he come for nothing? Still, it had seemed like the right thing to do. Were one of his sisters receiving attention from a man like Bunderson, he would want to know of it, social expectations of privacy be hanged.

Evan stood. "I thank you for your time, sir."

Mr. Wilton stood as well and put out his hand, which Evan shook. Mr. Wilton did not look away from Evan's face. "You must see how this appears."

"I do," Evan said. "I can only hope that *you* can see how my coming here does nothing to improve my situation. I am not and will not pursue Cassie, Mr. Wilton. I gave you my word and I will not break it. Only I feel she deserves a man who would be true to her, that is all." *As I would be*, he thought.

"Perhaps you would prefer she not find happiness with any other man. Perhaps you assume that if she does not find interest elsewhere I will relent in my opposition."

Evan was startled by the accusation and fell back half a step. "N-no. I expect nothing to change on my behalf, and I *do* want Cassie's happiness." He swallowed. "With a man who deserves her and will protect her, body and soul."

"Good," Mr. Wilton said with a nod. "Then we understand each other." He led Evan to the door.

"Good day to you, sir," Evan said, replacing his hat as he stepped over the threshold.

"Good day, Mr. Glenside. I assume if there is any other information I should know for the good of my daughter, you will inform me."

Evan turned to look at the vicar, confused at what seemed to be contradicting positions the man had taken. He seemed unimpressed that Evan had come, and yet he was inviting him to come again should he have reason? Evan could only nod, agreeing to share information that would be in Cassie's best interest.

The vicar nodded and promptly closed the door.

Chapter Forty-Eight

They did not have tea at the vicarage every day, but today, Mrs. Glenside and her daughters, as well as the Glanchard women, would be joining Cassie and her mother. Cassie was anxious about how Rebecca would treat the Glensides but hopeful that the afternoon would be pleasant for everyone. She helped prepare the tray and had just popped one of the miniature macaroons into her mouth when Papa came in through the kitchen door. She attempted a smile, then chewed quickly and swallowed.

"Good afternoon, Papa," she said. "Would you like a macaroon?"

He said nothing but kissed her on the cheek, something he used to do often. She had not realized until that moment how much she had missed the token of affection. When he pulled back, he held her eyes. In the months since the broken engagement, Papa had kept his distance. She found his sudden attentiveness unnerving.

"Is everything all right, Papa?" she asked.

"Well enough, I suppose." His attention moved past her to the tray. "Are you entertaining today, my dear?"

"Mrs. Glenside and her daughters, as well as Mrs. Glanchard and Miss Rebecca, are coming for tea."

"Ah, yes, you said as much last night." He picked up a finger sandwich, but did not eat it right away. "You are getting on well with Mrs. Glenside and her daughters?"

"Yes," Cassie said cautiously. The Glensides were not often a topic of conversation at the vicarage.

"You seem to visit with the girls quite often."

"I have been working with them on elocution and etiquette. They've borrowed some of my books."

"Do you find them teachable?" he asked.

It was an odd question, but Cassie did not mind answering it. She wondered why her father was suddenly interested. "Very teachable and eager to learn. Their reading is behind, which is why I've encouraged the books, but they are bright girls."

"And are they well-mannered?"

Cassie couldn't help but laugh. "You have met them, Papa, and dined with them, surely you need not ask as though they are strangers to you."

"They *are* strangers to me. A dinner and few greetings after church do not make them known to me." His voice was rather flat, and he let out a breath. "But then there are those you can know all your life and still find that they are strangers, can you not?"

"I-I suppose so." Cassie cocked her head. Was he talking about her? "Are you certain everything is all right?"

"Have you had any contact with Mr. Glenside?"

The question startled her even as the sound of his name made her chest warm. "Yesterday, I was riding with Mr. Bunderson, and we encountered Mr. Glenside in town. He was waiting outside of Buttons and Bobs while his sisters bought ribbon. I did not speak with him, only accepted his greeting from where I sat in the carriage."

"Did Mr. Bunderson talk with him?"

"Yes."

"What about?"

"Well," Cassie said, thinking back. "About London. He wanted Mr. Glenside to visit with him next time he goes; he had visited East End, where Mr. Glenside was from."

"And what did Mr. Glenside say regarding a trip to London with Mr. Bunderson?"

Cassie felt as though she were being tested. "He did not seem to like the idea, though I don't know why. I would assume he has friends he would want to see, but he said he had no interest in returning to his old neighborhood. He did not direct conversation toward me, Papa, and he left as soon as he could politely do so. I suppose I should have told you of the encounter, I-I wasn't sure."

"It is all right," Papa said, sounding tired. "I would like future accountings, though."

"Of course," she said. "I promised you I would not have private communications with him, and I have kept my promise."

"I have your word?"

Cassie nodded, but she was beginning to worry. Something was pressing upon her father, that much was certain. "What is wrong?"

"Nothing," he said, shaking his head and looking around the room as though in need of distraction. He seemed to remember the finger sandwich in his hand and put it in his mouth. After chewing a few times, he swallowed and met her eye again. "I have been thinking. I do not feel it is the right time for you to be out, even unofficially, after all. I know we made an exception for the Allens' ball, but upon further consideration, I feel it would be better for you to not be so involved, socially, that is. At least not for now."

"Have I done something wrong?" Cassie said. "I did not instigate that meeting with Mr. Glenside, Papa. I promise I didn't."

He shook his head. "No, my dear, you have done nothing wrong. It is only that I do not feel right about you being out when Lenora is still without a match. I might reconsider next spring. We shall simply have to see."

The rebellious part of Cassie considered posing an argument, but Lenora would be home in another week, and Cassie worried how her sister would feel having both of them attending social events. And while Cassie had enjoyed herself at the ball, she had been too mindful of Evan to make the most of the evening. Surely if she waited another six months, or even a year, she would not be so aware of him.

"All right," she said.

"You are not angry?"

Cassie shook her head. "I don't want to upset Lenora any more than I already have."

"Huh," he said, obviously not expecting her answer. "And what about Mr. Ronald Bunderson? You will not be able to go about with him any longer."

"That is all right, too." She had tried to get to know Mr. Bunderson better, but she did not long for his company. Especially after the carriage ride yesterday when he'd been such an arrogant braggart.

"You are not particularly attached to him?"

"He is agreeable enough, but I am not *particularly* attached."

She didn't understand why her answer made the lines around his eyes soften. He placed his hand against her cheek. "You're a good daughter, Cassie."

The sentiment brought tears to her eyes, which she tried to blink away. "I am trying to be," she answered in a soft voice.

Papa smiled, then removed his hand from her cheek. He started to turn away, but then looked at her again. "Are you happy, Cassie?"

Cassie did not know the answer. Lenora was still angry with her, Evan was lost to her, and though she was learning much, she still did not feel complete. Finally she gave him the most honest answer she could think of—the same thing she'd said a minute earlier. "I am trying to be."

He held her eyes a moment longer, then exited the kitchen. He was gone before Cassie realized she'd never learned the reason he'd come home in the first place.

Chapter Forty-Nine

Thank you for walking with me, Evan," Mama said as they rounded the corner onto the cobbled sidewalks of High Street. Shops lined the road, and large trees created dappled shade. There were not many people out this early in the morning—in London it would be unheard of for gentry to be out before ten o'clock—but they were not in London, and the entire Glenside family was becoming more and more comfortable in Leagrave. It was getting harder to remember what life was like in Mile End.

"It is my pleasure," he said. "I had supposed now that I am no longer employed and we are once again living in the same house, I would see more of you than I do."

Mama laughed. "Yes, I had thought so, too."

"It seems, however, that I have to compete for your attention these days."

She laughed again, and he cast her a sidelong look, grateful that she could laugh so easily. "I am just so very busy," she said, lifting her chin in a display of exaggerated airs. "There are visits and shopping and socials and . . ." She sighed and patted his arm with her free hand. "But at least I can meet you for a morning walk now and again."

"So glad I can be of service, m'lady."

Mama laughed again. "I hope I won't see less of you once we are moved over to the cottage."

Uncle had said the Dower House would be ready the first of next week, only a few more days.

"You'll still dine at the manor most evenings, won't you?"

Mama shrugged. "I don't know the way of things, but I hope so."

"And I shall send round cards inviting you for these morning walks and hope that you can fit me in."

Someone called out a greeting. "Good morning, Mrs. Glenside."

Evan and his mother both turned to see a woman from church—Evan did not know her name—on the opposite corner, going the opposite direction, and yet she'd made a point to greet his mother. He smiled and nodded while his mother waved back. "Good morning, Miss Shrives."

"Will we see you at ensemble tonight?" Miss Shrives asked.

"Of course."

"Ensemble?" Evan asked as they continued their walk.

"It's like a choir, I believe, only smaller. They are working on some music for the Christmas service."

"It is not yet August," Evan pointed out.

"It's never too early to learn one's parts," she said. "And the company is delightful." She sighed, a delicate, delightful sound. "I like it here very much, Evan. I thank the good Lord every day for bringing this blessing into our lives."

"I am glad to hear it, Mama," Evan said, as content as he could imagine being.

"And you? Are you grateful for this circumstance?"

"Of course I am," Evan said, but he felt the muting of his mood.

"I wonder if you are sometimes." She didn't say it as a reprimand, but Evan wasn't sure she could say such a thing without it feeling as though he were being taken to task. Especially since she had just commented on what a great blessing it all was. "There are times I feel you are merely tolerating this place." She swept her hand through the air, indicating the narrow streets and squat buildings of the village.

"Perhaps I am not as effusive as I ought to be, but that has never been in my nature, and you can't expect everything to change so quickly."

"No, I suppose I can't. You are so very much like your father—serious and careful about everything. Only I hope you can find enjoyment here, and I wish you would stop pining for the Wilton girl."

Evan felt himself tense. "I am pining for no one." Pining suggested hope, and there was no hope. Hadn't Mr. Wilton reminded him of that fact just last week when Evan had warned him about Bunderson's character?

Evan was still unsettled about that meeting, sure that if he'd thought longer and harder he could have found a better approach. And yet Monday night, Bunderson had told Evan at a dinner party that he'd received a letter from the vicar explaining that Cassie was unable to receive his attentions.

"They've sent her out and then pulled her back in again," Bunderson had said, rolling his eyes. "It's a wonder that girl knows what direction is up anymore. Do you know she would not even give me a kiss for good luck when we rode out last week? My cousin may have been wrong about vicar's daughters." Bunderson then launched into plans regarding a hunting party he was putting together for September and asked if Evan would like to join. "I'm sure the six of us together could make a quick study of you with a rifle. What do you say?"

Evan was not interested in the least and had an easy time excusing himself by explaining he would need to help oversee the last of the harvest. He'd ended the night grateful that Mr. Wilton had put Bunderson in his place without tipping his hand.

"Evan?"

He shook himself back to the present moment and repaired his smile.

"I am not pining, Mama," he said again. "There is simply a great deal to be done and a lot for me to learn. I am choosing to be focused, which requires serious and careful attention."

"Touché," she said with a nod. "Perhaps, however, you should also be serious and careful about finding a wife."

"I don't want a wife." Evan winced at how blunt his words sounded. He should have acted as though he were considering the suggestion rather than rejecting it outright. "I have far too much to do now to think of such a thing and . . . it is too soon."

"Is it?" Mama waved to another acquaintance on the other side of the street. "No one speaks of the engagement."

Not to you, Evan thought to himself. He had little doubt it would be whispered about through the village forever. "Which is all I could wish for. Perhaps next season I will reconsider things. For now, it is all too fresh for me to make another attempt. For her sake if not my own."

"Miss Wilton's returned from Bath, did you know?"

Evan glanced at his mother. "I didn't know."

"A few days ago. Her sister is due to deliver any time, and she's returned to stay with her for the duration."

"She is not at the vicarage, then?"

"Apparently not. Mrs. Gibbons was telling me of it the other day. From all reports, Miss Wilton enjoyed her time in Bath."

"I'm glad," Evan said, but his responsibility to Lenora weighed in his chest. Their paths would cross at some point. What would he say? How would he act? It was unfair that she'd been so disgraced, and yet it would have been more unfair to marry her. He felt the continued awkwardness whenever he and the Wiltons shared one another's company and imagined how much worse it was going to be with Lenora part of the equation. Then he hated to be directing even more negativity toward her. She had more than she deserved already.

"Anyway, you had better prepare yourself for a great deal of motherly encouragement come spring. What kind of gentlewoman would I be if I didn't push my son to marry? I understand that is to be my primary occupation, in fact."

Evan smiled good-naturedly but was already dreading the spring when Mama would make good on her threat.

They finished their walk just as the day was becoming warm. Evan retired to his study where he transcribed last month's reports and then caught up with some correspondence.

It was some time later when he heard footsteps approaching. He looked up as Leggit appeared in the doorway, a silver tray in hand.

"A letter for you, sir."

"Thank you, Leggit." As soon as Evan held the letter in his hand a rush of familiarity washed through him.

The size.

The shape.

The paper.

The handwriting.

He turned it over and stared at the seal, a simple circle with a cross inside—the very same seal from the letters he kept in a corner of his desk drawer.

Why is Cassie writing me? Evan broke the seal and unfolded the paper.

> *Dear Evan,*
>
> *I must speak to you, and I hope you will agree to meet me in the glen behind the barn where we have met before. Please come at four o'clock this afternoon; my parents will be visiting my sister for tea.*
>
> *Cassie*

Evan read it one more time and then dropped it on the desk. He scrubbed a hand over his face and let out a heavy breath.

Chapter Fifty

Cassie was feeding one of Mama's shifts through the ringer when she heard the back door bang shut. She looked over her shoulder to see Young approaching. It was hot today, and she felt as though she were melting. The sooner she finished the task, the sooner she could escape into the house and find reprieve from the stifling heat. It was a halfhearted hope to think that Mama had sent Young to help her and Mrs. Ashby; Young never helped with the wash.

"A note for you, Miss Cassie," Young said, holding out a paper. "It was on the doorstep when I went out to sweep."

Cassie pulled her eyebrows together as she looked at the note in Young's hand.

"I'll see ta this," Mrs. Ashby said, gathering the wrung-out items from the basket so she could hang them on the line. "You bin hard at it since mornin'. Take yerself a minute."

"Thank you." Cassie wiped her hands on her apron before taking the note from Young. Young held Cassie's eyes a moment and then glanced at the letter with nervous significance. Confused, Cassie looked at it again and then caught her breath at the familiarity of the letter addressed to the servant. Her eyes jumped back to meet Young's. "Thank you," she said again. She began walking away from the maid while turning the paper over in her hand. There was no stamp on the seal, but Cassie knew it was from him. Who else would write to her through Young?

She looked at Young's name scrawled across the front. Was that Evan's script? She remembered it being . . . finer than this. But it had come from the manor. No, Young said it had been on the doorstep. But who else could it be from?

She was about to break the seal when her hands stilled. She had promised her father she would not correspond with Evan, and she was determined to live with integrity. But it was *right here* in her hands.

It was not *her* corresponding with him.

What could he have to say to her?

The conflict kept her frozen for several seconds. To take this to Papa would be a betrayal to Evan. To *not* take it to Papa would break the promise she had made. Her stomach was tight, and she closed her eyes and took a breath while saying a silent prayer for help in this decision. A measure of peace came to her mind, and she opened her eyes and looked at the letter in detail. The words did not look right. There was similarity in the looping letters, but they did not precisely match the lovely script of Evan's practiced hand. If this letter was not from Evan, then it was not a betrayal of him to take it to her father. Surely Papa would not fault her for seeing what it said.

Despite her fear that what was written inside might only add to her troubles, Cassie turned the letter over and broke the seal. She unfolded the letter and then furrowed her brow as she read the lines that were even less similar to Evan's writing, though the signature gave him ownership.

> *Dear Cassie,*
> *I must speak to you and I hope that you will agree to meet me in the glen behind the barn where we have met before. Please come at four o'clock this afternoon. I must see you.*
> *Evan*

"This is not from him," Cassie said under her breath.

"Miss?"

Cassie looked over her shoulder at Mrs. Ashby, not realizing she was close enough to overhear.

"Nothing." Cassie's heart was racing. Only a handful of people other than Evan even knew of the letters: Mama, Papa, Rose, Lenora, Evan's mother, Mr. Glenside, and Young. None of them seemed likely to have sent this letter, but someone had. Why? And who knew of the significance of the glen? Was someone trying to get her in trouble?

Lenora.

Cassie swallowed, but the possibility quickly rose to the top of the short list of suspects. Lenora had returned to Leagrave a few days ago, but she had gone directly to Rose's house. Rose was confined to her bed, the midwife and doctor agreeing that the longer she could remain pregnant, the greater good for her baby—or babies, as everyone had come to expect. Lenora had come to the vicarage for dinner the day after her arrival. She had been more pleasant than she'd been before her visit to Bath, but she had not engaged with Cassie directly.

Cassie forced her mind to remain calm. She had to think clearly. It was just after one o'clock. That gave her a few hours to determine what this letter was about and if she were correct regarding Lenora's interference. What a spiteful thing that would be—and yet did Cassie not deserve her spite? Perhaps Cassie confronting her sister, without anger, would provide the opportunity for them to discuss their feelings and even make repairs. On second thought, she had no time to waste.

"Mrs. Ashby," Cassie said. "I am afraid I have an urgent appointment I must see to. Would it be possible for you to finish the wash and leave the items on the line for me to remove?"

The woman made a face but she nodded.

"I am very sorry," Cassie said, shoving the note into her apron pocket. "I promise to make it up to you."

Mrs. Ashby grudgingly accepted the apology, allowing Cassie to turn in the direction of Rose's farm some half a mile away and walk as fast as she could.

Chapter Fifty-One

When Lenora opened the door of the farmhouse and her eyes went wide with guilt, Cassie's suspicions were confirmed. She withdrew the note from her pocket. "We need to talk," she said evenly, then forced enough of a smile to reassure Lenora that she was not there to ring a peal over her head. "Can you get away?"

Lenora swallowed and gave a quick nod. "Give me a minute to come up with an excuse," she said softly, then shut the door and left Cassie to pace upon the porch and prepare what she would say.

By the time Lenora returned, Cassie felt she had found the right words for this conversation. Lenora stepped gingerly onto the porch and closed the door behind her.

"How can I make this right?" Cassie asked before Lenora could speak. "I have made such a mess of things, Lenora, and I hope you can believe me when I say that I have tried to make things right here in Leagrave. But I have not been able to determine how I might make things right with *you* and that causes me a great deal of pain. If going to the glen and being reprimanded will work toward your relief, I will do it, but if there is some way I might make amends without endangering Mr. Glenside, I would prefer to take that direction."

Lenora looked at Cassie with confusion. "Reprimanded? What are you talking about?"

"You're trying to get me in trouble with Papa." It was the only possible motivation. "And I deserve that, but Mr. Glenside does not. He has been a victim of my idiotic behavior all along."

Lenora blinked but looked no less confused. "You think I was trying to get you in trouble with this note?"

"Papa has forbidden me from having any contact with Mr. Glenside." Cassie held the note higher. "Why else would you want me to go to the glen at four and make it appear to be at Mr. Glenside's bidding?"

Lenora's expression softened. "I was not trying to get you in trouble. I was . . ." She began wringing her hands and stomped her foot. "Oh, I am making such a mess of this too."

It was Cassie's turn to be confused.

Lenora let out a breath and raised her hands for just a moment before dropping them and giving Cassie an entreating look. "I was trying to arrange for you and Mr. Glenside to be together so that I might talk to both of you."

"What?" Cassie shook her head. "Why?"

"So that I might apologize," Lenora said, sounding embarrassed. "And give you my blessing."

The world froze. The birds did not sing. The wind did not move the leaves on the trees. Cassie let go of the letter, and it fluttered to the ground. "Your blessing?" she repeated in a breathless voice.

Lenora moved forward and took Cassie's hands in both of hers. "I have been selfish, Cassie. I have refused you the forgiveness you have asked for and held bitterness in my heart."

Cassie swallowed against the lump in her throat while Lenora continued. "Rose told me of your feelings for Mr. Glenside—feelings she sensed were very real and that Evan returned for you. I have heard all you've done for his family here in Leagrave, and how it has changed people's reception of them, and it caused me to evaluate my own actions and ask if I have been as good in my behavior as you have been in yours."

"Lenora," Cassie breathed, shaking her head. "I have only tried to remedy in some small way the pain I have caused. There is so much I cannot do."

"Yet you have made every repair you possibly could."

Cassie looked at the ground. "I am unworthy of your praise."

"No, you are not," Lenora said, giving Cassie's hands a squeeze. "I have undertaken my own evaluation of the situation and my actions in it, and I am not without blame. I see that now."

"You did not know I was writing to him on your behalf, and you would never have condoned it if you had."

"Yet when I did learn of it, I was pleased to continue the deceit. I was relieved to be spared the discomfort. I let you do the work on my behalf but benefitted from the spoils. I knew you had interest in him but I did not care, certain it would fade. I knew when you went to Mary's that it was to avoid seeing us together, and I still thought only of *my* future and *my* interests. I gave no consideration toward you or, for that matter, Mr. Glenside, who was treated the most unfairly of any of us. Now that I have faced the truth, I know it would be wrong for me to prevent the two of you from being happy with one another, and so I did what I felt was very brave. I invited you to be together so that I might explain myself clearly to you both and not risk any misinterpretation of my thoughts." She turned toward the house and waved. "I even wrote down what I wanted to say so I would not bungle it like I am doing now."

Cassie raised her eyes to meet Lenora's, overwhelmed and unsure if she could trust the joy that rose in her heart. After so long convincing herself that there was no hope, it was difficult to make room for it now.

Lenora smiled nervously. "If Evan is what will make you happy, Cassie, I will not stand in your way."

Tears filled Cassie's eyes, but she attempted a smile even though she felt as though her heart was breaking all over again. "I cannot tell you what it means to me to hear you say this, Lenora, and I thank you from the bottom of my heart for forgiving me and being so good and pure, but those things are not enough to repair this. Mr. Glenside is lost to me, and I have accepted it. Papa has renounced any possibility."

"Because of me," Lenora said, putting a hand to her chest. "To preserve my feelings."

Cassie hesitated. To hope again and have it foiled was too much risk. "In part, perhaps, but there is public opinion to consider. I have caused enough embarrassment. To have any kind of connection between me and the man who jilted you would never do. Papa has been very clear that the allowances he has granted between our families does not include a connection between Mr. Glenside and me."

"Papa would not keep you from your heart's desire if he knew I was content with it," Lenora insisted.

Cassie wiped at her tears. "I wish that were true, but I don't believe it is."

Lenora looked away, lost in her own thoughts and regrets.

Cassie was touched by her sister's consideration and grateful for all she had done, yet there was one more question that needed to be discussed.

"Lenora?" Cassie said. "Did you send a letter to Evan, then?"

Lenora nodded. "I thought it would be . . . romantic. The two of you would meet and then I would announce myself and explain."

And it would have been romantic. Cassie could imagine seeing Evan there, in the glen, waiting for her. Their first private moment since he'd walked away from her. She was tempted to be at the glen at four o'clock just in case he came, but she couldn't do that.

"He has promised Papa no correspondence with me just as I have promised," Cassie said. "If he acts on this letter, he'll be breaking his word. I cannot let that happen."

Perhaps he would not act on it, but Cassie knew how tempting it had been for her when she thought the letter was from him. Could he resist? What might it mean if he could?

Cassie looked at Lenora. "In truth I do not know where Evan's heart is. He has every reason to want nothing to do with me. I could not blame him should he feel that way, but I also cannot risk him getting in trouble for this. If he comes to the glen . . ."

"What can we do?" Lenora asked, her face reflecting the same desperation Cassie felt.

Cassie searched her mind, instantaneously weighing out every possible course. Only one seemed reasonable, though it was also the most uncomfortable. "I think we must confess the whole of this to Papa."

Lenora's eyes went wide, and her breath shuddered out of her. But she drew her shoulders up and nodded. "I will go with you."

While Lenora explained to Rose that she had to go to the vicarage, Cassie's anxiety seemed determined to propel her the opposite direction. Would this additional complication push Papa past all reason? Would this confession affect Evan negatively?

Cassie picked up the letter from the porch and refolded it carefully along the creases. She imagined Evan receiving his letter. Would he be glad to have it? Or angry to think she might entice him to such a meeting?

Lenora came out the front door while tying the ribbons of her bonnet beneath her chin. Cassie had no bonnet and was surely going to be pink from the sun come tomorrow. She was also dressed in her washing clothes, her hair curled with her sweat around her face. They had to explain before Evan possibly acted on the letter he received.

The sisters turned toward the church, walking together with commitment and purpose. By the time they reached their father's office door, the letter was nearly burning through Cassie's hand.

She took hold of the door handle, shared a look with Lenora, and pushed the door open without knocking. "Papa," she said as she walked in, Lenora a single step behind. "We need to talk to you about—" She stopped as every other thing fell away, and she stared into a pair of blue eyes she had resigned herself never to see up close again. "Evan?"

Chapter Fifty-Two

Evan stared at Cassie, as surprised to see her as she seemed to be to see him.

"Evan?" she asked again.

He couldn't help but smile. To be so close to her after all this time was invigorating. She wore a gray dress with the sleeves pushed up to her elbows. Her apron was stained and sweat had turned the hair around her face into soft curls that would wrap perfectly around his finger if he should reach for them. Her cheeks were pink, and her brow wet with perspiration—beautifully undone.

"Good afternoon, Miss Cassandra."

She opened her mouth but said nothing, just stared at him in a way he completely understood. Then she flicked a glance behind her and Evan realized she wasn't alone. He straightened and swallowed, attempting to keep his smile in place when he saw Lenora.

"Miss Wilton," he said, bowing slightly. "I'm sorry, I didn't see you there."

She smiled nervously and shut the door without saying anything. Evan took the chance to meet Cassie's eye again only to have Mr. Wilton clear his throat. Evan faced the vicar but had no idea what to say. It had been hard enough to come; if he'd known Cassie and Lenora would be here as well he could never have done it.

"Cassie," Mr. Wilton said, looking hard at his youngest daughter. He was holding Evan's letter, or rather Cassie's letter to Evan. "Did you send this to Mr. Glenside?"

"No, Papa," Cassie said.

No? Evan repeated in his mind.

Cassie continued. "But please let us explain."

Us?

Lenora stood shoulder to shoulder with Cassie, who held an envelope in her hand.

"Perhaps I should go," Evan said, feeling sure he would be unwelcome at a family council.

"Please don't, Mr. Glenside," Lenora said rather bolder than he'd expected. "As this involves you, I wish you would stay."

Evan looked toward Mr. Wilton, who did not look happy with this turn. "Apparently my daughters have no consideration for propriety at all anymore," he said gruffly, then leaned back in his chair and folded his arms over his chest.

After a moment, Lenora cleared her throat. "I wrote that letter," she said, nodding to the envelope in Mr. Wilton's hand. "And this one." She took the envelope from Cassie and handed it to her father. Then she clasped her hands tightly in front of her, her knuckles turning white.

"You?" Papa said, sitting forward. He looked between the three of them but then locked his eyes on Lenora. "Explain."

Lenora took a breath and then the words poured out of her. She explained her bitterness toward Cassie, and then her understanding of what Cassie had done in her absence. She explained her discussion with her sister, Mrs. Capenshaw, and her idea to write two letters that would bring

Evan and Cassie together in the glen—the place where their paths had been separated several weeks ago.

"I wanted to do for them what Cassie had done for the Glenside family," Lenora said. "I wanted to make things right, and I . . ." She paused for a breath. "I wanted to be brave to make up for my lack of courage, which was what spurred Cassie toward writing Mr. Glenside in the first place. I didn't know Cassie was forbidden to have any contact with him, or he with her. I didn't know I was putting them both at risk of your anger or displeasure. I thought I was making everything better, not worse."

Mr. Wilton rubbed a hand over his forehead as though exhausted. After a few seconds, he looked up at Evan. "You did not write this letter to Cassie?"

"No, sir, I did not write it."

Mr. Wilton turned to Cassie. "And you did not write this letter to Mr. Glenside? Lenora is not taking responsibility for something she did not do?"

"No, Papa," Cassie said. Was it Evan's imagination that she seemed disappointed that her father could think her deceptive again?

"She recognized it was not Evan's script," Lenora offered, "and felt I was trying to exact revenge on her by creating a situation that would bring trouble to both her and Mr. Glenside."

"By meeting in the glen against my wishes?" Mr. Wilton clarified.

"I did not know of your wishes, Papa. I assumed the reasons they were kept apart was because of my feelings, not yours."

"And now you are hoping I will change my feelings?"

Evan caught his breath and glanced at Cassie, who also seemed to be holding her breath. Would Mr. Wilton change his mind? And if he did, what then?

"I do," Lenora said with a nod. "I bear neither of them any ill will and, in fact, I very much want them to find happiness with one another, if that is possible."

"He broke an engagement to you and damaged your reputation, perhaps beyond repair."

Cassie cringed.

Lenora, however, spoke, and her voice was strong. "Do you remember the Bible story of when the Pharisees brought the woman caught in the act of adultery to Christ and asked Him to pass judgment on her? Christ was in an impossible position because he could not overstep Roman jurisdiction nor could He go against Mosaic law. He could give no right answer, so he asked the accusers to look inward rather than to either of the laws, which he could not satisfy. Mr. Glenside was put in an equally impossible place."

She paused for breath, and perhaps strength. Evan sent a silent prayer in her direction in hopes to help her. As it was, he had never seen Lenora speak with such confidence. He'd never heard her say so many words at one time.

"He could not marry me when his heart was somewhere else, but neither could he follow his heart due to his proposal *to* me. He did the only thing he could, which was to turn away from us both."

"My dear Lenora," Mr. Wilton breathed.

"Don't do that, Papa," she said in a softer tone. "Do not let me be the victim of myself any longer." She waved toward Cassie, who was blinking back tears.

Evan wished he could reach for her hand. He hated that she felt responsible for all the pain.

"Cassie did for me what I couldn't—what I *wouldn't*—do for myself. She was trying to help me, Papa, and I believe that her intent was pure at the start."

Papa shook his head. "She was trying to satisfy herself. She wanted you married so that she might be out in society."

"She was trying to make up for my deficits—as you all have done all of my life."

Mr. Wilton straightened, and Evan considered once more that he should leave. The things being shared were far too personal for his ears. But to interrupt was unthinkable.

"In Bath, I was forced to speak with people, answer questions about myself, and interact differently than I ever have before. Aunt Gwen did not protect me, and I had to find my own way with people I'd never met before. Cassie once gave me advice on how to hold myself, and I used it every day I was away. Though it hasn't been easy, I have improved, Papa, more in the last weeks than in all the years ahead of it. I am disappointed in how I have behaved until now—so quick to let others attend to me and make things easy—and I am determined to be better. The first step is to make this right. I want you to lift whatever sanctions you have put upon Cassie and Evan and let them follow their hearts."

The room fell silent. Evan could do nothing but blink.

"Perhaps it is not proper," Lenora said after several seconds of silence, "but it is *right*, Papa, and I think you know it is. They have my blessing, and I hope, from the bottom of my heart, that they shall have yours as well."

Chapter Fifty-Three

Cassie could barely breathe. Between the astounding things Lenora had said and being so close to Evan, she feared she was dreaming. She kept her eyes trained on Papa, fearful that when he spoke, the fragile hope she had dared build would shatter. The room was still, like the morning after a heavy snowfall, and she wished she knew what to do. Should she state her opinion and beg for Papa's mercy, or would her eagerness appear vulgar? None of what Lenora had said could discount the fact that Cassie was still the culprit of this mess, and she dared not try to offer a defense for fear that the prejudice against her would be even further ignited.

"Cassie," Papa said, his tone unreadable as he turned his eyes to her. "Mr. Glenside." He moved his gaze to Evan. "Please leave us. I would like to speak with Lenora alone."

Cassie's hope froze in her chest. Did that mean he wanted to speak more candidly than he would with her and Evan there? But he was dismissing them . . . together. "Yes, Papa," she said, turning toward the door while her heart thundered in her chest.

"Yes, sir." Evan stepped past Cassie so he could open the door for her. She glanced at Lenora before leaving. Her sister stood opposite Papa's desk, her neck red and her hands clasped behind her back while she stared at the floor.

"Thank you, Lenora." If Lenora was going to get in trouble once the door was closed, Cassie wanted to make sure she knew she had Cassie's gratitude.

Lenora glanced up and smiled nervously.

"Cassie," Papa said as Cassie stepped over the threshold. She turned even faster. Evan quickly stepped out of the way so she might meet her father's eyes.

"Papa?"

"Gather your mother." He looked at Evan. "Call your uncle and your mother and meet us in our parlor at four o'clock. We shall all be there."

"Yes, Papa," Cassie said at the same moment Evan said, "Yes, sir."

Then Cassie exited and Evan shut the door. She turned to face him. He was so close to her she could see the tiny white stars in the blue of his eyes.

"What will happen in that parlor, do you think?" she whispered.

One moment he was looking down at her with those eyes, and in the next, he cradled her face in his hands and kissed her. She startled, but then grasped his wrists in case he tried to pull away. They both stood there, lips touching still and silent for the space of time it took a starling to dart from beneath the eaves. Then she tightened her grip on his wrists and kissed him back. Her hands slid up and around his neck as though they belonged there, and he lowered his hands from her face to her shoulders and around her back. Her mind, which was so often spinning, became blessedly still. No thought existed save for him and for her and for what might be. What could be.

Finally he drew away, allowing her to look into those beautiful blue eyes again. "Let us pray that is not the only affection we ever share," he whispered.

"I shall pray it with every beat of my heart," she whispered back. She looked at his lips, eager for another kiss to seal such sentiments, but her mind was moving again. They were standing beside the church, mere feet from her father on the other side of the door and in full view of the vicarage across the graveyard.

Evan took a step back but held onto both her hands as though determined to remain connected. "I so feared I would cause more damage by turning in that letter."

"I so feared you would go to the glen."

He smiled with one side of his mouth. "I nearly did."

"But you were a man of your word and that may very well have saved us."

He smiled fully and leaned forward for one more kiss, which she savored for the moment it lasted.

"I shall fetch my uncle and my mother," he said, finally releasing her. "And I will see you in the parlor at four o'clock." He tapped her on the nose, then turned and fairly ran for the front of the church. Cassie waited until she heard the thundering hooves of his horse before she turned back to the vicarage, lifted her skirts, and ran for the back door.

It is the meek and the mild who will inherit, Mama had said. How she hoped she had been meek enough and mild enough to prove the proverb right.

Chapter Fifty-Four

Papa may have summoned what could be the most important conference of Cassie's life, but Cassie had promised Mrs. Ashby she would take responsibility for removing the wash from the line. One would think there would be a reprieve, given the circumstances, but Mama was Mama, and she'd been quick to remind Cassie of her responsibility. Mrs. Ashby had left, and Cassie started on the driest linens in hopes that by the time she reached the wash most recently put on the line, those items would be dry too.

By the time she finished, it was half past three. She scrambled toward her room, calling for a basin of warm water as she darted through the kitchen. She dearly wanted to change into a more suitable dress. While there was something endearing about Evan not being put off by her wretched appearance that afternoon, she would very much like to make a better presentation.

Young did not arrive for ten minutes. Cassie spilled water from the basin down the first dress she put on, then caught her hair on the clasp of the next dress, and finally banged her shin against the dressing table so hard that she lost her balance and jarred her wrist when she fell. Suffice it to say, her preparations for the afternoon meeting were a fair representation of all the mishaps and difficulties she had faced throughout her acquaintance with Mr. Evan Glenside.

By the time Young had applied a tight bandage to reduce the swelling in Cassie's aching wrist, it was a quarter after the hour. Cassie hurried down the stairs and threw open the parlor door with more strength than she meant to, causing it to bang against the wall behind it. Every eye in the room turned to her, and Evan, Mr. Glenside, and Papa all rose to their feet.

"I am so sorry I am late," she said, wishing she were not out of breath. She hurried into the room, taking the empty space beside Mama on the settee. "Please, continue."

Mama laughed. "Continue? It is done."

Cassie looked at Mama, then at Papa, whose expression was rather blank, and finally to Evan, who was still standing and smiling at her in such a way to give her hopes flight. Even Lenora, quiet and still in a chair beside the settee, had a smile on her face.

"What is done?" Cassie asked.

"I think to say 'it is done' gives too strong an impression," the older Mr. Glenside said. "Perhaps we ought to excuse ourselves."

Everyone seemed to agree and exited the parlor, leaving only Evan, still standing, and Cassie, still in her seat. Once the door shut, he came to sit by Cassie. He took her injured wrist in his hand, turning it gently, but perhaps not gently enough. She winced slightly, and he handled it even gentler still.

"What happened?" he asked, looking into her face.

"I'm ridiculous," Cassie said. "If you are to marry me, you should know that. . . . Not that you are . . . or . . . goodness." Her face felt like a kettle left on the stove too long, and she tried to pull her hand away. He wouldn't release it and lowered his head and kissed the skin just above the bandage. It was no longer just her face on fire.

He looked up at her through his lashes. "What else must I know about you if I am to marry you?"

He kissed her arm just below her elbow. She shivered.

"I . . . I have opinions about everything."

"Everything?" He kissed just above her elbow.

"Yes," she said. "Everything."

He kissed her again, further up her arm. "What about horses?"

"I love horses."

Another kiss, this one below the hem of her sleeve. "Parsnips?"

"I-I love parsnips."

"Spiders?" He kissed her collarbone, and her eyes fell closed.

"I don't care for spiders, but I can kill them when I ha-have to."

She felt his breath against her ear before he spoke next. "And what do you think of a common-born man, ill-equipped for high society, who jilted your sister and then wished every day for a way to see you despite promising your father he wouldn't?"

The kiss he placed on her jaw sent pure fire through her veins, and she reached for him while moving her lips to meet his with a kiss of such passion that her mind was still again. "Is he particularly devoted to his family?" she asked between breathless kisses.

"He is."

"And a man of his word in every way?"

More kissing. "Nearly to his detriment."

"And does he love me despite knowing the very worst parts of my character?"

Evan laughed low in his throat and kissed her again. "He does."

"Then I have no objection to such a man." Cassie pulled back and looked him in the eye. The adoration she saw there, pure and unmasked, made her throat tight with emotion. "Am I to assume my parents gave their blessing?"

"It seems Lenora can be quite convincing when she's of a mind to. And it seems she was very much of a mind to."

So many poor choices on Cassie's part. So much hardship endured by so many people because of her actions. But, then, so many prayers. So strong a desire to make things right. Never again would she regret the need to copy a Bible verse so that the voice of God might imprint itself more indelibly upon her heart. Only, as a married woman, she would not face that discipline ever again. *A married woman.*

"I can't believe it," she breathed.

"Then let me convince you further," Evan said, kissing her until she had no doubt at all that he was meant for her and she was meant for him.

Chapter Fifty-Five

The daughter of a vicar would never be married by special license, therefore Father read the banns in church as required for the next three Sundays. Not everyone in the village approved of this turn, but the entire Wilton family held their chins up high and ignored the whisperings that accompanied the readings. A united front gave little soil for the complaints to grow.

While wedding preparations took place at the vicarage, Evan's mother and sisters took residence of the Dower House, allowing the apartments they had been using to be available for the newlyweds. Cassie's wrist healed without incident, and Rose was delivered of two beautiful, although small, baby boys. Cassie reminded herself, almost daily, that this was truly happening, and yet there was little time for such ponderings. Even a simple wedding required a great deal of preparation.

The church was cleaned top to bottom, and the vicarage was humming with sewing, baking, packing, and a hundred other things that Mama managed gracefully. She had done this four times before, after all.

Christopher and Percy returned from school on the Monday prior to Wednesday's ceremony, along with Cassie's sisters not already residing in Leagrave. There was barely a moment for anything other than wedding work and wedding talk, and a great deal of attention for Rose and her babies.

Lenora had continued to stay on with Rose, but she returned to the vicarage the night before the wedding so that Mary's family might stay with Rose. It was easier to fit her family of six there than it was at the vicarage, which was overflowing. The evening was loud and chaotic until finally, blessedly, everyone began retiring to their rooms.

Lenora, quiet as always, was making her exit from the drawing room when Cassie hurried to catch up with her. After her impassioned plea to Papa, Lenora had quickly retreated to her shy disposition. Cassie took Lenora's arm. "Walk with me in the yard?" she whispered.

Lenora looked as though she might object.

"Please," Cassie added.

Lenora swallowed whatever she might have said and nodded.

Cassie steered them past the stairs toward the back door. Everything had happened so quickly that Cassie had had little time to talk with her sister. She suspected that Lenora preferred it, but Cassie could not in good conscience make her vows tomorrow before speaking privately with Lenora. Without Lenora's mercy, this turn in Cassie's life could never have taken place, and yet the guilt Cassie felt about her actions still haunted her.

Soon enough the sisters stepped into the quiet yard, lit by a half-moon. The night was pleasantly cool.

"Are you all right?" Cassie asked amid the sound of night birds and crickets.

"I am," Lenora said, patting her sister's hand and giving her a reassuring smile.

"But you would not tell me if you weren't," Cassie said. "In fact, no one would be able to tell because you keep your thoughts so very much to yourself."

"That I keep my thoughts to myself does not mean I am not all right."

Lenora looked Cassie in the eye. "I have no regrets of what has happened, and I *truly* want you and Evan to be happy. Please do not let assumptions of my feelings detract you."

Cassie looked deeply into her sister's face and saw her heartfelt sincerity. "I don't doubt that you want us to be happy—that is what is so remarkable."

"It is not so remarkable," Lenora said, shaking off the compliment. "This is right, and my knowing it gives me peace."

Cassie felt her heart soften as she cocked her head and regarded her sister. How had she missed the strength of her sister for so long? "And what shall you do, now? What will your future hold?"

Lenora took a deep breath. She stepped away from Cassie and looked across the yard to the trees that surrounded the glen. She said nothing.

Cassie filled the silence. "I have sensed that you do not plan to stay in Leagrave once the wedding is over."

Lenora gave her a surprised glance, then looked back at the trees. "I do not want to detract from the wedding."

"So you will not stay?" Guilt burned brighter in Cassie's chest. Had she chased Lenora away from her home?

"Aunt Gwen left me with an open invitation to stay with her in Bath and . . . I am different there."

"You mentioned that when you spoke to Papa."

"I attend Aunt Gwen, and rather than speaking around me, she pulls me in to conversations and forces me to share my opinions. It was overwhelming in the beginning, but in time I realized that I was capable." She turned back to Cassie. "It began with your advice to smile and focus on my breathing, and then, though it was ill-fated, my time with Mr. Glenside forced me to step further out of the circle of my comfort. I thought any progress to be worthless when I left for Bath, but in fact that became a starting point."

Cassie felt absolved to hear that there had been healing for Lenora. She wondered also if there might be something, or someone, in Bath that was drawing Lenora back there. Would Lenora tell Cassie if there were? "And so you will seek your future in Bath?"

"For now. I have no regrets of what has happened, Cassie. I see the place it has taken each of us, but I hear the whispers too. I feel the pity. It will take time for the gossip to settle, I think, and perhaps even longer for Papa to fully agree that this was the right choice." She shrugged. "Beyond that, I have come to realize that I was raised with one expectation for my future—a husband and children. I never doubted it would happen or that it was the only path for happiness. I am twenty-three years old, and I have had one man cry off from his engagement and marry my younger sister. My prospects are poor."

Cassie winced at the sting of so bold a summation.

Lenora put her hand on Cassie's arm and smiled sympathetically. "I have *no* regrets," she repeated, "but society will keep its score. For so long I have lived amid panic that if I do not marry, I shall have no joy or purpose at all." Her smile brightened. "I no longer feel that way, Cassie. I have seen another side."

Cassie could not believe what she was hearing. Perhaps she didn't understand. "What side?"

"One of independence, confidence, and comfort in my own company."

Cassie gasped. "You are not spurring marriage?" She thought of how happy she was with Evan and how much she wanted that same happiness for Lenora.

"I am no longer *expecting* marriage to define my future," Lenora said. "In fact, I have looked into a position as a music teacher at a girl's school in Bath. Aunt Gwen has been helping me. We met with the headmistress just before I left."

Cassie was stunned, and her mouth fell open. An occupation? Though it was not unheard of for a woman to have an occupation, especially a woman of Lenora's age, it was generally not accepted amid the gentle class. A woman's primary responsibility was to find a husband, and then care for her home and family once she was married. To reject that was . . . uncivilized. And yet if this was truly what Lenora wanted, was Cassie in any position to pass judgment?

"Mama and Papa will not be pleased."

"No, they will not," Lenora said, her smile falling. "Which is why I will wait until after the wedding to tell them. I hope to return to Bath by September so I might be situated at the school in time for the new semester."

"But if you become an independent woman . . ." Cassie trailed off, unsure how to complete her sentence without giving offense. She knew firsthand that society kept score of such things, and it would mark such a thing heavily against Lenora.

"I may never marry," Lenora finished for her. "I know that, and I am at peace with it."

"Are you truly?" Cassie said.

Lenora took both of Cassie's hands and smiled. "Truly. I have come to realize that if I cannot be pleased with myself, I cannot be pleased with anyone else. A husband cannot make me whole. I must do that for myself."

"And you think teaching is the answer to finding that wholeness?"

"I do," Lenora said. "For now."

Cassie blinked back tears. "I feel responsible for this."

Lenora smiled. "Then I hope you take pride in that responsibility because I have never been more excited about my future. I get to fill my days with music and make my own way in the world. I want you to be happy for me."

"Then I shall be," Cassie said around the lump in her throat. "I feel that after spending our entire lives together I am only just now beginning to know you."

Lenora laughed. "I feel the same." She took Cassie's arm and turned back toward the house. "I hope amid your wedded bliss that you will find time to write to me so we might become the sisters we ought to have been."

"I shall write to you every week," Cassie said.

They walked in silence until they reached the back door, then Cassie turned to face Lenora one last time, searching her heart to make sure she had said everything she wanted to say. "I can never thank you enough for forgiving me and giving me the chance to be with Evan. It would not have happened without you."

"You can thank me by soaking up every bit of happiness you can."

Cassie shook her head. "You are too good, Lenora. What else can I do? Surely there is something else."

Lenora paused a moment and her expression turned sincere. The moonlight lit up the blue of her eyes, making Cassie think that if the right man could see Lenora in this moment and see the strength she had just demonstrated, he would have no choice but to fall in love with her. Could she truly find the happiness she craved in teaching? Might there be a man in Bath who could capture her heart and restore to her the expectation of her youth?

"You can pray for me, Cassie," Lenora said. "Pray that I find the same happiness you have found, one way or another."

"I shall do so every day," Cassie said.

Lenora gave Cassie's hand a final squeeze. "Then be happy. It is everything I want for you and Evan both."

Epilogue

A warm fire crackled in the grate of the Glenside drawing room and Cassie looked up from her sketchpad as the moment struck her anew. The scene was ordinary—a repeat of many evenings played out just this way—but the very comfort of it pressed upon her mind and heart.

One year ago, Evan, Mama Glenside, Natalie, and Camilla lived in a poor section of London. Evan worked as an accounting clerk and owned one pair of shoes. Uncle Hastings drank himself into a stupor every night, his heart stuck in the past.

One year ago, Cassie was pining for Mr. Bunderson, angry at her parents, and exasperated by Lenora.

Now, some eight months after she and Evan had exchanged vows in the church she'd attended all her life, everything was different. Uncle Hastings had a single glass of wine with dinner and nothing more. Mama Glenside sang in the choir, quilted with friends, and had a light in her eyes Evan said he hadn't seen for years. Camilla was preparing night and day for her debut, and regardless of whether Camilla had made a match this season, Natalie would have her debut next year. How things had changed. And would change again.

"What are you sketching tonight?" Mama Glenside asked Cassie from the writing desk Uncle Hastings had moved near the fire. She was fanning the most recently finished invitation so that the ink might dry.

"I'll show you when I finish. Tomorrow, perhaps." Cassie pulled the sketchpad closer to her chest. "How are the invitations coming?"

"One more evening's work ought to finish it." She placed the invitation on the stack and squared the corners.

"And then we shall have Camilla's coming out ball!" Natalie said, her eyes dancing.

"In a fortnight," Camilla said, always the steadying influence. "There is much to be done before then." She'd made a list of all the things that needed to be ordered, arranged, cooked, purchased, and organized. She would make a very fine wife, especially if the fortunate man needed help putting his life in order.

Mama Glenside smiled at her daughters and returned the pen to the stock before she stood. "We'd best get back to the cottage. Come along, girls."

Uncle Hastings, who had been reading, clapped his book shut with a snap and stood. "I shall escort the three of you, then turn in myself. We've an early morning tomorrow if we hope to have pheasant for dinner, Evan."

"Yes, Uncle. I shall meet you in the stables at seven."

It was still dark that time of morning, but now that Uncle Hastings didn't drink himself to sleep, he liked to beat the sun when he could. He'd completed Evan's shooting education, and they went out at least twice a week together.

"You're very kind to escort us, Hastings," Mama Glenside said.

"Of course."

The first few times Uncle Hastings had offered to escort the ladies to the Dower House, located exactly thirty steps from the main house, Mama Glenside had protested, but he was intent on doing the gentlemanly thing, and some months ago she had stopped complaining. No one said there'd been a change in Hastings Glenside since her coming to Leagrave, or that the two of them might be perfect for one another, but Evan and Cassie shared a knowing look as everyone left the room.

"It is only a matter of time," Cassie said with a smile.

"It is none of our business, but wouldn't a match between them be something?" Evan replied.

He returned to his chair by the fire and picked up the stack of farm reports.

Now that they were alone, Cassie took a breath she hoped would settle the butterflies in her stomach, which had been decidedly uncomfortable for two full weeks now. She swallowed and then cleared her throat. "Evan, will you look at this sketch and tell me what you think?"

Evan smiled at her in that way that made her melt inside. "I can already tell you what I think—it's amazing." Still, he stood, put the reports on his chair and came around the back of the settee where she was sitting. Before looking at the sketch, he kissed the back of her neck, adding a shiver to the melting and *almost* making her forget the drawing. He lifted his head and, though she couldn't see his reaction, she felt him freeze and inhale quick and sharp.

Cassie allowed the silence to hang between them a moment. "I'm hoping you can build this." She tapped her pencil on the paper.

"A cradle?" he said in a reverent tone.

She turned so she could look into his face. "A cradle."

In an instant, he came around to sit beside her, his eyes going to her belly, the sketchpad, and her face. "You're certain?"

She nodded and blinked back tears. His reaction was everything she'd hoped it would be. "I don't want you to feel overwhelmed by the project. You've six months to have it ready. I think it would be lovely in walnut, or would you suggest oak?"

He rested his gaze upon her and took her hand, rubbing his thumb across her knuckles. "Do you understand what's happened, Cassie?"

She laughed. "I know very well what's happened, believe me. I am sick for hours each morning and . . ." Evan's expression was too serious for her jesting, and she fell silent.

"You've made us a family."

"We were a family already," Cassie said.

"What I mean . . ." He paused as though to collect his thoughts. "My mother and sisters are safe and well-cared for, my uncle is teaching me everything he can to help me make a success of this estate, and now you have given me a family of my own—something I dared not hope for such a long time."

"You certainly can't give me all the credit," Cassie said, though she was deeply touched. "There is fate and God and entailments to thank."

"And you."

She fell silent, and he held her gaze. "Thank you, Cassie, for being who you are, for loving my mother and sisters, for managing my uncle and his household, and, mostly, for making me the man I could never be otherwise."

"I could say the same things about you, Evan. Without your dedication and integrity, none of this would have happened."

He smiled in acknowledgment of her compliment, then placed his hand over her belly. "Promise me that we will never take what we have for granted."

In the space of a breath, the crooked paths they'd trod played out in her mind, and she marveled all over again that they could have come so far. "Never," she breathed. "And we will cherish every day."

He pulled her to him, wrapping her in strong arms and holding her close. In that moment, Cassie saw the path laid out before them. A path they would take together, hand in hand, with grace, humility, and gratitude. Every day.

Acknowledgments

This story originally began as a novella to be featured in one of Heather Moore's Timeless Romance Anthology collections. As I got into the story, however, it grew into something much more complex. I wrote a *different* novella for Heather ☺. Big thanks to her for the many opportunities she's brought my way through her entrepreneurial spirit and generous nature. She does so much good for so many people and is directly responsible for inspiring this story.

Thank you to my agent, Lane Heymont, who encouraged and supported this project, and to Heidi Taylor and Lisa Mangum at Shadow Mountain. Thank you to Donna Hatch for answering some of my questions about the time period and to my writing group for their priceless feedback: Nancy Campbell Allen (*Beauty and the Clockwork Beast,* Shadow Mountain, 2016), Becki Clayson, Jody Durfee (*Hadley, Hadley Benson,* Covenant, 2013), Ronda Hinrichsen (*Betrayed,* Covenant, 2015), and Jennifer Moore (*A Place for Miss Snow,* Covenant, 2016).

I could never do what I do without the unfailing support of my sweetheart, Lee, and the cheerleading—and extreme patience—of my kids, Breanna, Madison, Chris, and Kylee. I am blessed to have so many remarkable people in my life, and I thank my Father in Heaven for each one of them.

Discussion Questions

1. Have you ever struggled with anxiety? If so, did Lenora's descriptions resonate with you? Why or why not?

2. Cassie struggled with her position in the birth order of her family. Where do you fit in the birth order of your family? How do you feel it has affected you?

3. Have you ever lost anyone close to you, as Uncle Hastings and Mrs. Glenside did? How have you coped with the loss and continued forward?

4. Have you ever found yourself in a situation like Evan where you were expected to fit into a world you were unfamiliar with? How did you approach the challenge?

5. Was there a particular scene you especially enjoyed in the book?

6. Do you feel that every inherent strength—like Cassie's assertive nature or Lenora's dedication to music—comes with a corresponding weakness?

7. Have you ever found yourself in need of forgiveness? How have you sought out that relief? How did you know when you found it?

About the Author

Josi is the author of twenty-five novels and one cookbook and a participant in several co-authored projects and anthologies. She is a four-time Whitney award winner—*Sheep's Clothing* (2007), *Wedding Cake* (2014), and *Lord Fenton's Folly* (2015) for Best Romance and Best Novel of the Year—and the Utah Best in State winner for fiction in 2012. She and her husband, Lee, are the parents of four children. You can find more information about Josi and her writing at josiskilpack.com.